W9-AXZ-913

Open Your Heart

Also by Cheris Hodges

The Richardson Sisters series

Owner of a Broken Heart

Won't Go Home Without You

Open Your Heart

The Rumor series

Rumor Has It

I Heard a Rumor

Deadly Rumors

Just Can't Get Enough

Let's Get It On

More Than He Can Handle

Betting on Love

No Other Lover Will Do

His Sexy Bad Habit

Too Hot for TV

Recipe for Desire

Forces of Nature

Love after War

Strategic Seduction

Tempted at Midnight

Open Your Heart

CHERIS HODGES

Kensington Publishing Corp.
www.kensingtonbooks.com

This book is a work of fiction. Names, characters, businesses, organizations, places, events, and incidents either are the product of the author's imagination or are used fictitiously. Any resemblance to actual persons, living or dead, events, or locales is entirely coincidental.

To the extent that the image or images on the cover of this book depict a person or persons, such person or persons are merely models, and are not intended to portray any character or characters featured in the book.

DAFINA BOOKS are published by

Kensington Publishing Corp.
119 West 40th Street
New York, NY 10018

Copyright © 2021 by Cheris Hodges

All rights reserved. No part of this book may be reproduced in any form or by any means without the prior written consent of the Publisher, excepting brief quotes used in reviews.

If you purchased this book without a cover, you should be aware that this book is stolen property. It was reported as "unsold and destroyed" to the Publisher and neither the Author nor the Publisher has received any payment for this "stripped book."

All Kensington Titles, Imprints, and Distributed Lines are available at special quantity discounts for bulk purchases for sales promotions, premiums, fund-raising, and educational or institutional use. Special book excerpts or customized printings can also be created to fit specific needs. For details, write or phone the office of the Kensington special sales manager: Kensington Publishing Corp., 119 West 40th Street, New York, NY 10018, attn: Special Sales Department, Phone: 1-800-221-2647.

The DAFINA logo is a trademark of Kensington Publishing Corp.

ISBN-13: 978-1-4967-3191-3
ISBN-10: 1-4967-3191-3
First Kensington Mass Market Edition: August 2021

ISBN-13: 978-1-4967-3192-0 (ebook)
ISBN-10: 1-4967-3192-1 (ebook)

10 9 8 7 6 5 4 3 2 1

Printed in the United States of America

There are always so many people to thank
when you enter into this writing life.
The family who listens to you talk about
some bright idea that may fizzle in the end.
The family who understands that you're going to sit
in the corner and type all day because
you've just got to get this idea in that document.
The friends who support you and talks you off the ledge
when you spill water on your laptop.
And every reader who picks up your book and allows
you to be a part of their world.
Thank you to each and every one of you.

Prologue

It was a warm May night and Yolanda Richardson had spent more time in her Richmond boutique than she'd planned. But the summer dresses and suits that had just come in were beyond beautiful. The yellow, pink, and purple outfits just popped. When she'd opened the shipment, she knew she wouldn't rest until she put those items on display.

And that was what set her fashion boutique apart from every other store in the city. Yolanda dealt in one-of-a-kind items from up-and-coming designers. Her plan was to add some of her own designs to the fold at some point. But believe it or not, the outspoken wild card of the Richardson family was fearful to share her work with the world. Her youngest sister, Nina, had seen a few of her sketches, but Yolanda hadn't shared them with anyone else.

There was something about your baby sister telling you that the work was good that eased Yolanda's ego for a while. She looked up at her display window and smiled. She had the mannequins dressed in the amazing sundresses and had sunflowers surrounding them. It looked like one of those fields that people stopped at on the side of the road to take pictures. But instead of a sun lamp, she had a spinning disco ball in the corner, just to add a little quirk to the scene. And because she'd accidentally ordered the silver ball two years ago and had no idea what to do with it.

Now it had found a home that would call attention to the store. She was proud of her work, even if it was super late and she still hadn't eaten dinner. Her stomach growled, echoing the point that she needed food.

Just as she was about to take a picture of the display for her Instagram feed, Yolanda heard a couple of loud pops. She thought it was fireworks at first, but it was May. There were no celebrations going on in the middle of the night.

Then there were more pops. Louder this time and Yolanda realized they were gunshots. She took off from the sidewalk in front of the shop and ducked behind the trash cans on the side of the building and watched a car speed into the alleyway. She closed her eyes and prayed this was a bad dream.

Yolanda was frozen in place as the door to the white Chrysler 300 opened and a man was pushed out of the back of the vehicle.

Another two men hopped out of the front seat, both holding guns. Their faces filled with anger and malice burned in her brain and she prayed they didn't notice her quivering in the corner.

"You think you can steal from me?" the tallest man growled. "There is always a consequence for every fucking action."

The man cowering on the ground threw his hands up.

"Danny, man, you got it all wrong. I'll get you the money. Things are hard right now, but I'm trying."

Danny took a step closer to the begging man and all Yolanda noticed were his shoes. Patent leather church shoes. Who wears their Sunday best to threaten someone? She held her breath and tried not to move as she watched the drama unfolding in front of her.

"Don't do this, man. I'll get you the money."

"Too fucking late. You probably can't even come up with the interest." Danny pointed the gun at the man's head and fired three shots. Yolanda covered her mouth with her hand. Seeing death in person was nothing like the movies. Blood oozed into the street; parts of that man's skull littered the road. The smell of gunpowder filled the air and her nostrils.

"Pick him up," Danny ordered the other man as he crossed over to the car and popped the trunk. The other man, who was medium height but built like a muscular bulldog, picked up the dead man as if he were a pile of trash and tossed him in the trunk.

When Yolanda saw brain matter ease out of the man's head, her knee quivered and bumped the plastic trash can. Since it was empty and the street was silent, the thump echoed.

Danny and the bulldog turned toward the trash cans and Yolanda closed her eyes as she curled up into a ball. Did they see her? Was she going to join that man in the trunk with several bullets in her head? She held her breath.

"You think someone is out here?" the bulldog asked.

"Let's move," Danny said as they got into the car. Yolanda waited until she heard the car pull out of the alleyway before she dashed into the boutique. She was too shaken to call the police. So, she hid in her office until the sun came up. To say she was afraid would be the understatement of the year.

As Yolanda left that morning, she kept looking over her shoulder for the mysterious Danny and that bulldog-looking man. Perhaps she was being unfair to bulldogs. That man looked more like the devil than an animal or a human. If she was lucky, those men hadn't seen her and knew nothing about who she was.

Now she regretted ignoring the security warnings the Business Neighborhood Association had sent out over the last few months. But she'd told herself that she was too busy getting ready for the summer season to pay attention to scare tactics. Crime wasn't a problem in downtown Richmond these days. Well, until last night. Yolanda took the long way home, trying to wash the memories of murder out of her head. But she kept seeing that man's brains oozing out of his head after he begged for his life. What would happen to her if she reported this to the police? The killers already knew where her shop was. It would only take a simple Google search to find out who owned it.

Doesn't mean they would know you had been there last night. Yolanda may have known going to the police was the right thing to do, but she couldn't do that today. All she wanted to do was go home and try to forget with the help of a bottle or two of wine.

Once she got home, Yolanda called her boutique manager, Kelly Coe, and told her that she wasn't feeling well and wouldn't be in today.

"You've been working too hard, boss lady. Do you need me to call Uber Eats and have some food sent over to you?"

"No, no. I have some soup and crackers here. Just take care of the orders for me, and if any of my sisters call, don't tell them I'm sick," Yolanda said, trying to keep her voice light.

"All right. Hope you feel better."

Yolanda told her good-bye, then curled up in her bed. She tried to close her eyes, but the images of last night's brutality played in her mind over and over again.

Yolanda tossed and turned until about noon. When her stomach growled and she knew she wasn't going to get any sleep, she headed for the kitchen and made a tuna salad sandwich, poured herself a glass of wine, and headed for the den to watch the news. Before she could take a bite of her sandwich, she saw his face on the TV screen.

"A local businessman was found dead in the James River." The man's face popped up on the screen and Yolanda dropped her wineglass. It was him. She listened intently as the newscaster finished the story.

"Affectionately known as Bobby G., Robert Gills owned a few restaurants and a couple of clothing stores in Regency Square. Police say he suffered multiple gunshot wounds before being dumped into the river. Two fishermen found the body this morning and called the police."

Yolanda shut the TV off and headed for the kitchen to grab a mop, broom, and dustpan. This was becoming all too real. This man's death wasn't going to go away and those killers weren't going to disappear. She said a silent prayer that they'd never connect her to what they had done. Yolanda was still too afraid to talk to the police about what she'd seen, even if she knew it was the right thing to do. Her lawyer sister, Robin, would be ashamed of her inaction. And her father, Sheldon Richardson, would tell her that she needed to do the right thing.

She had no idea who Danny and the bulldog were, but they didn't look like the kind of people you'd testify against in court. She tried to reason that the police would find the killers without her help. Yolanda had seen enough *Law & Order* and true-crime shows to know that police solved murders all the time without an eyewitness.

At some point, you're going to have to do the right thing, her voice of reason said. Yolanda closed her eyes and wondered why her voice of reason always sounded like her older sister Alex.

After sweeping up the broken glass in her den and mopping up the wine, Yolanda had lost her appetite and decided to check in on her youngest sister, Nina. She hadn't talked to her globetrotting sister in a couple of weeks and Nina, who was a freelance sportswriter, always had something going on.

But what Yolanda really needed was someone to hold her and tell her everything was going to be fine, or better yet, wake up and find out that last night had simply been a nightmare. She grabbed her phone and started to call her sister when the phone rang. It was her boutique. She had already told Kelly in no uncertain terms not to bother her. If you can't play sick at the company you own, then what is the point? Yolanda reluctantly answered the phone.

"Hello?"

"Yolanda," Kelly said. "I know you're not feeling well and I didn't want to bother you, but I noticed a couple of our security cameras were off-line and then I saw something disturbing from last night."

Yolanda inhaled sharply. "What did you see?" She knew she should've deleted the video. Unlike Yolanda, Kelly paid attention to the business neighborhood watch newsletters. Made sense that she checked the security camera feed every day.

"Two men shooting someone in the alley. Should I take this to the police?"

"N-no," Yolanda stammered. "We're just going to keep this on the hard drive and not say a word about it."

"But, Yolanda, don't you think. . ."

"Kelly," she said quietly, "I was there and I'm afraid they're going to come back. If no one asks for the video, then we don't say anything about it." *And maybe all of this will go away*, she added silently.

"You were there? Oh my goodness, Yolanda! Did anyone see you?"

"I don't know and I don't want to discuss it further."

"All right. Well, if you need anything call me."

Yolanda ended the call and tossed her cell phone across the room. What was she going to do now? Since someone else knew what happened, Yolanda knew she had to do the right thing and go to the police. But first, she needed a little liquid courage.

A bottle and a half of Chardonnay later, Yolanda was

asleep on her sofa. The right thing was just going to have to wait.

The ringing of her cell phone woke her up a few hours later. She smiled when she saw the face on the screen: a great distraction, Harrison Moore, her off-and-on boy toy, who could cook. If he wanted to come over today, she would definitely let him spend the night. Just so she wouldn't be alone.

Chapter 1

Two weeks had passed since the murder outside of Yolanda's shop and she hadn't been back. She'd given Kelly all of the excuses she could muster, from being sick to going out to do some meetings with designers. All she'd really done was hide out in her house and talk herself out of going to the police about what she'd seen. Yolanda had called the Crime Stoppers hotline, but when she was put on hold three times, she'd lost her nerve.

Today, she made the decision to head back to the shop. Kelly had taken on a lot of responsibility for the summer sale and the end-of-the-day reports proved that she'd been working hard. Yolanda couldn't keep leaning on her store manager like this. As she drove to downtown Richmond, she felt as if every car was following her. Then when she saw a Chrysler 300, she yelped. Thankfully, there was an older man driving and not giving her a second look. Arriving at work, she parked in the garage across the street and headed into her boutique.

"Aww, the prodigal owner returns," Kelly said as she folded shirts for a display in the middle of the shop.

"I'm here and you can go home for the day."

"Are you sure?"

Yolanda nodded. "I can't thank you enough for holding this place together over the last two weeks."

"It's been my pleasure. And that display window has brought so many people in. I think it's the disco ball."

Yolanda shuddered inwardly. That damned window had been why she couldn't sleep at night. But since the story had left the headlines and the evening news, maybe the killers didn't care who saw them.

That made her feel a little better about not calling the police. Though, she'd never tell another person that she'd seen the killing. It was bad enough that Kelly knew.

"Hey, Yolanda," Kelly said before she headed out the door. "I meant to tell you, the neighborhood watch leader, Walton Kennerly, came by and said the detectives on the Bobby G. killing want the videos from the security cameras."

Yolanda's breath caught in her chest. "Um, what did you do?"

"I told Walton he'd have to talk to you." Kelly took a deep breath. "I think you should just give it to them. There are a lot of people who want to know what happened to Bobby G."

"Let me ask you something," Yolanda said. "If I give Walton the video, is there anything on it that identifies our shop?" She closed her eyes and watched the scene in the alley play out in her head all over again.

"I don't think so, it just has the time stamp and the alley. Have you been all right, being that you . . ."

The bell above the door rang, indicating that they had a customer. Yolanda was about to smile until she saw it was Walton.

Walton was the kind of guy who had gotten passed over for hall monitor in middle school and used his adult life to make up for that slight. She shook her head as she watched him walk in, dressed in dad jeans and golf shirt. His bald head glistened with sweat as he crossed over to Yolanda. He always looked as if he had tasted sour milk.

"Yolanda, glad to see that you're here," he said, then wiped his mouth with the back of his hand.

"What's going on, Walton?" she asked as she folded her arms across her chest.

"We're trying to help the police solve Bobby G.'s murder and I heard you all might have some video of what happened that night."

Yolanda shot Kelly a cold look. There went her bonus. Kelly turned away from her and looked down at her feet.

"Yeah, possibly," she said.

"I'm collecting the videos to give to the police, so, what do you have?"

"Give me a second to download the security video," Yolanda said as she started toward her office. "You can keep him company, Kelly."

"But I thought," she started. Yolanda rolled her eyes and headed for her office. She grabbed one of the USB drives she kept in her desk and downloaded the video. Watching it again made her stomach lurch. Maybe this was enough. Walton could be the hero and no one would know that she'd been in the alley.

Moments later, she returned to the showroom, where Kelly was helping a few customers. The two girls from Virginia Union University whom she'd hired as clerks and Instagram influencers were on the floor as well. Fine, Kelly could leave. "All right, Walton, here you go."

"Thanks. You never noticed the things that happened on this video before Kelly told you about it?"

"I don't check the feed every day."

Walton expelled a frustrated breath. "I asked all of the businesses here to do that in the last three newsletters that I sent out. Does the safety of the district not mean anything to you?"

Yolanda closed her eyes and squeezed the bridge of her nose. "I don't need your attitude right now. You have the video, now please leave."

"I'm sorry, I wasn't trying to give you 'attitude,' as you say, but it's scary to know that someone was murdered here."

Who the hell are you telling? she thought as she offered him a plastic smile. "Well, Walton, I have customers."

"Just a quick reminder, the next neighborhood watch meeting is Friday. Diamont's will be providing the refreshments."

Yolanda was tempted to go to the meeting to sample the new bakery's goods, but listening to Walton go on and on for hours was enough to make her decide to skip the meeting. Then again, Yolanda figured she needed to see if any other business owners knew about the murder. In her heart, she hoped someone else had seen Danny and the bulldog, then called the police. The more time passed, the more her conscience gnawed at her.

Bobby had a family and she knew she'd be devastated if someone killed . . . She wouldn't allow the thought to fester in her mind.

"I'll be there," she finally said. Her response was enough to get Walton to leave. Yolanda greeted her customers before heading back to her office. Sitting at her desk, she glanced at the phone and thought about calling the police. Fear paralyzed her as she placed her hand on the phone. Her name would be public record, her address and her phone number. What if they came after her?

And who was this Danny person? How dangerous was he? Yolanda wasn't willing to find out. She figured if she kept quiet, she could stay alive. So far it had worked, and if it wasn't broken, she wasn't going to fix it.

Chapter 2

The summer moved quickly for Yolanda and despite looking over her shoulder every time she left the house, things had been good for her. The business had been booming, and Yolanda had been creating sketches and designing outfits for her own fashion line that she'd launch one day. She thought they were good. And she was actually going to have one made. A snow white leather jumpsuit. Just like Nina and their father, Sheldon, Yolanda was a fan of movie star Pam Grier. The jumpsuit reminded her of the blaxploitation movies she'd watch when Sheldon wasn't looking. If she were taller, she'd make some bell-bottoms.

Yolanda still avoided Walton's meetings, even if she did go to the one he held shortly after giving him the video. She'd been surprised that she hadn't seen the video on the local news. One thing TV news was good for was showing the death of a Black man, no matter who the killer was.

Had people forgotten about Bobby G.? Unsolved murders weren't new when it came to people of color. Could she exhale or would she feel guilt for the rest of her life knowing that she could've done something to put two criminals behind bars?

Yolanda pulled out her sketch pad, which she had been doing a lot more lately. It was as if designing made her focus on everything except what she knew.

"Knock-knock," Kelly said from the doorway. "Look who got roses."

Yolanda looked up from her pad. "Really? I wonder why my dad felt the urge to send me flowers," she said as she took in the dozen red roses in Kelly's arms.

"You can hold out on me all you want," she quipped. "There is some man in Richmond who is mad about you."

"And you didn't look at the card?"

"I try to mind my business," Kelly said with a wink as she set the roses on the edge of the desk then headed out of the office. Now, Yolanda was curious. Where did the flowers come from? She picked up the crystal vase and sniffed one of the fragrant roses. Then she saw the card. At first she thought it was a red ink slosh on the outside of the white envelope. But as she looked at the card, it looked like a bloody fingerprint. *Okay, this is weird,* she thought as she opened the card.

When she read the card, her knees quaked and she dropped the vase to the floor. Yolanda screamed and Kelly came running into the office.

"Yolanda, what's wrong?"

"Shut everything down. I have to get out of here," Yolanda stammered.

Kelly looked at the broken vase and the roses and water on the floor. "What happened?"

"Just shut everything down," Yolanda said as she grabbed her purse and sketch pad. She dashed out the back door and ran to her car. Yolanda started her car and sped out of the parking lot. The words on that card echoed in her head.

Talk and bitch you're dead. We know who you are and you're not safe. There was no way she'd go to the police now. She was going to the one place where she could be at peace for a little while: She was going to the Richardson Bed and Breakfast in her hometown of Charleston, South Carolina.

The Richardson Bed and Breakfast was a crown jewel in the Charleston landscape. Sheldon and Nora Richardson built the historic bed-and-breakfast at a time when Jim Crow ruled the South. They turned their property into a place where everyone was welcomed and treated like royalty. Yolanda loved that her family brought so much joy to people. And she was even happier that Sheldon didn't expect all of his daughters to follow in his footsteps. Besides, her older sister Alexandria had filled those footprints and made them her own. She was Sheldon's right hand and good at her job. Though all of the younger Richardson sisters knew Alex needed a life that went beyond the doors of the bed-and-breakfast, too bad she didn't see it that way. If Alex wasn't hard at work, she was deep in Nina's business or judging Yolanda for her choices that didn't line up with what Alex thought she should be doing. At least that's how Yolanda always saw things with her older sister.

Alex and Yolanda were always at odds with each other. Sheldon nicknamed them oil and water. But when things really mattered, all of the Richardsons stood together. Yolanda wondered what her sisters would say if they knew she was being threatened. Would they talk her into going to the police or would they stand by her decision of self-preservation?

It didn't matter because she was going to hide this from her family as long as she could. And since the card in those roses said she was being watched, Yolanda decided to check in to a hotel for the night, then decide when she'd go to Charleston. She drove to Petersburg, which was about a half hour outside of Richmond, and hoped that no one had followed her. Part of her wanted to call her sister Robin, who was an attorney, and ask her what she should do. But knowing Robin, Yolanda figured she'd make her go back to Richmond and meet her at the police department to make a statement.

And what if telling Robin put her in danger? She knew something was going on with her sister and her brother-in-law, Dr. Logan Baptiste, but no one would tell her what was happening. *Guess that's how things roll when people think you're the family firecracker*, she surmised as she pulled into the parking lot of the Ragland Mansion B&B. Since it was the middle of the week, she prayed the property had at least one vacancy. Heading into the lobby, she couldn't help but compare this place to her family's bed-and-breakfast. She could admit that the mansion was beautiful, but the Richardson B&B had an ocean view and the win in her book.

After checking into her room, Yolanda hated that she hadn't grabbed some clothes from the store, but at least she had her toothbrush and toothpaste in her bag. Was this going to be life from now on? On the run, looking over her shoulder and dreading being alone? Yolanda built her life spending time by herself, but that was because she wanted to get lost in drawing and making clothes for her dolls. Then Nina came along and it was as if she had a doll who grew into her best friend. The two youngest sisters of the Richardson clan had their own language and own ways of getting on Alex's nerves when they were growing up. And Yolanda was sure Alex would think that they still did.

Flinging herself onto the soft bed, Yolanda buried her face in the pillows and tried to quiet the fear in her head. After twenty minutes of tossing and turning, she knew she was going to need wine to get any rest.

Before she headed for the bar, Yolanda decided to turn on the local news and see if there was any news about an arrest in Bobby G.'s murder. She thought it was cute the TV's start-up channel was ESPN. After all, it was about time for college football to start and then NFL preseason had kicked off about a week ago. She was about to flip the channel when she heard Nina's name.

"What the hell?" she muttered. Nina Richardson was a freelance sportswriter based out of Charlotte, North Carolina. The joke around the bed-and-breakfast had always been that Nina got into sports to keep from doing chores with her sisters. The fact that Sheldon let her get away with it never ceased to amaze Yolanda. Especially since she didn't get away with much growing up.

"Social media is blowing up after Panthers QB Cody Cameron called sportswriter Nina Richardson *sweetheart* in the middle of the postgame press conference after he threw three INTs, got sacked three times, and lost a fumble."

"Asshole," Yolanda muttered as she watched the exchange. How Nina kept her poise, she'd never know. Must have gotten that from their father. Yolanda would've slapped the fashion-challenged quarterback. But she'd almost pay him to let her design some clothes that would celebrate his body and style instead of having him look like a carnival hustler looking to sell snake oil.

Yolanda knew how hard Nina worked to be taken seriously in a male-dominated industry. Another testament to her sister's professionalism: She never dated a player, never commented on the number of men she'd seen naked in the locker rooms other than saying, "It's just a body. And it stinks in there."

Yolanda was proud of her sister and if people were on social media calling her baby sister names, then she was going to clap back, because she knew Nina wouldn't. First, she needed to talk to her sister. And secretly, Yolanda was happy for the distraction. She called Nina and closed her eyes as she waited for her sister to answer the phone.

"What is it, Yolanda?" Nina asked dejectedly.

"Why do you sound like somebody stole your dog?"

"Because somebody did! This whole Cody situation has gotten me suspended. . . ."

"What? That is some bullshit. You should've told his ass off since you still got in trouble anyway. You can do better than writing for some local rag anyway. Why aren't people jumping on your side like they do when a white girl gets treated like this?"

"Because I'm not a white girl and . . ."

"Them Twitter trolls are out of pocket and before I pop off . . ."

"Look, Yolanda, I got to go. I'm tired of talking about this and everything else."

Now, Yolanda was worried. Something didn't sound

right in her sister's voice and it was clear to her that it wasn't about social media and football. "What else is going on? Spill it, Nina."

Her sister sighed into the phone, then launched into what sounded like a tear-filled story about the guy she was dating, Lamar Geddings. Nina said that after the game she'd gone to a diner and seen Lamar on a date with another woman and he'd had the unmitigated gall to introduce Nina to the woman he'd been eating with. Yolanda was pissed. Who did this loser think he was? Though she'd never met Lamar in person, Nina had sent her a picture and that man was average at best. And he thought he could do better than Nina Richardson? Smart, beautiful, and built like a brick house.

"Oh, girl, I'm . . ."

"We'll talk later," Nina said, then hung up the phone. Yolanda wanted to head to Charlotte and fight that overgrown man child for making her sister cry and throw eggs at Cody Cameron. But she was going to have to figure some things out first. Like, if had Danny and the bulldog been arrested. Walton acted as if the videos from everyone's security tapes were so important in solving the crime. Yet, nothing had happened and those killers were still on the streets.

When she finally made it to the local CBS channel, she noticed that there wasn't a word said about Bobby G. or the murder. If these killers saw that she hadn't been to the police, why were they threatening her? She wasn't a threat to them. Still, they wanted her dead.

After spending two nights in Petersburg, Yolanda found the courage to go home. Perhaps the heat had died down and she could rest in her own bed. She could reopen her shop and return to some kind of normal life. But when she arrived at home, there was a white floral box on her doorstep. Since her last experience with flowers ended up being a death threat, Yolanda wasn't happy to see the box. She wasn't dealing with anyone who sent flowers and Sheldon only sent his daughters bouquets on their birthdays and Valentine's Day. It was neither of those days. She started to pick up the box, but every Investigation Discovery show about bombs in boxes and flowers hiding poison that could kill with one touch flashed in her head. She kicked the box down the steps and waited to see if it would explode. It didn't, but roses spilled down the steps. Then she saw the note underneath the spot where the box had been.

Die Bitch, written in big red letters. Yolanda looked at the door to see if anyone had been inside while she was gone. She reached for the doorknob and was happy to see that it was still locked. But she wasn't going to stick around and wait for these people to come back. Yolanda unlocked the door and dashed inside the house. As she frantically packed a bag, Yolanda looked around the house to see if anything was out of place. It hadn't seemed as if anyone had been inside and she was thankful for that.

Taking a deep breath, she decided to call Nina and let her know that she was going to come to Charleston this weekend. But she needed to keep things light with her sister. She didn't want to tell anyone in her family about the threats and what she was dealing with. She just needed to feel safe for a few days and figure things out.

But did these people know about her family in South Carolina? Would she be followed and put her father and sisters in danger? What about the guests at the B&B?

Yolanda decided that she'd drop her car off at the airport and rent a car. Maybe that would give her time to get her shit together and build up enough courage to report what she saw and the threats that she was facing.

An hour later, she was heading to the Richmond International Airport. Yolanda parked in the long-term lot and took the shuttle to the Enterprise counter. Even though she knew she was probably going to pay a pretty penny for this last-minute rental. She decided to rent a Maxima, something totally different from the Lexus she normally drove. When the clerk handed her the keys, she decided to tell anyone who asked that her car was in the shop for a recall.

After she got into the black sedan, she called Nina to check on her sister's drama. Nina was still upset about her breakup with Lamar and Yolanda used that as a reason for her to come to Charleston. Why tell her sister that she was running from killers?

"Listen, don't tell Alex that I'm coming. I want to surprise her," Yolanda said.

"Promise me that you will be nice to Alex. I don't want to play referee between you two all weekend."

"I'll be on my best behavior," Yolanda said without laughing, but she was sure Nina knew that wasn't true.

After hanging up with her sister, Yolanda focused on the road and made sure every car on her bumper wasn't following her. She arrived in Charleston about seven hours later, but instead of heading directly to the bed-and-breakfast, Yolanda decided to check in to a hotel along the interstate and wait to head over to Richardson Bed and Breakfast on Friday morning. She hated being this close to home and not being able to go there immediately.

She wanted to hug her father. She wanted to just be around him and feel safe for the first time in months. But she had to make sure that her family was safe before she went over there. That meant seeing if she received any additional threats here.

Chapter 3

For the next few months, Yolanda made every excuse in the book to be in Charleston at the bed and breakfast or in Charlotte with Nina. She hadn't gotten anymore threats, but that had a lot to do with the fact that she'd been anywhere but Richmond. After Clinton Jefferson, the B&B's marketing manager and the man whom Nina was now falling for, had gotten Sheldon featured in *USA Today,* Yolanda used the photo shoot as a reason to extend her stay. And then, Nina needed a makeover, so she had to oversee it.

It wasn't long before Alex noticed and cornered Yolanda at breakfast one morning. "What's going on with you?" Alex asked as she took Yolanda's bowl of grits from her hand. "I know you can't run your boutique from here."

"That's why I trust the people who work for me."

"Yolanda, I know you and that little boutique of yours is . . ."

"Stop right there. Every time you talk about my successful business, you have to throw in a jab. Just worry about yourself and leave me the hell alone." She snatched her bowl back and stormed out of the dining room.

A smarter person would've taken that moment to tell Alex what was going on, but in that moment, Yolanda wasn't ready to confess what was going on. And since Nina had returned to Charlotte, Yolanda thought it was time to head there.

After she returned to her room, she started packing. When she heard a knock at her door, she figured it was Alex and started to ignore it.

"Yolanda, are you in there?" Sheldon asked.

She crossed over to the door and opened it. "Hey, Daddy," she said as she gave him a hug.

"Alex said you two are being oil and water again," he said as he walked into the room.

"She said that?"

"Not in those words, but what's going on with you? I know this is a busy season for you. And while I love seeing you visiting more, is there something going on in Richmond?"

She shook her head. "I'm just trying to figure out my next move. I want to do a fashion line of my own. So, I've been sketching and considering if I can afford to do it." Yolanda hated lying to her father. She'd never been good at it. And she wasn't technically lying because she had been considering doing just what she'd said.

"Well, I've seen your books and it doesn't look like that's a bad idea. But I thought you wanted to open a second location first."

She turned her back to Sheldon, because looking him in the eyes was a truth serum and she wasn't ready to tell him about everything that was happening in Richmond. "Maybe I can do both?"

"Am I going to need to make another investment?"

"No," she said as she turned to face him. "Dad, I appreciate what you did to help me, but I will not keep asking you for handouts."

"That check I got last month doesn't seem like I'm just giving out handouts. If you need help, just ask."

Yolanda fought back her tears. She needed help and wanted her father to tell her that everything was going to be all right. Of course, she'd have to tell him what was going on and she wasn't ready to do that.

"Oh, Daddy, thank you for believing in me."

"Baby girl, I believe in all of my daughters. But I need you and Alex to fix this argument before you leave. Where are you going? Back to Richmond?"

"Um, I was thinking about going to Charlotte. If I do a second location or move my whole business, Charlotte is a great place."

Sheldon shrugged. "You know fashion and retail. I'm sure you've done your research and will make the best decision."

"That's what I'm trying to do, Dad," she said.

"I know you're going to make the right decision. You have always done that and I don't see it changing," he said.

Yolanda smiled. "Thank you."

"And when you get to Charlotte, try not to cause too much trouble with Nina. I know how you two can get without supervision."

"Daddy, we're grown-ups now. We don't need supervision," Yolanda said with a laugh.

"Sure you don't. Drive safe, honey, and let Alex know that you're leaving," he said in a tone that meant it wasn't a suggestion.

"Yes, sir," she replied.

It took her an hour to prepare to see Alex. Not because she was angry or anything, but just like with her father, lying to Alex was hard. Yolanda always hid it behind an argument. But she didn't want to leave on bad terms today. So, she was going to hug her sister, pretend she had a meeting with an investor in Charlotte, and then shift the focus to Nina. What could go wrong?

Yolanda headed to Alex's office and stopped short when she heard her sister having a curt conversation with someone in her office. Through the cracked door, she saw that Clinton was on the receiving end of Alex's venom. Yolanda didn't understand why her sister didn't like Clinton Jefferson.

He was a smart man; he'd obviously been qualified for the job or Sheldon wouldn't have hired him. And that *USA Today* article had been a boon in business for the B&B. What was so wrong with him?

"Knock-knock," Yolanda said as she walked in. "Sorry to break up this meeting, but, Alex, Dad wanted me to tell you that I'm leaving."

Alex faced her sister, then rolled her eyes. "Where are you going?"

Yolanda smiled and glanced at Clinton. "Charlotte."

She could tell he was trying to hide his smile.

"I'm going to head back to my office if we're done here," Clinton said.

"We're done," Alex said, then waved him off as if he were an annoying gnat.

When they were alone in the office, Yolanda closed the door and shook her head. "Why are you so rude to him? Even for you this is mean."

Alex rolled her eyes. "I'm sorry that I'm not easily impressed by someone who used to work for Randall Birmingham and was in here not too many months ago trying to buy the bed-and-breakfast. I haven't found a reason to trust him."

"Not even the fact that Nina likes him?"

"Yeah, because Nina has the best . . . I'm not trying to fight with you or have you go to Charlotte and tell Nina what I said. I'm praying he is everything he says that he is."

"You and me both. Alex, about this morning. . ."

"Let's just let it go. I can't talk to you about your business without you taking it as a dig, so I'll just mind my business."

"Or you could let me refresh your wardrobe."

Alex scoffed. "I don't think so. But I'll keep it in mind when I go on vacation."

"Um, so that means never, okay then."

"So funny. Anyway, thanks for letting me know that you're leaving and drive safe. Why are you going to Charlotte?"

"Researching some things," she said. "And I want to make sure Nina doesn't make a mistake and do something dumb."

"Good idea. She'll listen to you."

"Sounds like you have a message you want to pass along," Yolanda said.

"No, I don't. You'd better get going if you want to get ahead of the traffic."

"See you later," Yolanda said as she left the office. When she got to the rental car, Yolanda called Kelly and told her that she was going to send her a severance package because she was closing the Richmond store.

"Why? We were doing so well here," Kelly said, her voice filled with confusion. "What's going on?"

Yolanda cleared her throat. "There are a lot of factors in this decision. I want a bigger space and I've kind of outgrown Richmond."

"And this has nothing to do with . . . you know . . . what happened?"

"That is a factor in it. But I've been researching the Charlotte market for a while and it seems like a booming place. If you want to relocate here when I get everything up and running, I'd love to have you."

"No," Kelly said. "I appreciate you for making the offer, but Richmond is home for me. Yolanda, forgive me for saying this, but if you're running scared about what you saw then maybe you should go to the police and let them handle it."

"They know where I live," Yolanda said quietly. "The threats haven't stopped. I just have to start over and hope this all stops."

"I don't think it works like that. You're going to be running forever if these men don't go to jail. Is that really how you want to live your life?"

"Kelly, I just want to live and you have to understand that."

"The police have come by my house and asked me questions about the video," Kelly revealed.

"And what did you tell them?"

"Just what was on the video. They seemed really concerned about if I was an eyewitness or who was in the alley."

"Can they see me on the video?" Yolanda asked nervously.

"I'm sure if the police enhanced it they can."

"Shit," Yolanda muttered.

"What?"

"Nothing, I'll get the funds transferred to you. Kelly, did you tell anyone I was there or my address?"

"I told the police where you live, but . . ."

"Okay," she said. "Talk to you soon."

Yolanda hung up the phone and banged her hand against the steering wheel. Did this mean these killers had an in with the police department? How else could those people get her information? Did that mean they could find her family, too? There was no way she could go to the police and put everyone in danger. But could she get as far away from Richmond as she could without raising questions with her family?

Yolanda knew that she was going to have to spend a lot of time in Charlotte and she couldn't always camp out at Nina's place. Her journalist sister would ask too many questions and get to the truth too soon. Besides, Yolanda figured the less anyone else knew about her situation, the more she could keep everyone safe. How could anything go wrong?

Chapter 4

Months Later

Yolanda was frantic because her worst nightmare had just come true. Nina was in the hospital because Yolanda's killer stalkers had finally found her in Charlotte. She'd hoped hiding out in North Carolina would've put her family in the clear. But that wasn't true. Nina may have been known to drive like a bat out of hell, but she'd never had issues before. What if she had told her father what was going on? Then Nina wouldn't be in the hospital.

How was she going to face her family knowing that she was the reason Nina was fighting for her life? Looking at the worried looks on the faces of her father and sisters, Yolanda prayed for the floor to open up and swallow her.

"Yolanda, are you all right?" Alexandria asked as she wrapped her arms around her sister's shoulders.

She shook her head and leaned on Alex.

"Don't worry about Nina. She's strong and we're not going to lose her."

Yolanda wanted to believe her sister, but the last time

she was in a hospital, she went home without her mother. Facing Alex, she was about to tell her that she was responsible for Nina's accident. But before she could say anything, one of the nurses walked over to the family to update them on Nina's condition. The words went over her head and she felt as if her knees were going weak.

A supportive arm from Clinton Jefferson, now Nina's fiancé, kept her from hitting the floor. "This was all my fault," he said again. Yolanda had been numb when he'd said it before because she knew her tormenters had found her family and they were all in danger.

"What do you mean?"

Clinton told her about the argument he and Nina had before her accident. Now, her fear turned to anger. It must have been written on her face as her father, Sheldon Richardson, crossed over to the duo before they could further their conversation.

"We need to pray for Nina, so whatever is happening here isn't important," he chided.

Looking into her father's eyes, she wanted to tell him that she was in trouble and had put the family in danger. But was now the time? Two hours after the last update on Nina's condition, the sisters huddled in the corner, hugging each other. Yolanda felt needles of guilt stabbing her in the heart. Running hadn't helped and her family was still in danger.

Charles Morris woke up in a cold sweat. The nightmares had returned. Her pleas for help and him being too far away to save her. Hillary's name burned on his lips. His greatest failure, his deepest love. The owner of Morris

Protection Agency broke every rule of engagement when he fell in love with a client. Vulnerable. He'd left her vulnerable.

Today wasn't the day to think about past mistakes. Business was booming again at his security company since he had ended his exile. Charles, known to many as Chuck Morris, was a sought-after personal bodyguard. The former marine was a hand-to-hand combat machine. After his medical discharge from the corps, he started the agency to help out in his hometown of Charleston, South Carolina.

He'd be picking that mantle up again—instead of just securing contracts for the business. Shortly after Hillary's murder three years ago, he'd lost confidence in doing the work. For a year he'd traveled and tried to dull his memories with expensive whiskey and yoga. It took seeing a woman in Singapore who looked like Hillary from a distance to realize that he needed to get his life back in order. Besides, he needed to do everything in his power to make sure Maynor Kingsley, Hillary's ex, paid for what he'd done. He'd testified at the trial and watched as the sorry bastard was sentenced to twenty years for killing Hillary.

Sitting up in the bed, he ran his hand across his face. *Time to go to work,* he told himself as he headed to the bathroom. Stepping in the shower, he turned the water on full blast and let it beat down on his muscles. He had to let his memories of Hillary go, especially today. While he'd learned a lesson from loving her, he could no longer be haunted by her. As the water beat against his muscles, Charles thought about reclaiming his life and how he was never going to allow his feelings to ever get in his way again.

It was time to take his life back and he was happy to do it.

Chapter 5

Weeks after Nina was released from the hospital, Yolanda was convinced that she'd overreacted about those killers finding her. Nina's car accident was just that, an accident. Perhaps they'd forgotten all about that night in the alley and she was going to be fine. Yolanda still wanted a fresh start just in case. So, that had been one of the reasons why she'd signed a lease in Charlotte for her boutique. Out of sight, out of mind.

Nina and Clinton had been spending most of their time in the family wing of the Richardson Bed and Breakfast while Nina was rehabbing from the accident. The fact that Clinton stood by her said a lot about him and Yolanda couldn't wait to welcome him into the family.

Maybe seeing her sister safe had lulled her into a false sense of security. And ignoring the investigation into Bobby G. made her feel as if everything that had happened outside of her shop had been just a dream. Charlotte meant a fresh start and no need to worry about threats and being tracked down by the devil and the bulldog.

Yolanda walked up to her new shop space and smiled. She was going to name it Lux and Posh. Her demographic was going to be the wives of the professional ball players in Charlotte. Nina may have had her issues with a certain quarterback, but Yolanda wanted him to come to her shop just one time and post it on social media.

A post like that would put her at the top of the food chain and she'd have everything she would need to stay away from Richmond. Looking down, she saw a long box at the entrance. Picking up packages made her nervous. She figured the delivery service had left the package for the previous tenant.

All she wanted was to start over and be at peace with her life. Holding the box at her side, Yolanda unlocked the door and looked around her space. She was going to bring the flair from her Richmond store into the heart of Charlotte. Especially the disco ball. She wanted to look different from the other shops in the center. While they were following a trend, Yolanda was going to set them.

After all, she had a blank slate and she could do what she wanted to do. Yolanda set the box on the counter, then stood in the center of the showroom. She looked down at the box and sighed. The label was faded and she couldn't tell when it had been delivered or where it came from. Maybe it was her decorations or something that she needed for the walls. Yolanda opened the box and held her breath. Then she smiled when she saw the long-stemmed roses were from her Realtor.

Roses were no longer her favorite flower. Whenever she saw the buds, she immediately thought of the threat she'd gotten wrapped in a beautiful bouquet. The threat that sent her running from Virginia to North Carolina.

She closed her eyes and said a silent prayer for peace of mind and safety. She hadn't put her house in Richmond on the market yet, but she did have a moving company pack her things and put them in storage.

She'd been in the shop for about an hour when the bell chimed. A FedEx delivery driver walked in with three boxes and an envelope. She set the boxes, which contained her decorations, on the counter then opened the envelope. There was nothing on the paper inside. Yolanda shrugged it off. She had work to do so that she could open her shop and start her life over.

After she'd set up her showroom, Yolanda logged on to her computer and started ordering the season's fashion for the shop.

Yolanda had been so engrossed in her work that she hadn't noticed someone standing at the door. The knocking startled her and Yolanda tumbled from the edge of her seat. "What the hell," she muttered as she locked eyes with the tall police officer waving at her.

She crossed over to the door and wondered how smart it would be to open the door. Just because he was dressed like a cop didn't mean he was one. Yolanda opened the door a slight bit.

"Is there a problem, officer?"

"No. Sorry if I startled you. I'm one of the patrolmen for this district and I wanted to introduce myself and see if you needed an escort to your car this evening."

She shook her head. "Thank you, officer . . . I didn't catch your name."

"Oh, I'm so used to everyone knowing me around here. Kenny Treadwell."

Yolanda dropped her guard a little as she drank in the

officer's uniform, badge, and muscular frame. *Well, it can't hurt to be friends with the police.* "I'm Yolanda Richardson and this is going to be my shop."

"Are you new to Charlotte?"

She nodded. "My sister raves about how great this place is and I decided to give the Queen City a shot myself."

"Had I known you were brand new here, I would've gotten some salted caramel brownies from Charlotte's favorite bakery."

"I tell you what, Officer Treadwell," she said as she looked down at his left hand and noticed his glittering wedding band. "Just come to my grand opening with your spouse and we'll be friends forever."

"I can do that. And I can still bring you the brownies. It's always good to know the sweet side of my city."

"Well, thank you." She extended her well-manicured hand to the officer. He shook her hand, then told her that the area where she'd set up was generally safe, but the weekends could get a little rowdy because of the nearby clubs and bars.

Yolanda thanked him for the heads-up and told him good night. A few moments after the officer left, Yolanda decided to pack up and head to Nina's place. She'd been staying there since she left Richmond, and so far, she'd been able to keep the details about her sudden move to North Carolina a secret for now, but how much longer would she have to live in fear? Yolanda hated to admit how much she missed Richmond. She had a good thing with her shop in that city. But there were just too many bad memories there and she didn't want those killers coming back hoping to find her.

She just hated putting Kelly out of work. But the Richmond native had already said she had no desire to move to Charlotte. What other choice did she have?

You could go to the police and end this drama, her voice of reason whispered. Yolanda sighed and wished she had the courage to do that. But every time she thought about going to the police, she saw that man's face as he pulled the trigger. In her nightmares, she was the one dead in the parking lot, not Bobby G.

Yolanda had hoped the move to Charlotte would've stopped the nightmares. She'd put distance between her and the killers. And most importantly, she'd kept her mouth shut. That should've been enough for them to leave her alone, right?

Shaking her head, Yolanda decided to focus on her future and try not to be afraid of her past.

Since her inventory wouldn't be in until the beginning of the week, Yolanda decided that she was going to head to Charleston and check on her sister, after she went home and packed a bag and took a shower. Yolanda didn't want to be alone tonight and she still had a nagging feeling that Nina's accident had been her fault. The thought of putting her family in danger was almost too much to bear.

That had been one of the main reasons why she'd been spending so much time with Nina and Clinton. Yolanda tried to clear her mind of the carnage she'd seen in the alley. Then she'd be hit with guilt of not reporting the crime. There was a family missing their son, brother, and loved one. A community mourned for him and his killer was running free and terrorizing her. She couldn't bring herself to do the right thing and risk putting her family in danger.

Out of curiosity, Yolanda pulled out her smartphone and entered Bobby G.'s name in the search bar. Link after link about the dead-end investigation populated on her phone. Could she breathe now?

Would the guilt ever go away? *Daddy would be so ashamed of you.* Yolanda paced back and forth, then tucked her phone in her pocket. She was going to Charleston and try to ignore the dull throbbing in her chest.

Charles had been in the gym for two hours. It wasn't because he was that much of a workout junkie; he was on a case. The owner of Bright Fitness was sure that someone was selling steroids out of her workout center.

Charles had spotted the suspect as he worked his deltoids. After setting the weights at his feet, he grabbed his phone and called his guy outside.

"Chuck. What's up?"

"Left exit. Neon shorts and a tall blond guy. Get the pictures and leave."

"Got it, boss."

Charles ended the call then headed for his car. He spotted Nate in the parking lot looking like a tourist soaking in the Charleston skyline. Charles unlocked his car and sat behind the wheel. The man who was selling the drugs looked familiar to him. Then it clicked like a lock: that was Brandon Ellis, the mayor's son. Brandon stayed in the media for all of the wrong reasons. Charles liked the mayor, but he wasn't going to ignore this or let his client down. Bright Fitness was a new facility and Shelby Miller deserved to run his place without the reputation of a 'roid shop. Besides, Pilar Bright, the owner of the gym, wanted to take the chain national and this would ruin her chances if news of drug sales got out to investors.

Once Nate put his camera away and got into his car to leave, Charles called 911. It was a good thing that Brandon was a talker and arrogant enough to carry his drugs in the trunk of his car as if it were a showroom.

Charles called his client and reported what he had discovered and that the police were on the way.

"Chuck," Pilar Bright said with a relieved sigh. "I can't tell you how much I appreciate this."

"The last thing you want is for the wrong element to ruin your business before it even gets off the ground."

"Right. Do you still provide security for businesses?"

"Nah. But I have some recommendations I can send you with my invoice."

"Oh, yes. I appreciate that. If they have your seal of approval, I know they must be awesome."

"I'd like to think so. I have another call coming in, we'll talk soon."

"I certainly hope so," she said, her voice taking a seductive lilt.

Charles ended the call without a response or taking another call. Pilar had been making overtures at him since he'd taken her case. It started with their first meeting, where she was wearing a sports bra and a pair of barely there shorts. Then there were her double entendres every time they spoke. But Charles had learned his lesson; he'd never get involved with another client—even if she was a former MMA fighter.

Heading back to his office, Charles decided that he

needed a vacation—away from the beach. That was the only thing about living in Charleston: The beach got old quick. A nice mountain getaway would give him some solitude and let him relax.

Then he could refocus what he wanted his security company to be now. Did he still want to work in personal security or run more undercover stings like the one he'd just wrapped up? Could he trust himself to never make the mistake he made with Hillary again?

Shaking his head, Charles turned his attention to his ringing phone. He recognized the number as the Richardson Bed and Breakfast's. Charles had done security with the historic bed-and-breakfast in the past. Like most people in Charleston, he had a deep admiration for Sheldon Richardson, the owner of the picturesque bed-and-breakfast.

"This is Charles," he said.

"Chuck," Sheldon said. "I need to talk to you about a security assignment."

"Is there a problem at your B&B?"

"No, there's a more personal problem I need your assistance with. Can we meet later today?"

Charles looked down at the calendar on his Apple watch. "Yes, my calendar is clear."

"I don't mean to rush you, but do you think you can be here in an hour?" Sheldon asked.

"Yes, sir." Charles was about twenty minutes from the bed-and-breakfast. "It may be sooner than that. I'm not too far away."

"Thanks, Chuck. This is really important. My daughter is in trouble."

After hanging up the phone, Charles started toward

the bed-and-breakfast. His mind raced with questions. Which one of his daughters was having issues? Was it the sportswriter? What about the executive at Sheldon's company? Then there were the other daughters whom Sheldon said lived in Virginia. He'd just save the questions for when the two men would meet. Traffic was light and he made it to the bed-and-breakfast without any delays.

Charles walked in and looked around the charming lobby. He'd always thought this place felt like a set from one of those cheesy Christmas movies that he'd done security on the set of years ago. The muted gold and yellow colors whispered that Thanksgiving was coming. Charles loved the cornucopia on the front desk with apples and small pumpkins surrounding it.

There was a soul to this place that made the Richardson Bed and Breakfast one of the most visited places in Charleston. Crossing over to the front desk, he smiled at the clerk before telling her that he was there to see Sheldon.

"And here I thought you were here to sweep me off my feet," she said with a throaty laugh as she picked up the phone. "What's your name, handsome?"

"Charles Morris."

She nodded, then said his name into the phone. "I'll send him right up." She turned toward the elevators. "He's waiting for you."

Charles strode to the elevators, ignoring the lustful looks of some of the women in the lobby. He was used to it. He'd been told that he was a cool drink of water, the kind of man women went crazy for. He thought he was average, but standing at six three and muscular because of his years in service and five a.m. workouts, he had a solid frame that some people said made him look like he should be in a superhero movie.

Charles wasn't a conceited man, so he always took the compliments with a silent smile.

After all, she'd said the same things to him and it didn't have the same energy coming from someone else. Part of him wondered if he'd ever get over Hillary and let another woman get close to him again.

As he rode the elevator to Sheldon's office, Charles put on his game face. He was ready to find out how he could help this legend.

Yolanda glared at her little sister and promised herself that she wouldn't tell Nina anything ever again. But when she'd gotten a phone call from a robotic-sounding voice that had said she was a walking dead woman and Nina had been in the room, she had no choice but to tell her what had been going on in Richmond.

Now they were standing in Sheldon's office and Yolanda felt as if she was about to get a spanking like the time when she'd broken a five hundred–dollar crystal vase and tried to lie about it.

Sheldon Richardson sat behind his desk and shook his head. "Why did you think you could keep this from me after everything we've been through?"

"It's not that big of a deal," Yolanda exclaimed. "I'm not even in . . ."

Sheldon held up his massive hand. "Someone wants you dead. It is a big deal and I can't believe you tried to keep this from me."

"That's why I didn't want to say anything. We have enough drama going on right now."

Nina rolled her eyes. "Maybe you will take this seriously now. I'm going to find Clinton," she snapped as she rose to her feet. As Nina stormed out of the office, a man walked in. Yolanda's breath caught in her chest. Who was this Adonis with green eyes?

"Chuck," Sheldon said as he crossed over to the man Yolanda couldn't tear her eyes from.

She looked at him as he shook hands with her father. This man was fine. He had a quiet quality that made her wonder what he was hiding. He looked like the kind of man who would make you scream in pleasure and pain. But why was he in this office? Clearly he wasn't . . .

"Thank you for coming so quickly," Sheldon said.

"No problem. I want to see what I can do to help."

Sheldon turned to Yolanda, who quickly averted her eyes from Chuck. "This is my daughter Yolanda. She's been getting death threats."

Chuck gave her a slow look that should've made her blush. Instead, Yolanda flashed a flirty smile.

"My father is overreacting," she said.

"If you're getting death threats, there's no such thing as an overreaction." His voice was filled with the bass of a quiet storm DJ and the concern of a knight in shining armor. Yolanda wanted to say something, but his eyes were hypnotizing and she found herself lost in his spell.

"Chuck, I know this is asking a lot, but I want you to protect her, maybe even help her report what she knows so the people trying to kill her will stop this madness."

"Wait," Yolanda said, rising to her feet. If she thought Chuck towered over her while she was seated, standing up, she realized what it felt like to be in a redwood forest. And those arms on that man looked like the strongest branches of those historic trees. Or maybe he was mythical, an Egyptian god come to life.

No matter what he was, she didn't need his protection. She'd just keep a low profile, get away from her family, and never return to Richmond again. If she pretended that she didn't see or hear anything, maybe Danny and his killers would leave her alone. She wasn't going to testify or even talk to a Richmond police officer. As far as she was concerned, she knew nothing.

"I don't want anything to do with this case, and I'm sure whoever is sending these little love notes will stop once they see I'm not a threat and I have no plans to go to the police."

Chuck and Sheldon shot her a cold look. "Do you think this is some sort of joke?" Sheldon boomed.

Yolanda took a step back. This was why she didn't want Nina to say a word to their father about the threats or what she saw. Sheldon was overprotective and he worried about his daughters too much, in Yolanda's mind. She didn't want to give him another reason to worry or be on the other end of his uber concern. When Sheldon saw a problem for one of his daughters, he would stop at nothing to fix it.

Since Nina made things sound so dire, which they were, Sheldon had gone overboard with this bodyguard, Yolanda decided. Her plan was to get away from her family. That way the bed-and-breakfast wouldn't be in the line of fire. Since she'd closed her shop in Richmond, Yolanda had no intentions of going back there. How long was it going to take for Danny to lose interest in her once he saw that she wasn't a threat?

Although she tried to act tough, Yolanda felt guilty that she wasn't helping another family get justice for their dead loved one. She knew that if it had been one of her sisters or her father she'd hope the community would rally together and find the killer. She'd be the first one to go on the news and beg for help.

Was someone from Bobby G.'s family making those same pleas? Yolanda had been ignoring the news of what was going on with the case because she didn't want to get involved. Knowing that people were hurting, she'd do the right thing. But how much would she have to risk to do that?

And how did a bodyguard even figure into her life? She looked up at Chuck. "You do know that I'm not based out of Charleston, right?"

"I was planning to get all the details from you, Ms. Richardson. Your father is concerned about your safety and my job is to keep you safe—it doesn't matter if it's in Charleston or New Zealand."

Sheldon gave him a nod of approval, and Yolanda wondered what kind of relationship he had with this man. She'd never seen Chuck before and she would've remembered a man who looked like that. What had Chuck done to earn her father's trust like this?

"Ms. Richardson, do you think we can talk outside?" Chuck asked. His voice was as seductive as a chart-topping R&B singer and she would've said yes to anything he asked her. But she needed to get him to understand that she didn't need his help.

Chapter 6

Charles watched Yolanda as she walked toward the elevator. She was the definition of a firecracker. A fine one, but she was dangerous. The kind of woman who would be a distraction, but he'd already made a promise to Sheldon.

He should've asked a few more questions because this was the kind of case that he'd promised himself he wouldn't take again. It seemed as if she didn't want help, despite how much her father wanted to protect her.

Charles knew he wasn't going to be able to make her understand how important it was to protect herself from the killers if she didn't put something on the line, like reporting what she'd seen to the police. Had she done that and was this why she'd been getting the death threats?

"Chuck, right?" she said as the doors to the elevator opened and they stepped on.

"Charles, actually, but most people call me Chuck."

"Mind if I ask why?"

He chuckled as he locked eyes with Yolanda. She had beautiful eyes. Expressive and intense. The gold specks in her brown eyes sparkled as she spoke and made her face glow like the sun. Was it possible for a woman in a package that small to be a goddess? *Calm down*, he thought. *This is not why you're here.*

"My last name is Morris."

She brought her hand to her mouth, covering those full lips that he'd been trying to ignore. "Chuck Morris," Yolanda said after she stopped laughing.

"Heard it all before," he said. "But Chuck Norris and I have one thing in common: We both kick ass."

"It's a good thing that I don't need you to do that for me," she said.

"Do you think that death threats end because you ignore them?" Chuck rocked back on his heels and folded his arms across his chest.

"Why wouldn't they?"

"Tell me what's going on, the truth that you probably didn't tell your father."

Yolanda sucked her teeth. "Listen," she began. "I was in the wrong place at the wrong time. But I never told anyone, meaning the police, what I saw."

"It doesn't matter. Yolanda, I've seen people killed for less. Do you want to live?"

"What kind of question is that? Who wants to die?" She pursed her lips.

"Clearly you do, since you don't want to hear what I have to say."

"Chuck, I just want to keep my family safe and the only thing I need to do is keep everything separate from the family."

He sucked his teeth and shook his head. "That's not enough."

"Then what do I need to do?" she asked.

Chuck looked at her and shook his head again. This woman was low-key frustrating. "The question is, are you going to do it?"

"What do you mean?"

"I mean that my job is to keep you alive. But I can't do it if you aren't going to listen to what I have to say."

She furrowed her eyebrows and tilted her head to the side. "What do you want from me?"

"I want to help you."

Yolanda took a deep breath as the elevator came to a stop. "But I don't need your help."

"Do you want to live?"

"Is it really that serious?" Her voice was flippant and Charles wanted to shake her until she understood how much danger she was in.

"Yes, it is. Yolanda, do you think this guy is going to believe you're not a threat because you disappeared?"

"Why wouldn't he?" She shrugged her shoulders and Charles tried not to focus on the naked flesh that flashed before him. Keeping her alive was all that mattered. But how much did it matter to her?

"Yolanda, how much have you told your family?"

She sucked her bottom lip between her teeth and focused her stare on him. Charles was almost mesmerized by her eyes, but he knew that being bewitched by a beautiful woman was the path to disaster. Turning away from her, Charles pretended he was looking for a stalker watching them. When he felt Yolanda's hand on the small of his back, he nearly jumped out of his skin. But the moment he turned around to face her, he looked in control and ready to be in charge.

"I don't want any harm to come to my family."

"Then you are going to have to follow my instructions."

She furrowed her brows and sighed. "First of all, I need you to watch how you talk to me. I'm not good at following direction and I don't take well to being given orders as if I'm a child."

"That's fine. Just do what I say and you don't have to worry about orders. Yolanda, I'm not here to make your life hard. You've done a good job of that yourself. But keeping you safe isn't going to work if you start off fighting with me."

"Oh, this isn't a fight, Chuck." Her words flew out of her mouth like bullets.

"Then what do you call it?"

She folded her arms across her chest, calling attention to her amazing breasts. Charles turned away and released a low sigh. "Listen," Yolanda said. "I just want this to stop."

"What's going on? Why does someone want you dead?"

Yolanda expelled a frustrated breath and tossed her head back. "I saw something that I shouldn't have seen."

"What was it?"

She looked up at him and he noticed fear clouding her face. "It . . . I saw a murder." Her voice was low and shaky.

"And you never reported it to the police?"

She shook her head. "The security cameras outside my shop caught the whole thing and maybe me hiding behind the trash cans." Yolanda slapped her hands against her thighs. "I knew I shouldn't have given that video to the neighborhood watch people."

"That's how the killer knows about you?"

"I guess. There have been notes left at my house and the shop. Now this phone call. Someone called me using a voice distorter and that's why Nina went running to Daddy."

Charles stroked his face, wondering if those people had gotten access to the video from the police or the media. "Did you trust the person you gave the video to?"

She shrugged. "Walton Kennerly was the head of the program, and to hear him tell it, he was all about keeping downtown safe. I was hoping that the video would've gotten the police the leads they needed and my part would've been done."

"What do you know about the men who committed the murder?"

Yolanda ran her fingers through her hair. "I heard a name. Danny."

"Do you know who this Danny person is?"

Yolanda closed her eyes and hugged her waist. "Listen, Chuck," she said. "I'm tired of talking about this. Just give all of this time to blow over."

"It's been how long since the murder? Tell me how that blow over thing is working."

Tears shone in her eyes as she turned away from him. Charles reached out and placed his hand on top of hers. "We're going to get to work," he said. "When we find the people who did this, then you can stop running."

"All right."

Yolanda felt comforted by Chuck's touch and his voice. This was too intense. He needed to go do something else and not remind her how much she'd risked coming to Charleston and putting her family in this psycho's sights. What if Danny and his goon squad decided to use her family to keep her quiet? That's how things happened in the movies, right?

But this wasn't a movie; it was real life. "How about this," Chuck said, breaking the silence. "Where are you based out of?"

"Charlotte. My sister is moving back to Charleston and I'm taking over her home in Charlotte and opening a boutique in down—Uptown."

He looked down at his watch as he removed his hand from hers. "I need to pack a bag, then we can head to Charlotte. I want to check out your security at home and work."

Yolanda lifted her perfectly arched eyebrow and stared at him. "Today?"

He nodded. "Can we just agree that this is serious and you've been dealing with this for months? We don't have time to waste. If you're being watched or followed, then I need to know that and then I can make the necessary moves to keep you safe and get these killers arrested."

Yolanda cleared her throat and looked away from him. "You make it sound so easy and we know it won't be," she said. "Do you understand that I'm trying to just disappear in the shadows and pretend . . ."

"That's not going to work, Yolanda. These people, whoever they are, will not let you live when one word from you could put them in prison for life." Chuck placed his hand on her shoulder. "We can meet here around six and head across the border."

"All right, but my sister's getting married soon. I don't want to be too far away. . . ."

"I got you. Wait for me inside," he said, then turned and left the room.

* * *

Yolanda closed her eyes and expelled a deep sigh. She had questions about how this protection plan was going to work. Would he be living with her? Going to work with her?

How in the hell was she going to worry about safety when she'd be trying her best to keep her knees together?

"Are you speaking to me yet?" Nina asked, breaking into Yolanda's lustful thoughts.

"Nope. Why did you . . ." Yolanda shook her head. "I knew you were going to run off at the mouth; this is all on me."

"Did you think I was going to sit back and watch . . . Yolanda, I don't care if you're mad. I just want you to be alive so I can take all your shit for talking too much."

Though she was mad, Yolanda drew her sister into her arms and hugged her tightly. "You do talk too damned much. Now, I have a whole new set of problems."

"What's that?"

"Keeping my hands to myself when Chuck and I go to Charlotte."

Nina rolled her eyes. "Can we focus on the fact that someone is sending you death threats?"

"That's why I left Richmond. I'm sure this will all die down once these people realize that I'm not a threat. And if anything, you've called more attention to me and anyone who was watching me."

"Because you're a punk and won't do the right thing?" Nina hitched her right eyebrow up and glared at her sister.

Yolanda rolled her eyes. But Nina was right. She was afraid to do the right thing and was doing the one thing she and her sisters said they'd never do: She was running.

But this was different, right? It wasn't because of heartbreak or a job. She was running for her life. "Why don't you do me a favor and put those reporter skills of yours to use," Yolanda said.

"What are you talking about?"

Yolanda offered her sister a sly smile. "Find out who Chuck Morris is."

"Wait." Nina threw her hand up. "His name is Chuck Morris?" Nina burst into laughter. "I really need a back-story."

"Then get busy, sweetheart."

Nina glared at her sister. "Too soon, jerk."

Yolanda winked at her little sister, who was now anti-sweetheart after the viral exchange with a quarterback who called her sweetheart in a press conference. Because she'd gotten suspended from covering the team after the incident, Nina returned to Charleston and met Clinton Jefferson, the man who'd stolen her heart.

Yolanda watched their love grow and was excited about their upcoming wedding that Christmas, which was one of the reasons why she was trying not to allow the people who were threatening her to cause any more problems. Was she being naïve about how much danger she was in? What if someone tried to get her at Nina's wedding? It was time to start taking things a lot more seriously if she wanted make good on her promise to keep her family safe. But until Nina's wedding was over, she wasn't going to the police with any information.

While she waited for Chuck's return and Nina had gone off to hang out with Clinton, Yolanda meandered around the property and tried to wrap her mind around what was going on in her life. Everything seemed to be in shambles. Though she'd closed her shop in Richmond, Yolanda had loved her life there.

Starting over in Charlotte wasn't going to be easy, and it now seemed as if it wasn't going to be safe either.

Her father was scared and now she had a bodyguard. A fine one that she was going to have to coexist with for the foreseeable future. How in the hell was this going to work?

She walked toward the beach but stopped when she heard someone call her name. Turning around, she locked eyes with Chuck. He was early.

"Why are you out here alone?" he asked as he jogged toward her. She drank in his image, clad in a pair of black joggers and a black sweatshirt. Her eyes traveled down to his thighs and stared. If this was a snack, she wanted to take a bite.

"Yolanda!" Chuck called out.

"Huh?" she said as she met his angry glance.

"I'm sure I asked you to wait for me inside."

Yolanda smirked. "I have this thing with doing what I'm told."

"Do you want to live? Because you're going to have to follow my instructions to a tee."

Yolanda smirked again and shook her head. "Whatever."

Chuck planted himself in front of her and a breeze blew off the ocean and mixed with his clean Irish Spring scent. Yolanda was nearly brought to her knees. "Why are you fighting this when your father hired me to protect you?" he demanded. "There are people who want you dead. They could be anywhere."

"Not fighting anything, Chuck. But I don't like being ordered around."

"Asking you to stay inside so a sniper or some other killer won't get you isn't an order." He placed his hand on her shoulder. "Can we go inside and talk about the rules before we head to Charlotte?"

Yolanda smiled. "You work for me, right? So that means I make the rules."

Chuck didn't crack a smile as he stared into her eyes. "Technically, I work for your father. And it doesn't matter who signs my check—if you want to live, you will do what I say."

She rolled her eyes and shrugged his hand off her shoulder. "Where do you want to have this discussion?"

"Someplace private where we won't be interrupted."

She offered him a wily smile. "I know the perfect place. But if you wanted to be alone with me, you could've just asked."

Charles followed Yolanda as she walked toward the pool at the edge of the bed-and-breakfast building. This woman was dangerous and going to be a huge problem. As much as he'd been trying to downplay the bronzed beauty's sensuality, he was beginning to see that she was a tempting proposition. He needed to get off this assignment sooner rather than later. He respected Sheldon too much to hand this job off to his partner. He'd trusted him to take care of his daughter and he couldn't let him down. And he couldn't get beguiled either.

Yolanda opened the door to what looked like a storage area. Charles hitched his right eyebrow.

"You said you didn't want to be interrupted," she said as she caught his stare.

"Didn't expect this."

"It's the honeymoon suite," she said as she walked in.

Charles looked around the room and thought it was a romantic little spot. Maybe even a great panic room. *Focus,* he told himself. *You're here to build a safety plan.*

Yolanda pointed to the settee behind a coffee table. He sat down and leaned back on the soft seat.

"Do you have the blueprints for your business and your home?"

"Not with me," she said. Her voice was low and slightly seductive. "Why is that even important?"

"One of the first things we have to do is set up a security system in your home and business. I'm sure you're on social media, right?"

She nodded, then ran her tongue across her bottom lip. Charles looked away and tried to ignore the tightening in his pants.

"I need social media for my business."

"You're going to have to adjust your settings."

"What do you mean?"

"No addresses, no geotags, don't go live and . . ."

"Hold up," she said as she waved her hand. "How am I supposed to run my business?"

"You're creative, I'm sure you will figure out how to market your business in another way."

"Yeah, I'm marketing my business on social media." She pouted and folded her arms across her chest.

"And you're giving the people looking to kill you direct access to you at all times."

"And my customers. You know most people shop because of ads they see online and especially on social media?"

"Yolanda, you can't spend money if you're dead."

"You think I'm that shallow and I'm doing this for money? How dare you. I'm not trying to simply keep a business open. This is my life and I want some normalcy," she snapped, then turned her back to him.

"Yolanda, that's not what I meant, I just . . ."

Her mouth dropped open and Charles waited for a smart comment to follow. Instead, he saw fear flicker in her expressive eyes. That made him believe everything had been an act she'd been keeping up too long. A single tear dropped from her eye and she wiped it away quickly.

"Tell me what's going on, Yolanda."

She looked up at him, her face contorted with fear and defiance. Underneath all of her sarcastic quips, she was afraid. He could almost see her heart racing.

"I just want this to end. I left because I . . ." Her voice trailed off as she began to sob.

Charles stroked her hair and stopped himself from brushing a kiss across her forehead. "I'm going to protect you. But you have to trust me, Yolanda."

She looked up at him and blinked. "Chuck, I'm scared. I'm so scared."

Chapter 7

Richmond, Virginia

Danny stalked across the floor in his penthouse suite and glared at his two associates. Two men who should have done the work he'd hired them to do.

"Why is this bitch still breathing?" he demanded.

"Boss, she hasn't gone to the police and . . ."

Danny pointed his bony finger at the stout man. "Dead bitches can't talk. She saw everything and I'm not going to jail for taking out the trash."

The man looked away from his boss. "There was a better way to handle Bobby G. Too many people are looking into who got him."

"And I'm not going down for this bullshit. That fashion bitch got to go. Especially since your dumb ass called my name that night." Danny pushed the man to the floor. "You find her and remind her what happens to snitches."

The man nodded. "I don't think she's in Richmond anymore. That shop looks closed."

Danny shrugged. "Make sure you're right because you'll join Bobby G. if she ain't dealt with."

The man nodded then dashed out of the room. Alone, Danny pulled out his cell phone, a burner that was untraceable, and called his heavy hitter.

"Chase."

"It's Danny. You need to help me tie up these loose ends."

"What's going on?"

"There's a bitch on the run and she needs to be found and taken out."

"So, it's true then?"

"What?"

"You killed Bobby G. Heard the cops got a sketchy video of the shooting outside of that shop."

"That's why she has to go. Check your phone. You got seven days to make it happen."

Chase laughed. "I'll get it done in three days. You know my fee and how to pay me."

"I got you. But make it look like an accident or something."

"Extra work costs extra."

"Don't worry about the money." Danny ended the call and walked over to his desk, where his computer was set up. He tapped a couple of keys and transferred a hundred thousand dollars from his offshore account to Chase. The landline phone on his desk rang. Danny smiled when he looked at the caller ID.

"Branch Investments, Danny speaking."

To the greater Richmond community, Daniel "Danny" Branch was an investment banker from New York with a golden touch. He'd come to the city and made a lot of money for people. He had helped the University of

Richmond build its multimillion-dollar endowment. He worked with churches in the area to help fill their coffers through risk-free investments that paid them every month.

He sat on the boards of several charter schools in the area and often lobbied for those schools in Washington. But at his core, Danny was a loan shark—like the family he'd left behind in New York. He laundered drug money, hiding the dirty money as good returns on his investments.

Then there were his illegal gambling games. Especially high-stakes poker. That's where Bobby G. messed up. He'd gotten in too deep in Danny's games and couldn't pay off the debt. Danny had actually arranged for Bobby G. to lose because he'd wanted what he'd thought was a profitable business. Turned out that Bobby G. was on the verge of losing everything.

Since he'd been of no more use to Danny, Bobby G. was trash to be taken out. Just like anyone who became a liability. It was just like getting rid of Simone, his ex-wife. Maybe getting rid of her had been so easy that Danny had felt untouchable. She'd been gone for a year, and because he had accused her of stealing from his company, no one had bothered to look for her.

Killing Bobby G. was supposed to be simple, but that nosey bitch had to see and hear everything. Danny worked too hard to carve out his place in Richmond society to allow someone's loose tongue to derail all of that. There was a lot of money to be made in Richmond and he was going to make it. Without worrying about the cops or that woman opening her mouth. If she had to die, so be it.

It was after ten p.m. when Chuck and Yolanda arrived in Charlotte. She felt exposed after her breakdown at the bed-and-breakfast. He probably thought she was some emotional wreck. And now she was never going to be able to prove that she didn't need him and he should take his fine ass back to Charleston. She'd flipped the radio station every five minutes, looking for something to do with her hands while he drove. Chuck only stopped her once when she'd found a public radio station.

"So, you're a brutal nerd?" she'd quipped as they listened to a story about reforming schools in rural America.

"I like to be informed without politics brought into the middle of it."

"This woman's voice is making me want to go to sleep."

"Then please change the station for the seven hundredth time," he quipped back.

"I never realized how boring this ride is when you're not driving." She'd tilted her head to the side and watched him as he drove. Strong jawline. He looked as if he was sculpted from a golden stone. He was the kind of driver who kept his eyes on the road. And he even put on a pair of glasses. She had wondered if they were the Google glasses that allowed you to see the GPS so he wouldn't have to look at his phone. Yolanda didn't understand why she'd given this man the backstory of Bruce Wayne from the comics.

"Did you always want to save people?" she'd asked as a beat passed.

"Something like that. Hey, you want to stop and get a snack?"

Another thing she'd noticed: Chuck didn't like to talk about himself. And she couldn't help but wonder why. Maybe he really was a superhero. Or some woman's husband. "Nah, I'm good."

When Chuck pulled into the parking garage across from the town house, Yolanda stretched her hands over her head. "Finally. You drive like an old man." Yolanda reached for the door handle and Chuck locked them.

"Let me look around first. How far is the walk to Nina's town house?"

"It's across the street."

"And do you park in the same spot every day?"

"We have assigned spots."

Chuck nodded. "What floor do you park on?"

"The third floor. What's with all the questions, I want to get inside and use the little girls' room."

"I get that, but there are security issues we need to go over before we just walk over to your place. There could be places for a sniper to hide. You'd be shot before you stuck your key in the door."

"Do you have to scare me, knowing I have to pee?"

"The last thing I'm trying to do is scare you, but you need to be more aware of your surroundings."

Yolanda sighed. "What are we going to see in the dark?"

"A lot more than you think."

Stroking her forehead, Yolanda expelled a frustrated sigh. "Fine, let's just get this over with."

Chuck shook his head. "I'd like to think that you're going to take this seriously."

"*Charles*, we just drove three hours. I'd like to think about fixing a nice cup of tea and going to sleep. You're my bodyguard, right? Can't you guard this body tonight and show me all the security stuff tomorrow?"

"You've got me confused with the Secret Service."

"Can we get out of the car now?"

As if he realized that she wasn't going to cooperate tonight, Chuck nodded and unlocked the doors. Despite saying he wasn't the Secret Service, Chuck walked in front of Yolanda as they crossed the street to her town house. It was hard for her to think of it as hers sometimes. But knowing that she might be under a killer's watch, she was glad Nina was safe in Charleston.

When they walked out of the parking garage, Yolanda placed her hand on the small of his back. Even though he said he wasn't the Secret Service, he walked as if he were—shielding her from invisible snipers. He was hot. His body radiated heat that flowed through her system. He was electric. Yolanda closed her eyes for a second and pretended this wasn't a bodyguard, but a booty call.

Even though she and her sister Alex fought like cats and dogs, they had similar ideas when it came to matters of the heart.

Love was a myth. They wouldn't find the fairy tale their parents had. And Yolanda didn't believe in love because it was cruel. As much as her father loved her mother, he still lost her to death. His heart was broken and he had four little girls to raise.

There was no way she could allow herself to be hurt like that. Give everything to someone and still have to deal with the universe taking him away. She'd have fun with a guy until he wanted something more than she could give. At least she wasn't like her oldest sister and burying herself in work. Yolanda had been having fun with fashion, being the toast of the town—on the guest list at all the major Richmond parties. Styling some reality TV stars in New York and raking up the sales and likes on her social media platforms. She'd remembered months after her styling of a certain housewife went viral, she'd briefly met Bobby G.

His urban apparel shop had been popular in the city. He sold the outfits that people saw in hip-hop videos and throwback jerseys that rappers and celebrities coveted.

Then that night happened. She needed that shot of her window display for Instagram but instead, witnessed his murder and heard the shot that vibrated through Richmond. Bobby G. had once asked her if he could partner with her boutique, but she wasn't looking for anyone else to help her.

This past year, she'd been able to pay her father back for his investment in her company and she'd vowed that she'd be her own woman from now on. Sure, Bobby had been a Richmond legend, but Yolanda was on her way to creating her own legacy. Until she saw his death. Now, she was starting over again. Why had her business been chosen that night?

"Yolanda, are you going to unlock the door?" Chuck asked, breaking into her thoughts.

"Sorry, I was just in another space. This is weird."

He nodded. "I get it. But think of me as your shadow."

She tilted her head to the side as she unlocked the door. "I thought shadows followed you."

"Tonight was different," Chuck replied. He crossed in front of Yolanda and walked into the town house. She and Nina were both afraid of the dark, so the town house was outfitted with motion detection lighting. Chuck nodded in approval.

"Was your sister having issues with someone?" he asked when they walked into the living room and all of the lights came on.

"The monster under her bed. Nina was always afraid of the dark."

"And you?"

"What?"

Chuck smirked. "Are you afraid of the dark?"

She shook her head then smiled. "Nope." She winked at him then yawned. "There was a time when I wasn't afraid of anything."

Chuck returned her smile and Yolanda's heart quickened. There was something about him that made her think about anything but death and snipers ready to take her out. She wanted him to be a guy who was spending the night for pleasure. A fine man who'd hold her in the moonlight and whisper naughty things in her ear.

Shivering at the thought of his big hands touching her between her thighs, Yolanda remembered her manners. "Would you like something to drink?"

"Water is fine."

She started toward the kitchen and was surprised when he followed her. "I don't think the boogeyman is hiding in the fridge," Yolanda said.

"I'm just trying to get a tour of the place for security purposes." Why did this man's voice send ripples down her spine?

"Um-huh." She flipped the light switch on and crossed over to the stainless steel refrigerator. Yolanda grabbed a bottle of water for Chuck and retrieved a half-empty bottle of Chardonnay for herself. "Would you like a glass?"

He shook his head. "I need to stay focused. You drink every night?"

"Not really. I'm not an alcoholic," she said. But Yolanda knew she needed this wine to keep her mind off the sexy man standing on the other side of the kitchen island.

"How many bedrooms are in here?"

"Um, three. The master bedroom upstairs, my room is downstairs, and there's a room upstairs that I've been using as a storage room. The master bedroom is my studio." She set the wine bottle on the counter without pouring a glass. "Being that you need someplace to sleep, I should probably make room for you."

"You don't have to do that tonight. I'm going to sleep on the sofa in the living room and get used to the sounds of the house."

You're going to be right outside my door. Damn. "Oh, okay. Well, um, do you want something to eat?"

"Why are you acting so nervous?" His smile lit up his green eyes. Eyes she could get lost in because they reminded her of the Emerald Coast in Destin, Florida. She loved Destin.

This man is not Destin. Pull yourself together.

"All of this is new to me and I'm still trying to get a read on you, Chuck."

"What do you want to know?"

Chapter 8

Charles knew he'd opened a door he wasn't sure he wanted to walk through when he saw the wide smile on her face.

"Why do you want to save people?" she asked as she poured herself a glass of wine.

"Why not?"

"Seems dangerous."

"So is living."

"Not a real answer."

"I thought your sister was the journalist?"

Yolanda shrugged before taking a long sip of her wine. "I'm a jack-of-all-trades."

Charles raised his right eyebrow but kept silent for a beat. "You like to pretend you're tougher than you really are, don't you?"

Yolanda pushed her wineglass toward the center of the counter. "We're talking about you, not me. Excuse me if I want to get to know my new roommate."

"I'm not your roommate. I'm here to provide security and keep you alive."

She rolled her eyes and picked up her wineglass. "As you keep reminding me. If they ever do another *Terminator* movie, then you definitely need to audition. 'Come with me if you want to live.' "

"And you don't need to get to know me. But I need to know more about you, Yolanda Richardson."

She rubbed her hand across her face. "And why is that?"

"Your father hired me to keep you safe. That's the only reason I'm here."

She snickered. "That wasn't my follow-up question. I want to know why you think I don't need to get to know you."

"Because you don't. This is a job and I'd love for you to take this seriously."

"Clearly I know that, but you sitting there judging me while you sip your water isn't going to help you save me, hero," Yolanda said then snorted.

"You've got me all wrong, Yolanda. I'm not judging you, I'm trying to understand you."

She rolled her eyes and drained the rest of the wine in her glass. "I told you everything you need to know."

He shrugged and sipped his water before saying, "You told me what you think I wanted to know. When you saw that man get killed, why didn't you call the police? Days later, what made you so fearful?"

Yolanda drummed her finger against the rim of her empty wineglass. "What part of 'I was scared' don't you understand? My life was super simple. Even when I was in Atlanta, I never saw violence up close and personal. My dad sheltered us from a lot."

"I'm sure he would've wanted you to . . ."

She threw her hand up and shook her head. "Don't tell me that I should've honored my father's legacy and run to the police department to report what I saw. You didn't see the coldness of that man who shot Bobby G."

"You knew the man who was killed?"

Yolanda shook her head and crossed over to the refrigerator to grab another bottle of wine. "Saw who he was on a news report. He was one of those people everyone in Richmond knew." She filled her glass. "And we had one brief meeting about him wanting to come on as an investor. But I didn't want his money and I didn't want to partner with his shop. I'm finally standing on my own and then this happens."

Charles made mental notes of what she said about this Bobby G. person. Maybe there was more to the story. Maybe she and this Bobby G. person had a personal relationship and . . . getting ahead of himself. *This isn't about her personal life. This isn't Hillary.*

"How do the killers know you were the one who saw them that night?"

"Clue number one, the death threats. Or maybe the video from my shop showed something more that I thought?"

"Can you tell me what happened that night?"

"How about in the morning? I'm tired."

"All right, but before you go to bed, let me check the locks on the windows and doors."

"Go ahead," she said, then yawned. Charles stood up and walked through the town house. He was unimpressed with the single locks on the windows and made a mental note to get better locks for the windows.

The dead bolt lock on the front door was promising. But the lack of a security system was a problem. Charles sighed as he headed for Yolanda's bedroom. If she was being stalked, the killer probably knew where she slept. He looked at the closed door and wondered if he should walk in or just wait until tomorrow morning.

Death doesn't wait. You need to check the lock now. Why was he acting like this? Yolanda was a client and he was doing a security check. He crossed over to the door and knocked gently.

"Yes?" Yolanda said.

"I need to come in and check your windows."

"It's open."

Charles gripped the doorknob and took a deep breath. For some reason, he expected to see Yolanda in a silky nighty, her face washed clean of her makeup and her lips glistening with a light gloss.

When he opened the door, he saw that she was sitting at her desk working on her computer. Still fully dressed, except for her shoes. And what beautiful feet she had. Obviously, she kept her appointments for pedicures. The purple polish on her toes made his mouth water. Looking away from her perfect feet, he crossed over to the window and was surprised to find that the window was unlocked and broken.

"Yolanda. Did you know the lock is broken?"

"No, but what can I do about it tonight?" She sounded annoyed as she glanced at him.

Charles knew he could rig the lock up so that if anyone tried to come in through the window they'd have a warning. But the look on Yolanda's face told him that he'd be better off replacing the lock in the morning.

Still, he knew he wouldn't sleep knowing she was vulnerable in that room. "I don't think it's a good idea for you to sleep in here with that kind of security issue. I can put something on the window that would rattle if someone tried to break in."

Yolanda rolled her eyes. "Whatever." She stood up and stretched her arms above her head. "Do what you have to do. I'm going to take a shower." Charles watched her as she sauntered out of the room. As she turned around, he focused on the window. He needed two nails and an empty can. It was a crude alarm system that he'd developed when he and Hillary first started out. She had a lot of windows where the locks had been purposely broken or removed so that her ex could have easy access to her. He'd put the nails and cans on the windows the first night and then replaced the locks the next day.

Thank goodness Yolanda only had one broken lock. Maybe her stalker hadn't found where she lived yet. But if these people wanted her dead, it wasn't going to take long for them to find her.

Charles headed to his car to grab his tool kit so that he could shore up the window. Since Yolanda had dropped her house key in a bowl near the door, he took it with him—not taking a chance on leaving the door unlocked. He crossed into the parking garage and dashed to his car. After grabbing his toolbox, Charles looked around the parking garage trying to locate the cameras and hiding spots where someone could sit in wait to attack Yolanda.

There were shadows where someone could hide and jump out to grab her. None of the cameras were pointed at dark spots in the garage, which defeated the purpose of having cameras in place. Part of him wanted to e-mail the company and outline their security flaws, but he wasn't there for those people. His job was to protect Yolanda Richardson.

Maybe he was overreacting or maybe he was trying to get over his greatest failure. He had ignored small things when it came to Hillary and he couldn't do that again. After rushing over to the town house, he entered, being sure to lock the door behind him. Since he didn't hear the shower going he estimated that she was out of the shower and was probably dressed for bed. What he didn't expect was to see half-naked Yolanda zipping out of the kitchen. Her skin was damp and the bath sheet she had wrapped around her body slipped down with every step she took. Charles knew he should've looked away. But fresh-faced Yolanda with dripping wavy hair took his breath away.

They locked eyes and Yolanda didn't seem embarrassed or shocked at all. She simply adjusted her towel and poured her wine.

"Um," Charles said, "I was going to fix the lock on the window."

"Go ahead," she said, then shrugged her bare shoulder. "I was wondering where you were. I'm glad you don't smoke."

"Why would you think that I smoke?"

"Isn't that why most people go outside in the middle of the night?"

"Just so you know, I'm not most people. And you should really take your keys into your bedroom instead of leaving them at your door."

"Does everything with you end with orders?" She took a sip of her wine and winked at him.

"It's a simple security suggestion. Does everything with you have to be a fight?"

Yolanda laughed. "If you think this is a fight, this is going to be a long assignment for you."

Charles shook his head. "Are you going to be in here with your wine for a while or do you want me to fix the lock after you get dressed?"

She raised her left arm with a flourish. "So, you did notice that your little talk was keeping me from getting dressed."

Charles was about to respond when the bath sheet fell to the floor.

Inside, Yolanda was dying a slow death. Her father would've told her that this is what happens when you show off. But she had to save face. Did she mean for Chuck to see her running around in a towel?

No. It was quiet and she wasn't used to having people in her house. Besides, Yolanda knew if she was going to get any sleep, she needed assistance. That's why she went for the wine.

She looked at him and saw his eyes travel the length of her naked body. She struck a pose like an Instagram model, then picked up her towel. "Take a picture next time," she said, then sauntered out of the kitchen with the towel over her shoulder.

As soon as Yolanda walked into her bedroom, she threw herself onto the bed. Even for her, that scene in the kitchen was a bit much. *What were you thinking?*

She hopped off the bed and pulled on a cotton romper. Yolanda felt as if she should go out to the living room and apologize for acting like a jerk.

But fear made you do stupid things and she was doing that right now. She knew the drinking would have to stop. She couldn't remember the last time she'd been able to go to sleep without a couple of glasses of wine. Part of her thought if she didn't hear the killers coming or feel whatever means they decided to kill her with it would be all right.

But you don't want to die. She paced across the room and stroked her face. "He's here to protect you. Let him do his job." Once again, she tossed herself across the bed and buried her face in a pillow. Seconds later, there was a knock at the bedroom door.

Yolanda got up and crossed over to the door. "Yes?" she said before opening it.

"Are you dressed?" Chuck asked with a slight laugh.

"Do you have your camera?" she retorted before opening the door.

Chuck smiled at her. "Sorry, I figured I'd missed my chance. I just want to secure the window."

She stepped aside and watched him walk in. "Chuck, I think I need to explain what happened."

He turned toward her and shook his head. "I get that you have a lot going on and maybe you don't want me here and you're trying to push me away. But I'm here to keep you alive."

Chuck made quick work of rigging the lock so that if someone came in they would hear the person. As he started to head out the door, Yolanda stood in front of him. Maybe the wine had lowered her guard and she could be honest.

"Chuck, I'm sorry. This whole thing has been a new and scary reality for me. I can't sleep for more than three hours when I'm here, and I don't know when someone is going to come for me. I just want to keep my family safe."

"And your family wants to keep you safe. You guys want the same thing."

She closed her eyes and fought back the hot tears burning behind her lids. When she felt his arms around her, Yolanda released the tears she'd been holding. He inched back toward the bed, then sat on the edge. Yolanda pushed out of his embrace and sat beside him.

"Sorry, I'm not usually like this. And . . ."

He placed a gentle hand on her knee. "These are unusual times and you're going to feel a lot of different emotions. And being scared isn't something to be ashamed of."

She snorted as she sniffed and wiped her eyes. "What are you? A bodyguard with a background in therapy?"

"I do have a psychology degree," he said with a low chuckle. "But believe me, I can understand how you're feeling. People don't need a bodyguard because they aren't afraid of something. When you're ready, you're going to have to face your fear."

Tilting her head to the side, she shot him a questioning look. "I'm afraid for my family. I'm afraid that these people are going hurt the people I love even though I've never told anyone what I saw. Why can't they just leave me alone?"

"Can I ask you a hard and serious question?"

She nodded as their eyes locked. Chuck sighed and moved his hand from her knee.

"If your silence still has these people after you, why won't you go to the police?"

Yolanda blinked and rose to her feet. "Are you crazy? That's a signature on my death warrant."

"It's already been signed. If you go to the police, you're going to have that many more people protecting you. And possibly your family. Better yet, you could make sure that these killers go to jail and no one else will ever be harmed."

She sighed as she paced in front of him. "I can't do that."

"I'm with you now, you can do it. We can go to Richmond tomorrow and make this happen. You're not going to be able to rest until you do the right thing."

Yolanda shook her head furiously, coming to a complete stop in front of him. "Not until after my sister's wedding. Then, maybe."

Chuck looked as if he wanted to say something, but he stood and nodded. "Have a good night, Yolanda."

She watched him as he walked out of the room. Graceful steps, meaningful stride. This man was going to save her life and star in her dreams. How in the hell was she going to make this work?

Chapter 9

Morning came too early and Yolanda had her now familiar headache. Stress and alcohol didn't mix. She knew that, yet every morning Yolanda had the same angry conversation with herself.

She smelled coffee and thought her mind was playing tricks on her, but then she remembered that Chuck Morris was in her home. Probably made the coffee this morning. She looked at her cell phone; it was ten-thirty.

Her plan had been to wake up at six, have breakfast, and go to her shop. It felt as if half the day was gone and she still wasn't ready to face Chuck. Between flashing him and crying like a little bitch, she wasn't ready to face him. But she had a business to run and a grand opening to prepare for.

Stop being a wimp and get out of this bed. You have work to do. She swung her legs over the side of the bed and stood up. It wasn't like her to act like this. This feeling of shame was new. After all, she walked across the Atlanta University Center quad naked as an undergrad to protest something.

Yolanda paused. Why had she done that? Really it was

about a boy. A certain running back on the Morehouse football team had made her mad because he thought he could control what she was going to do with her life.

She showed him that Yolanda Richardson did what she wanted. Of course, that was about ten years ago and Yolanda wasn't the same impulsive coed she was then. Now, she was just acting out because she was afraid and having Chuck in her home made everything real.

And reality wasn't her friend right now. She just wanted to open her shop, celebrate Nina's upcoming wedding, and get Chuck Morris's eyes out of her head. Grabbing her robe, she wrapped it around her body extra tight and headed for the bathroom.

After splashing water on her face and brushing her teeth, Yolanda pulled on a cotton dress that she kept on the back of the door and emerged from the bathroom with her bravado intact as she walked into the kitchen.

"Good morning," Chuck said.

"Good is debatable," she replied as she glanced at his empty plate. "You couldn't share?"

"You didn't respond to me knocking on your door and I don't know what your tastes are."

"I'm from Charleston; always go with grits."

"Noted and I'll keep that in mind next time."

"But can you cook?" Yolanda gave him a slow glance. "You seem like the type who has an army of women stocking your refrigerator and freezer."

"I don't roll like that and grown people should be able to feed themselves."

Yolanda snickered. "Don't let my little sister hear that. Nina can't cook to save her . . ." She stopped short. Even jokes were different now. "It's a good thing Clinton can cook. Otherwise, they'd starve."

"I read your sister's stuff all the time. I've always wondered why she wasn't on TV."

Yolanda shrugged. "Not white and blond enough? Nina knows more about sports than anyone should. But she got into football because she didn't want to do chores. Guess it paid off for her. I'd love to see her on a show where she'd put those so-called experts to shame because she knows way more than they do. But she can only do those shows if I'm her stylist."

Chuck picked up his plate and took it to the sink. Yolanda couldn't help but be impressed with him cleaning up after himself. The kitchen didn't even look as if it had been cooked in.

"Is there any coffee left?" Yolanda asked.

"There's plenty. I figured you would need it this morning."

She sucked her teeth. "And what is that supposed to mean?"

"You had a lot of wine last night after a trip that you said made you so tired. Everything is not a fight or a judgment," he said. "Give me credit for being courteous. Besides, a little body like yours can't handle all of that alcohol."

"Okay, let's start over. I'm not a morning person and I think breakfast is the most important meal of the day, even if you eat it at noon. Also, coffee is a meal."

"All right, I'll get out of your way so you can make your grits."

She crossed over to the cabinet and pulled out a half

bag of grits. Then she furrowed her brows. "Where did you get your breakfast ingredients from?"

"The store." Chuck took a seat at the breakfast nook. "I couldn't just come in here and cook your food without you knowing that I did it."

She grinned as she measured the grits and grabbed a pot. "Aren't you just so gallant."

"Yeah, I am."

"Are you going to join me or am I cooking enough for one person, which I find hard to do."

"I'll try those grits as long as you don't put sugar in them."

"Bite your tongue. People who put sugar in grits should be arrested."

"We finally agree on something," he quipped.

"Well, look at that. You do have a sense of humor."

Chuck laughed, a throaty laugh that took Yolanda to her bedroom. Made her think of the afterglow. *My God*, she thought as she looked away from him. Why did she yearn to have his arms wrapped around her? *Grits. Cook the grits.*

Yolanda busied herself preparing cheese grits with sausage and tomatoes. She was well aware of Chuck watching her every move. She almost dropped her spoon three times. Once she'd mixed the grits with her stewed tomatoes and sausage, she filled two bowls for them.

"Smells good," he said as he accepted the bowl from her. She focused on those hands. Hands that looked big enough to handle her body in ways that would make her scream hallelujah.

"Thank you," she said breathlessly.

He stared at her for a beat then cleared his throat. "Are we going to drink this?"

"Oh, damn." She crossed over to the dishwasher and grabbed two spoons. "The only person who makes grits you can drink is my little sister."

"My goodness, that actually sounds scary," he said as Yolanda laughed. "You said her future husband cooks, right?"

She handed him a spoon. "Yes."

Chuck took a small bite of the grits. "This is good."

For some reason, Yolanda beamed. This was her signature breakfast dish and the only person who didn't like it was Alex. And that's because she had no taste. It was the one thing she remembered about her mother. If she was honest, Yolanda knew that Alex didn't like the meal because of their mother and how she didn't want to think about what they had lost. Yolanda didn't want to think about it either. She didn't like it when Nina asked questions and Robin told stories. She'd always walk away, but when she needed her mother's hug, she made these grits.

And Yolanda had been making these grits a lot lately. Maybe she was just feeling good because he liked them. *But why does that even matter?* Yolanda looked away and dug into her meal.

Chuck cleaned his bowl and then gave Yolanda a slow glance. "If you can cook like this, why didn't your sister take lessons?"

"Because she was too busy watching sports and staying out of the way of chores. By the time she wanted to learn to cook, simply so she could impress some stupid boy, I wasn't even having it."

"That doesn't surprise me at all. So, basically it's your fault that she can't cook?"

"I will not take the blame for that." Yolanda reached for his bowl, but Chuck moved it out of the way.

"I'll wash the dishes and you can tell me about your shop and when we're going to see it." He picked her bowl up from the breakfast bar and headed over to the sink.

"You need a new outfit?"

"No, I need to run a security check. I need to see what you have in place and what we need to do to keep you safe."

Chuck washed the dishes and Yolanda rolled her eyes at him. "I don't want to spend the day at my shop going over security options and thinking about how I'm going to die."

"You're not going to die while I'm here," he said as he dried the bowls. Setting them in the dish tray, Chuck turned to Yolanda. Something in his eyes gave her pause. He looked like a man possessed, someone who had experienced loss and was determined not to lose again.

What in the hell was that all about?

There he was again. Charles was making promises that he knew he might not be able to keep. He'd told Hillary that she wouldn't be hurt and now she was in a grave. Looking up at Yolanda, he could see she had questions—real ones. Not her smart quips. But he wasn't in the mood to share. He needed to focus on his job. This breakfast wasn't going to change anything. He couldn't have another Hillary on his hands.

"When do you want to leave?" he asked.

"Can we pause for a minute?" Yolanda said. "You keep asking me why I won't go to the police, but why do you feel . . ."

"I have a job to do and I'm trying to do it. Anything else that you might be thinking right now doesn't matter; we have to stay focused."

Yolanda stormed out of the kitchen and Charles knew that he had been too casual with her this morning. But everything felt good earlier, like he was making a friend. He wanted Yolanda to see him as a friend. If she trusted him, this assignment would be so much easier.

Just don't make the same mistake you made with Hillary, he thought as he dried his hands on a dish towel. Just as he was about to seek Yolanda out, she walked into the kitchen. Charles stopped short as he drank in her image. She was dressed in a white leather jumpsuit with gold stripes. She had on gold ankle boots with three-inch heels, giving her a bit more height. She was about chest level with him now. The way that suit hugged her curves made him wish this wasn't a job and they'd met at a restaurant or bar. He could've sat with her and bought her a drink. They would've talked about music, food, and anything but death and security plans. How was it that Yolanda looked as good as she did with clothes on and without them?

"Well, let's go. If we're going to my shop, I can't be looking like someone in need of a makeover."

"No one would think that about you."

Yolanda did a 360 spin and smiled at him. "I know you didn't ask, but this is my own design. This year, I'm going to start Private Label."

"The name for your designs?"

She nodded. "It's time for me to live my dream and . . ."

"How are you going to do that if you don't face this situation head-on?"

"Can we have five minutes without you throwing this in my face?"

"When are you going to take death threats seriously? Yolanda, you don't want to go to the police and I understand the fear. But you clearly have a future that you want to build."

"And that's why I'm minding my fucking business. Do you know how I felt after Nina's accident thinking that my tormentors had done that to her? I just want to forget for a while and you are a constant reminder."

"But what are you going to do if they do harm your family?"

Yolanda closed her eyes. "Are we going to the shop or what?"

"Just so you know, I'm not going to let this go. But I don't want to fight with you anymore this morning."

"You started it," she mumbled as they headed for the front door. Charles knew she was afraid and that's why she was acting out and he had to figure out how to break down her defenses and get her to do the right thing.

You know the police don't always protect the people who need it. Hillary's ex should've been under the jail, but he still killed her.

They walked over to the parking garage and Charles took note of the surrounding area. The trees gave him pause. Bushes and trees were a stalker's favorite hiding place. A patch of azalea bushes had been where *he* had waited for Hillary. Yolanda's groan kept him from going back to that day.

"I left the keys to the shop inside," she said, then glanced at her watch. "I've really wasted this day."

"Just go grab the keys and we can spend as much time as you need in the shop. There are a lot of things I need to go over there anyway."

She pursed her lips as if she was going to make a smart comment but decided to hold her tongue. "You know what, I have an extra set in the car."

Charles closed his eyes. "Yolanda, do you realize how dangerous and stupid it is to leave those keys where . . ."

"Did you just call me stupid?"

"You're missing the whole point. And for the record, I didn't call you stupid, but you made a stupid decision."

She rolled her eyes and stomped toward her car. Charles followed in silence. They entered the car without saying another word to each other, and Yolanda reached over to open the glove box and pulled out a set of keys.

"Please tell me you don't have your house keys on there as well," he muttered.

"No, because that would be *stupid*."

"Yolanda, you can't keep holding everything I say to you against me because I want to keep you safe."

She rolled her eyes as she started the car. "Whatever."

Richmond, Virginia

Danny was beyond pissed off as he glanced at his phone, but he kept his thousand-dollar smile glued to his lips. Today was his quarterly meeting with the Future Business Leaders of Richmond, one of the groups he started for inner-city kids. A few of the graduates of the program were doing very well. One of his graduates had a food truck that Danny had invested in. And because of that investment, he kept his dirty money clean. This current class was full of lames, kids hoping to be the next Barack Obama. Folks who wanted to make Grandma proud. Hell, his grandmother was a hustler. She didn't carry a pearl-handled .22 because it was cute; she shot people. Put a hole in his grandfather's stomach when she caught him taking money from her hustle.

That's when he learned how to handle his cash flow problems with action. Bobby G. was a problem and he'd handled it. Too bad that Richardson bitch saw it. If she saw his face, how long would it take her to realize she had a cash cow on her hands? Or one of the biggest news stories in the city? That's why she had to be eliminated and Chase was taking too long to get the job done. Chase had more bodies than the largest graveyard in Virginia under his belt and Danny didn't get why he hadn't killed Yolanda Richardson. Sure, she was out of the city for now. But she'd be back.

She had a successful store and no one walked away from that.

"Mr. Branch," one of the students asked, breaking into his thoughts. "You don't know what this group means to us."

He turned to the young girl, who wanted to be a social media consultant, a business that would take years to grow and a market that was already flooded, and smiled. "I wish I had a group like this when I was growing up in Brooklyn. It's good to see successful people who look like you and have been through the things that you're facing," he said.

"I wouldn't be a future leader if I didn't ask: Do you have any internships at your company so that I can work on my SEO skills?"

Maybe she could be helpful. He was sure that Yolanda was going to have to keep her social media popping. Chase said she was in Charleston that last time he had a lead on her. Was that where she was trying to hide now?

"Remind me of your name again?" Danny said with a plastic smile.

"Brittany Johnson," she said, then extended her hand. Danny shook her hand and nodded.

"Send me a resume and a proposal. As a matter of fact, there is a boutique in downtown Richmond that I want you to do a social media report on. Get me information on the owner and tell me how you would make her shop go viral."

Brittany smiled as if she'd already had the job. "Thank you, Mr. Branch!" She dashed off and Danny's smile turned sinister. That little girl was going to be the key to tracking Yolanda down. And if she found that woman before Chase did, he was going to get rid of his ass, too.

Yolanda leaned against the wall in her shop as Chuck walked around as if he were looking for the devil himself. And he was annoying. With those black-rimmed glasses and those dimples. Lord, those dimples. Why was Chuck so slick and sexy?

"Yolanda, why do you have just one camera in the showroom?"

"What?" she asked, tearing her eyes away from his full lips.

"You need more cameras."

"Oh, all right."

"That was too easy," he mumbled.

"Thought you were tired of fighting?"

He threw up his hands and smiled. Yolanda nearly came undone. Yes, it was the dimples. She turned away from him and took a deep breath. "Why are you wearing glasses?" she asked as she busied herself with folding some of the T-shirts that had been waiting at the door when they arrived.

"Are you going to do anything with the other windows in the shop?" He stopped in the middle of the showroom and folded his massive arms across his chest. Yolanda couldn't turn away from him.

"Are those Google glasses that give you sight beyond sight?"

"You sound like you watch *ThunderCats*. They're just glasses. And you should consider getting some tint on the windows around the display area where you don't have items. That way people won't be able to look in your shop and see who's in here."

She expelled a sigh. "They also won't be able to see things that aren't in the window, clearance racks, hats, holiday items. I'm running a business, *Charles*."

"And running for your life. Yolanda, this is getting to be a broken record. You either listen and protect yourself or you're going to find yourself in even more danger."

Though she wanted to flip over the display of shirts, Yolanda decided that wasting her hard work would have been the ultimate act of stupidity. "All right then, we can just wrap the shop in black construction paper and hope the mystery of it all will make customers come in."

Chuck pulled his glasses off and shook his head. "We can make it work."

Yolanda sighed. "This needs to be more than making it work. This business is my livelihood and I need to be successful." She thrust her hand in his face. "Don't you say a word about me needing to be alive."

"You already know why I'm here and what I'm here for, so stop acting like we're just building a store in a highly competitive market."

Before she could reply, a boom broke the silence and Yolanda flung herself into Chuck's arms. He ducked into one of the dressing rooms and placed his finger to her lips as he sat her on the bench. He ran out into the main showroom as Yolanda watched him check out the surroundings. And where did he get that gun from? He disappeared into the back of the store for what felt like hours. Yolanda's leg bounced up and down like a rubber ball. Was this it? Had they found her?

Chuck walked into the dressing room and smiled, which she thought was odd unless he had killed the motherfucker who was trying to kill her and this ordeal was over.

"Construction."

"What?" she questioned.

"That was a slight construction accident and that's what the noise was."

Yolanda expelled a sigh of relief. "Oh my God, I thought . . ."

"I know what you thought," he said. And even though he didn't tell her that he had the same thoughts, she knew he did. That scared her. That made her realize that she did need to take things seriously.

"I can't live like this, just being so scared all the time." Tears streamed down her face and Chuck pulled her into his embrace. "I don't want my family hurt and I don't want to die."

He stroked her back and rocked her in his arms. And for the first time in a long time, she felt safe. Yolanda was ready to buy into what Chuck was selling. Well, everything except going to the police in Richmond. Somehow, she needed to convince him that was the worst idea since donut burgers.

Charles dropped his arms from around Yolanda. He was so close to crossing a line. The same line that got him into trouble. *But she's not Hillary.*

"I'm sorry to break down like this," Yolanda said. Her bravado was back in effect. That's dangerous. He knew she needed to protect her emotions, but acting as if she didn't have any made it easier for her to hide. To ignore the things she needed to do.

"It's going to happen and I understand it. It's not every day that someone is out to kill you."

"So, what security company do we need to get to come in here and set up your plan?"

Charles smirked. "How do you know I have a plan?"

Yolanda walked into the showroom and spun around. "Because you're a man with a plan. And I don't care what you say, those glasses are some kind of futuristic technology that creates security plans."

"You're really going to have to stop watching *Iron Man*."

"Never seen it, besides, I'm a Batman type of girl."

"That's sad. One IRS audit and your hero is just a regular guy with a big house he can't pay for."

She curled her hand and hissed at him. "And Catwoman would just steal some diamonds and pay for everything. Then the Batcave becomes another type of dungeon."

Charles shook his head. "Your imagination is top rate. Ever thought about putting it to use for something else?"

"My designs. But I'll leave the writing to Nina."

Charles pulled out his cell phone. "I'm going to call my friend Ethan and have him come over to look at the best options for a security system. And he's going to check the house, too."

Yolanda nodded, not giving him an argument for a change. Now he knew things had gotten real.

Chapter 10

After the scare at the shop, Yolanda decided that she wanted to be nice to Chuck, so she offered to spring for an early dinner.

"What do you have a taste for? There are a number of restaurants within walking distance."

"Do you go to the same restaurants all the time?"

Now, she was regretting her decision to be nice. "No. Can we just take a break for a second?"

"I'm just trying to figure out if you have a routine that someone might have picked up on and is now following you." He looked around the semi–empty streets. "There are a lot of places where someone could watch you from."

"No one knows I'm here."

"Social media says differently. You've geotagged your shop's location several times."

Yolanda stopped and tilted her head to the side as she looked at him. "You've been on my social media profiles?"

"Wouldn't be doing my job if I wasn't."

"Are you hungry or not?" She rolled her eyes.

"I can eat." He pointed to a Mexican-themed restaurant above them. "Are they any good?"

Yolanda nodded, remembering when she and Nina had had lunch there. "Do you drink?"

Charles shook his head as they climbed the stairs of the EpiCentre where the restaurants were located. "Not when I'm working. But that shouldn't stop you from enjoying whatever you like."

She would like to enjoy his lips pressed against hers. She would like to enjoy his hands between her thighs and his thumbs drumming against her throbbing clitoris. Her body was buzzing with resentment and desire. She didn't want to think about Chuck like this. He worked for her father. His presence in her life was an overreaction by her father and nosey little sister.

"Yolanda, are you all right?" Chuck asked, breaking into her thoughts. "You're not feeling the Mexican restaurant now?"

She hadn't even noticed that she'd walked right past the entrance. She turned around and headed back to the door of the restaurant. "Oh, no, this is fine. I was thinking about . . . you."

"Me? Do I even want to know?"

Yolanda stood in front of him and looked up into those emerald eyes. "Charles Morris, you're driving me crazy."

"Crazier than the fact that people are out to kill you?"

And there went her wet dream of seducing her bodyguard. He considered her a job and she wasn't about to make a fool of herself and tell Chuck that she wanted to . . .

"Okay, let's eat," Yolanda said as she turned and reached for the door handle. Chuck grabbed the handle at the same time and his fingers brushed against the back of her hand. Why did her body respond with such fierceness to his touch?

"After you," he said.

Yolanda sighed as she approached the hostess booth.

"Hi, how many?"

Yolanda held up two fingers. The woman nodded, then looked down at the seating chart. "Okay, follow me," she said. Yolanda started walking and she could feel Chuck's body heat on her neck. She turned around to see if he was that close to her and he was. She face–planted right into his chest. Chuck brought his hand down on her back. "You all right?" he asked as he took a step back.

"Yes, I was just checking to see if you were . . . Sorry," she stammered. He stroked her shoulder and nodded as if to say everything was all right. Why. Did. He. Have. To. Touch. Her?

"First date?" the hostess asked as she led them to a secluded table.

"Oh no, not a date at all," Yolanda exclaimed. What was it on her face broadcasting that she wanted this man? *Maybe you're just horny and ridiculous,* she thought as the hostess gave Chuck a demure smile. Yolanda fought the urge to roll her eyes. The hostess could flirt; she couldn't. But the hostess needed to drop off the menus and bounce.

Yolanda cleared her throat as the hostess smiled at Chuck and told him their server would be there shortly.

"Bet that happens everywhere you go," Yolanda said once they were alone.

"What is the *that* you're talking about?"

She picked up her menu and hid her grin. "Pretty girls

losing their shit over you. That hostess was ready to take your clothes off and put her body on you. Like a cheaply made suit."

"Didn't notice that at all. Besides, I've seen a naked woman this week."

Yolanda dropped the menu, her face flushed with embarrassment. "Listen, about that . . . Well, hell, I was in my house and the towel wasn't cooperating."

"No harm, no foul. But I wish you . . ."

"Would take things more seriously. Would admit that I'm afraid. Would go to the police. Blah, blah, blah. I've heard you."

"But did you listen?"

Before she could respond, the server walked over to their table and thank God it wasn't a woman.

The waiter introduced himself and took their drink orders before going over the day's specials. Yolanda noticed how even when Chuck sat down in a situation that seemed to be calm he seemed to be on high alert. He kept looking over his shoulder as they waited for the waiter's return.

"Are you ever off duty?" she asked.

"Nope. My job is to protect you at all times. This kind of work doesn't get a lunch break. Besides, the people looking for you aren't on a schedule."

She was ready to give up. Chuck was all about business; she just needed to accept it and move on.

Charles knew he was overplaying the role of a bodyguard. He wasn't just protecting Yolanda from her stalker, but from him as well. Did this woman realize that she oozed sexuality? Naked or fully clothed, Yolanda was alluring.

She was the kind of woman he should've stayed away from. Yolanda wasn't like any woman he'd ever known. She was so free. Granted, she was afraid right now, but he could only imagine what she was like when she wasn't being hunted. A load of fun. In and out of bed. Why did his mind have to go there? Charles turned to face Yolanda as the waiter returned to the table with Diet Pepsi and sweet tea. She had a beautiful smile, pearly white teeth framed by thick, kissable lips. Why was he now focused on those lips as she talked to the waiter about the quesadillas? She wanted chicken, spinach, and onions, as well as the hottest salsa. Of course she liked spicy foods. Matched her personality. Just like that suit she was wearing. Charles knew he couldn't let Yolanda distract him from doing his job. He had to keep it in his pants this time.

"What? Spotted the killer and now you're ready to spring into action?" she asked as she noted his silence.

Charles just smiled. He wasn't about to tell her that her eyes stopped him cold. Or that her smile made his heart beat like a steel drum during a party in Jamaica.

"Ever heard that if you stay ready you don't have to get ready?" he asked.

She rolled her eyes and smiled, highlighting her dimples. How had be missed that Yolanda had dimples? Why did he have to be weak to dimples? He should've known she had them. Sheldon Richardson had them on the occasions that he smiled. But he mostly spoke with the legend when he had a problem and he didn't smile that much. Yolanda smiled a lot. It was her nervous tic. Just like when that towel dropped. Her smile wasn't one of a woman who had done that on purpose. But she wasn't ashamed of that curvy body of hers. And why should she be?

"Hello?" she said as she snapped her fingers in front of his face. "Can we just eat?"

"Yes, we can just eat," he said after a beat.

She leaned back in her seat and folded her arms across her chest. He could tell she wanted to say something but was clearly holding back. Charles knew he should've sat there and waited for his food. Should've just watched her, but instead, he leaned back and said, "You plan on keeping me around for the rest of your life?"

Yolanda leaned back in her chair, her mouth dropped open, and her heart nearly leapt from her chest.

"Why would you say something like that?" she stammered.

"The people who killed that man belong in jail. And . . ."

She threw her hand up as her phone chimed. Seeing it was a text from Alex, she started to ignore it, but what if . . .

Just read the text and stop sparring with Chuck. She looked down at her phone and read the message. *Call me, it's about Robin and Logan.*

"I need to make a call." She rose to her feet and Chuck followed suit. She shot him a questioning look. "I'm just going out front to see what Alex wants."

"That's fine." He nodded toward the waiter and said they'd be right back. Yolanda groaned as she walked outside to call her sister.

* * *

Chase stood across the street from El Compo Mexican Cuisine watching his target. Who was that man with her? He'd seen him at the shop but figured he was a contractor. Now he wondered if they were dating or something. Didn't matter, she was the target and he was learning how she moved. Basically, in a small circle. Home. Work. Local restaurant and Whole Foods. Chase didn't understand why people wanted to spend their whole check in a store that was a farmer's market with name brand items.

But that was neither here nor there. He had a job to do and Danny wanted it done fast, but Chase wanted to do things right. If Danny had gotten him to take care of Bobby G., they wouldn't be here now. So, Danny was going to have to wait until he could do the job correctly. That meant no cameras. Some people should just stay in their lane. Charlotte, he noticed, was filled with cameras. It seemed as if those electronic eyes were on every corner. He was looking for gaps and he'd found one. The parking garage where she lived. But this guy was going to be a problem. Chase wanted her death to look like a robbery gone wrong. Those things happened a lot in Charlotte. He had already planned for a clean getaway and a dump spot for the cheap Kia Rio he was driving.

This guy was putting a wrinkle in his smooth plan. The way he stood watch over her like a sentinel. Chase wondered if he was going to have to make it a two-for-one deal after all. *Danny's dumb ass*, he thought as he started walking down the sidewalk. *He should've been smarter about Bobby G.*

The killing didn't make much sense, but it wasn't for Chase to unravel. He needed to make Yolanda Richardson go away. Perhaps killing her in Charlotte would keep things from rippling back to Danny.

Maybe he wasn't as dumb as he'd been acting lately—except for sending that lady threats, letting her know that someone was after her. Now that was stupid as hell. Surprises always made the job easier. Made planning the act easier. But Danny's actions made this hit harder than it needed to be. It should've taken him three days to scout this woman, kill this woman, and go home.

Danny with his flowers and threats were out of pocket. Though he was a good client, Chase's partnership with Danny was going to end after this job. Power had gone to his head and that was more danger than Chase could afford to deal with. He'd been a contract hunter for years, never been caught or implicated in a murder. He had more than thirty kills under his belt and he wasn't about to let this job be the one to take him down. He needed to make a decision quick as to how to handle this woman. Tonight would've been perfect—if she had been alone.

Another day wasted.

Yolanda tried to focus on Alex telling her not to ask Robin questions about Logan when she came to visit for Thanksgiving. She knew her sister and brother-in-law were having some sort of issue, but at the moment, she couldn't stop watching Chuck as he watched her. "Alex, I get it. But I have to go."

"Wait. Have you gotten your new shop open yet? We're going to have to help Nina pick a wedding dress soon and some sensible shoes. You know if she has her way, she'd try to wear some Chuck Taylors."

Why did she have to say *Chuck*? "Alex, I have a delivery to sign for."

"This late?"

Yolanda ended the call and turned to her protector, or was he her nemesis? "Can we go in now?"

"Yeah," he said, his eyes focused on a figure walking down the sidewalk.

Yolanda folded her arms and waited for Chuck to make a move. A beat passed and he started toward the door of the restaurant. Yolanda followed and inhaled deeply. That man's scent filled the atmosphere and she was caught in rapture of his aura. Why couldn't her father hire some fat white man to keep her safe? A man she didn't want to wrap her thighs around and feel deep inside her. Yolanda closed her eyes, took a deep breath, and tried to relax. She walked into the restaurant trying to pretend that no one was trying to kill her and that Chuck was a dinner date, not a bodyguard. She couldn't keep playing that role. The man wasn't interested in anything but doing his job and she needed to accept that.

They returned to the table and noticed the ice had melted in their drinks. When Yolanda reached for her glass, Chuck shook his head. "We need fresh drinks. You don't know if someone dropped something in here."

She closed her eyes and thought about how her new normal was always waiting for a killer to snuff her out. Why did she have to be there that night? She'd turned down a perfectly boring date to design that window scene.

Chuck seemed to sense Yolanda's unease. "I hate to sound like a broken record, but if you want to stop living in fear, you know what you have to do."

"All I have to do right now is get some food in my

stomach because I'm hungry. And you sound more like a CD on repeat." She laughed but her eyes still held fear. Chuck placed a comforting hand over hers.

"At some point you're going to listen to the song all the way through, right?"

"After Nina's wedding. Can we do it then? My sister has been through a lot and I want to be there to celebrate her day."

"You all are pretty close, huh?"

Yolanda smiled thinking about her sisters. Despite the fights and arguments they'd have every now and then, the Richardson sisters were close. And if she would cause them to be hurt because of this mess, she'd never forgive herself. "We have our moments. Do you have any siblings?"

Chuck nodded. "Two sisters who think I'm the worst brother in the world until they need someone's background ran." He chuckled softly.

Yolanda could only imagine what kind of brother he was. Stubborn. Overprotective. Basically, Alex with muscles and a gun. "Are you older or younger than your sisters?"

He smiled. Those damn dimples. "I'm the youngest. My sisters are twins and I was their cute little doll until they realized I was going to need a diaper change."

"Wow. You were actually a baby once," she quipped.

"Funny."

She couldn't help but get lost in his Emerald Coast eyes. A lot of people wondered why Yolanda liked the beach as much as she did. Most people who grew up in a coastal town would be happy to get away from the ocean and sand. But when Yolanda needed to recharge, she went to Destin. Or she'd go home and hang out on Folly Beach. Something about ocean waves gave her peace. But she wondered what Chuck would look like in some hip-hugging swim trunks running down the coast that matched his eyes. *Stop it*, she chided. *This is business and it doesn't matter if he is the most attractive man you've ever seen.*

"No more jokes about being a child?" he asked, breaking into her thoughts.

"Not right now. Give me time to eat and I'll put on a whole comedy routine for you," she said as she spotted the waiter walking over to them with fresh drinks and a basket of chips. Yolanda clasped her hands together.

"They make those chips fresh every day. So amazing."

"Are you a foodie as well as a fashionista? I didn't think those two could go together."

"Women eat and wear clothes. What's the problem?"

Chuck threw his hands up as the waiter dropped off the drinks and chips. "You're right," he said.

What in the hell am I doing? Charles thought as he looked away from Yolanda's full lips as she nibbled on a chip. He'd opened up a little too much and got comfortable with her when he shouldn't have. Charles had no intention of falling into the sense of ease he had felt with Hillary. Without knowing it, Yolanda had tempted him into believing they could at least be friends. When they weren't arguing, she was charming. But she was always beautiful. It didn't matter if she was smiling, frowning, or scowling, Yolanda Richardson was beautiful.

And that was a problem. Beautiful women came with

a different set of problems and he wasn't trying to get caught up again. Or put Yolanda in even more danger because he couldn't control his growing attraction to her. What if she had a man?

He's a sorry-ass man if he is allowing her to go through this alone. But knowing her, she hasn't even told him what's going on.

"Please, don't let me eat all these chips, because I will." She pushed the bowl toward him and Charles took one of the warm chips between his fingers. He took a quick bite and nodded.

"These are good."

Yolanda reached for another chip just as Charles did. Their fingers grazed and she looked as if she felt the same electric charge he felt as well.

"Sorry, I'm being greedy," she said as she took her hand away.

"These will make you do that. Maybe we should get another basket."

"Oh, accidentally touching me, is that gross?" she quipped.

He would've loved to tell her the truth, that her hands felt like silk, that he'd touch her all over if he could. But those words and his lustful thoughts were inappropriate. Why the hell did he take this job? Being this close to Yolanda was torture. That's why he needed to find the person who was trying to kill her, sooner rather than later. Then the temptation would be gone. She'd settle in with her new shop and new city. He'd go back to Charleston and run his business. Then he could invite her out for a drink. Hell, he'd take her to breakfast, lunch, and dinner if she allowed him to. But that would have to happen after. After this was over and she was safe. Once Yolanda got back to her real life, would there be space for him in it?

"So, you can only talk when you're trying to make me go to the police?" she asked, noting his silence.

"Since you brought it up," he said with a short sigh, "we need to go to Richmond and talk to someone about the murder investigation. We need some clarity as to where things stand."

She shrugged. "You can't just make a phone call or two?"

"That would alert the wrong people as to what we're doing. And I want to look around the area, just to see who the players are and how someone could send a killer across state lines to find you."

Yolanda nibbled on a chip. Charles watched her hand tremble. "The man, the shooter, his name is Danny."

"You know anything else about him?"

She picked up another chip and broke it in half. "I didn't want to interrupt him while he blew a man's brains out and ask him for his LinkedIn profile."

"Do you think you could pick him out if you saw a picture of him?"

Chapter 11

Yolanda closed her eyes. For months she'd been trying to forget Danny and the bulldog. But their faces were burned on her brain like a tattoo. She didn't want to spend any time flipping through pictures looking for those men. But if she wanted this nightmare to end, then she was going to woman up and face her ultimate fear.

"Yeah," she said with a sigh. "I can pick him out, but I don't know if I'm up to a trip back to Richmond right now."

"I know you're . . ."

She held up her hand. "No, if I go to Richmond right now I'm probably going to fight my soon-to-be former brother-in-law."

Chuck smirked. "Interesting, you'll fight your brother-in-law, but you won't fight for your life?"

Yolanda was ready to tell him how he was ruining dinner with all of his judging, but the waiter arrived at the table with their entrees. At least she could ignore him while she ate her gooey quesadilla. Glancing at his shrimp tacos and red beans, she wished they were on a date. She was never that girl who didn't take a bite of her mate's food. Chuck didn't seem like the sharing type, so she decided to stop herself from reaching for a juicy shrimp that had fallen from the shell.

Chuck caught her eyeing his plate. He reached for his fork and speared the shrimp. "I know the Charleston in you wants this, right?"

Oh, if he only knew everything she wanted that was sitting at the table. "Well, you offered," she said as she leaned forward and bit into the shrimp on the end of the fork. Their eyes locked as she ate the shrimp. Now, Yolanda knew the look of desire when she saw it, and Destin eyes over there looked like he wanted everything she craved and more. Or she was just being horny and ridiculous again.

"Good?" Chuck asked as he dropped his hand.

Yolanda nodded as she swallowed. "I don't know why I've never tried these before. I guess I just don't think of Charlotte and fresh seafood."

"I understand that. I mean, I won't fool with crawfish that isn't from the Gulf Coast."

Yolanda closed her eyes briefly, wondering if he was good at sucking . . . the crawfish. Why was she like this? "Crawfish, huh?"

"Mud bugs are the best. My granny was from New Orleans and she made the most amazing crawfish étouffée ever."

So, he didn't suck the heads. She could think about something else now. Chuck continued his crawfish memories, though.

"But there is nothing like a plate of crawfish fresh from the boil. Bite the heads off and suck on that sweet meat."

If she hadn't been sitting down, Yolanda would've passed out. "Um," she said as she twisted in her seat.

"Not a fan?"

"Maybe I just need to be convinced." Yolanda crossed and uncrossed her legs underneath the table, hoping to ease the throbbing between her thighs. Nope. It wasn't working because all she could think about were those lips sucking sweet meat. Her meat. Her pussy, to be exact.

"Yolanda? You all right?"

She gasped, realizing how deep she'd fallen down the rabbit hole. "I guess I'm just tired. It's been an eventful day and I'm starting to feel it."

"Want to take this to go?"

Yolanda smiled. "Yes."

Chuck waved for their waiter and asked for a couple of boxes. After they'd packed the food, he stood up and gave the restaurant a deep glance.

Yolanda knew the pseudo date was over. He was back to being Chuck Morris, the bodyguard. Or was he a security specialist? One of Charlie's Angels? She still found it hard to believe that she was walking around with this man because someone could be lurking in the shadows ready to take her out. It would've been so much better if he was taking her home for ninety-nine different other reasons.

After an uneventful ride back to Yolanda's place, the duo retreated to separate areas of the house, Yolanda heading to her studio upstairs and Chuck wandering the house and the small patch of yard. She didn't know where he had gotten the motion-detecting lights that he'd positioned around the walkway of the house. Maybe she needed to stop with the after-hours cocktails and wine.

But tonight wasn't going to be that night. Yolanda needed to pass out in her bed without thinking of walking toward the sofa, where Chuck would be sleeping, and mounting him.

Why are you like this? She thought as she started for the stairs.

"You should really close your blinds," Chuck said as she reached the bottom step. Startled, Yolanda stumbled and Chuck enveloped her in his massive arms. "Didn't mean to scare you."

She held on to him a beat longer than she should have and inhaled his crisp scent. How did he smell so good after being outside and walking around the property? Because he was clearly magical.

"Designs, I was thinking about my new designs and I forgot that you were here," she said as she pushed out of his arms.

"You really need to pay attention to your surroundings at all times."

She raised her right eyebrow at him. "Even in my own home?"

"Especially here. You're most vulnerable at home and this is likely where . . ."

"You want a water?" The last thing she wanted to hear was that she wasn't even safe at home.

"No thanks. I'm going to heat up the leftovers after I close the blinds in your studio."

She nodded and headed for the kitchen. Halfway there she stopped. That man could not see her drawings in her studio!

* * *

Charles closed the window dressing after checking the locks on the French doors. It was cute, but not the safest windows or doors in his opinion. Granted, it was better to have the windows upstairs rather than on the first floor. Clearly the room had been Nina's master bedroom. Made sense to him that Yolanda would use the space to be creative. He glanced around the room, taking note of the mannequin frames with lush material draped across them. Those could come in handy if they had to hide in the house. Was there more than one person gunning for her? He crossed over to the bright lamps and turned them off. The curtains were too thin and he'd suggest that she get black-out curtains or something to shield her from anyone looking at her.

He glanced over at the huge drawing table and took a deep breath when he saw the image on the paper. She'd been sketching him in swim trunks. Just as he was about to pick up the drawing, a breathless Yolanda burst through the door.

"Oh my God!" she stammered. "It's not what you think."

"What are you talking about?" he said as he turned away from her desk.

Yolanda folded her arms across her breasts and his mouth watered. She was sexy when she pretended to have an attitude. That bravado hid her fear and he understood where she was coming from. But this was a comical situation. And he should've let it go.

"You're really going to act as if your observant ass didn't look at my sketches?" she snapped.

"Men's line? Nice."

"Yeah, because men buy clothes and you'd be the

perfect model for my Emerald Coast line," she replied honestly. "I get that you're trying to keep me safe, but if you ever look at my sketches again, you're going to need protection from me."

"I don't know how all of this works," he said, fanning his arm around the room. "But you're talented. I'd hate to see you get snuffed out before you have a chance to make your mark."

Yolanda placed her hand over her heart and he could've sworn he saw tears spring into her eyes. "Are you serious?" she asked.

Charles picked up one of the sketches. "If I was in Miami, I'd probably wear these while I was surfing."

"You surf?"

He nodded. "Something I got into after watching *Point Break.*"

"Great movie, but I don't understand how you even got into surfing from that movie."

"I wanted to go into law enforcement from an early age. That movie sealed it for me and riding waves got me away from my sisters. They don't like salt water."

"So, you ran from them and into the ocean?"

Charles nodded and returned the sketch to the table. "I didn't know you designed for men as well."

"Just something I'm playing around with." Yolanda crossed over to the table and flipped her sketches over. Was she embarrassed? Maybe he shouldn't have looked at them, but it was interesting to see how she saw him. If the design business didn't work out, she could easily draw comics. She met his gaze and ran her tongue across her bottom lip. "Are we done here?"

"Yeah, for now," he said. "But you need to get some blackout shades for the windows up here."

"Um, no. This room has the best light and that's why I switched bedrooms," she said.

"And I bet you spend a lot of time up here working without noticing if somebody is watching you." He crossed over to the French doors and pointed to the trees across the way. "This city seems to be obsessed with a tree canopy. People can hide behind those branches and have a direct view in here."

"People? Like you think there's a whole gang of killers looking for me?" Her voice was filled with emotion.

"I don't know. But I'm trying to be prepared for anything."

Yolanda turned her back to the windows and slumped her shoulders for a moment. Charles placed a comforting hand on the small of her back. This wasn't what he needed to do. He couldn't get too personal or close to her. But Yolanda was drawing him in. He had to put a stop to that. "This just gets worse and worse," she whispered. Charles pulled her closer to him.

"We're going to fix this," he said. "You're going to have to trust me on that, okay?"

She nodded and he dropped his arms from around her tempting frame. "But, I'm not blacking out my studio during the day when I need the natural light."

Charles expelled a sigh and watched her head for the door. He started to say something about light not mattering if she was dead, but his phone vibrated in his pocket. Pulling it out, he smiled when he saw it was his contact in Virginia.

"Madison Slim, what's going on?"

She giggled in his ear at her nickname. "You know you're the only person who can call me that without getting a punch to the throat."

"Thank goodness for small mercies. You have lethal hands, Ms. MMA."

"I also have some news for you and your project. What do you call women you're guarding?"

"Her name is Yolanda," he said.

"Miss Yolanda is in trouble. Like bigger trouble than you thought."

"What do you mean?"

"Word on the street is that the person who killed Bobby G. is well connected."

"Do you know who this person is?"

"Yep, they say it's Daniel Branch."

"You say his name like I'm supposed to know who he is."

"I forgot, you left everything about Virginia behind after . . . Daniel Branch is a money man. He calls himself an investment banker, and since everyone who works with him makes money, no one complains. But I've heard he has a shady side, underground gambling."

"How do you know this but the authorities don't?"

"I've got friends in low places and his ex-wife was a friend of mine. She started asking questions when they got divorced and she hasn't been seen in a year."

Charles let out a low whistle. "And no one is looking for this lady?"

"When have cops ever cared about a missing Black woman?" Her voice was filled with bitterness. Charles understood and hated that this was happening to her again. Madison's youngest sister disappeared from Danville,

Virginia, ten years ago. No one wanted to look for the fifteen-year-old, assuming she was a runaway. A year later, her image appeared on a man's hard drive who had been busted for child pornography.

Madison had turned her anger into a career where she searched for missing children. First as a police officer in Danville, then in Greensboro, North Carolina. But something happened to sour her against law enforcement and she struck out on her own to help families find their missing children. Later, Charles found out that Madison had found out who the man was and she had been searching for him quietly for years. When he'd offered to help, she'd turned him down, telling him they were her bones to bury.

And then she became an MMA fighter, too, which Charles didn't understand. But she was good at it. He didn't ask her a lot of questions about what she did, but when he needed Madison, she was always there. That's all that mattered.

She was even there when he tried to push everyone away after Hillary died. She was the only person who wouldn't listen and made him go to therapy to get over losing her.

"Anyway," Madison continued, "if Danny knows where to find Yolanda, he probably sent someone to follow her. So, be careful and stay strapped."

"I'm always strapped. Got a question: Would going to the police be a good idea?"

Madison sighed. "Give me a couple of days before you talk to anyone. I've really got a feeling that this guy has some heavy hitters in his pocket and the last thing you or I want to do is get the wrong people looking at her."

"Facts. And she's already giving me hell about going to the police, so . . ." Charles looked up and saw Yolanda walking back into the studio. "I'll call you back."

"Be careful," Madison said before hanging up the phone.

Yolanda tossed her head to the side. "I hope you're not still going through my sketches," she said.

"No. I was on the phone."

"You didn't have to hang up with your boo because I walked into my studio," she quipped. "Tell her you're safe, I don't want you."

Charles shook his head. "You're funny. I'm working, so any calls that I get are going to be related to keeping you alive."

She nibbled on her bottom lip and Charles had to turn away so his dick wouldn't get hard. She oozed sensuality just doing simple things. "Listen," she said, "my sisters are coming here in a couple of days and I'd like to have some privacy with them. We're going to be picking out Nina's wedding dress and stuff like that. You'd be bored out of your mind."

"I know how to stay out of sight, but I'm not going to ignore the fact that my job is to protect you."

Yolanda hated that he was going to be around when she wanted to ream Nina out for bringing this temptation into her life. She also wanted to tell her sister what she'd do to him if given the chance. But not with him in earshot. "You know when we get together, we do a lot of talking, laughing, and drinking."

"All the more reason for me to be around. Sounds like you guys will be distracted."

He didn't realize how his presence distracted her, nearly turning her senseless. She needed to get a few minutes away from him. Okay, a few days. And she was going to make Nina sweep and mop her shop for putting her in this situation. Stuck with Chuck was almost as dangerous as the people who wanted to kill her.

How was she going to look out for a killer when she wanted to see her bodyguard naked all the time?

"Can I at least get some time alone up here to get a little work done?"

"As long as you close the blinds."

Yolanda sighed. "Fine." She crossed over to the windows and closed the curtains and blinds. When she turned around to ask him if he was satisfied, Chuck was gone. "Wow," she murmured, then sat down at her desk.

For the next three hours, Yolanda sketched more drawings of men in swimwear, but she kept looking at the door to see when her protector would return. It was after midnight before she decided to shut everything down and head to bed. Tonight, she vowed not to give him an accidental striptease.

Heading down to her bedroom, she noticed him on the sofa, his long body stretched against the cushions, shirtless. She stood in the shadows and drank in his image. He had a dragon tattoo that started on his shoulder and looked as if it wrapped around his back. His washboard abs rose slightly as he slept. She wondered what it would feel like if she ran her tongue up and down those abs, sucked his nipples, and mounted him like he was a wild mustang.

Her lustful gaze traveled down to his thighs. Too bad they were covered with a blanket. She imagined him looking like the great gorilla king from the *Black Panther* movie. She expelled a low sigh and shook her head.

"It's rude to watch people when they're sleeping," Chuck said, his voice thick with sleep.

"Um," she said, "I was heading to my room."

"You've been standing there for five minutes," he said as he sat up. When the blanket dropped, she saw that he actually slept in pants. Gray. Sweatpants. Sweet Jesus.

"How would you know that if you were sleeping?"

"How are you from Charleston and don't know the phrase 'every shut eye isn't sleeping'?"

"Good night, Chuck," she said, then dashed into her bedroom. Yolanda liked being the cat and not the mouse in her little flirty games. Normally, it worked, but these weren't normal times.

Someone was still trying to kill her and her life was in danger. Her libido would have to wait. Crossing over to her bed, she flung herself onto the soft mattress and closed her eyes, hoping sleep would come quickly.

Chapter 12

Restless nights were becoming normal, but when Yolanda woke up covered in sweat at 4:30 a.m., it wasn't because she was reliving the murder she saw or the brains pooling by her feet. No. Nightmares didn't keep her tossing, turning, and moaning. It was Chuck Freaking Morris. Well, at least in dream form. The sex was a dream. The banging on her door was real.

She stumbled out of bed and opened the door. "What?"

"You were screaming," Chuck said. She looked down at the gun in his left hand.

"I-I was?" Her face heated from embarrassment and that never happened to Yolanda Richardson. "Must have been the TV."

Chuck nodded toward the darkened set mounted on the wall. "Were you having a nightmare?"

She nodded, unable to tell him the truth. Chuck walked into her bedroom and she drank in his image like a glass of wine. That tattoo was more expansive and detailed than she'd imagined. It covered half of his back and seemed to stop at his hip. She wished he slept in shorts, but then again, he made every Internet meme about gray sweatpants the God's honest truth. It was like Victoria's Secret for women.

As he looked around the room, Yolanda's eyes fell on his backside. Salt 'N' Pepa played in her head and she thanked his mother for an ass like that.

"You want to talk about it?" he asked, breaking into her thoughts. She hadn't even noticed that he'd taken a seat on her bed.

"Um. No." She walked over to the bed and tilted her head at him. "I'd like to go to sleep."

"All right," he said, rising to his feet. "But I'm here if you need to talk."

Yolanda cleared her throat. "That's good to know. But I just want to go to sleep."

He headed for the door and Yolanda felt drawn to follow him. "Charles," she said. "Wait."

He turned around and Yolanda pressed her body against his. He was hot. His body was on fire and she knew the only way to calm those flames was with a rejection or a kiss. Chuck glanced down at her and Yolanda's heart throbbed. "You don't know what you're doing and you should probably stop."

"What if I don't want to?"

"Then, I'm going to make the decision for you." He took a step back and walked out of the room. Now she was clear on what she needed to do—wrap up her emotions and hormones. No one had ever pushed her away. Was she really thinking about seducing this man? All because he had the good sense to focus on saving her from killers and not giving in to what she wanted. He wanted it too because what she felt against her thighs wasn't his gun.

Charles knew things had gone too far in Yolanda's room. Damn it, he wanted to kiss her. Hell, he wanted to do more than kiss her—he wanted to strip her naked and make love to her until the sun came up. Until he came. Until she came—several times.

Why was she tempting him? Was this her way of masking her fear? He needed to put a stop to this now. But how could he when he wanted to get lost between her thighs?

He plopped down on the sofa and dropped his head in his hands. Flashes of Hillary clouded his brain and guilt filled his soul. He loved that woman and allowed her to die. He couldn't let lust make him fall into that same trap again. Tomorrow, he'd felt that lush body against his and had the chance to do what he'd wanted since the moment he'd met Yolanda Richardson. For the next hour, he'd dream about what could've been.

Sunlight seeped inside the living room and Charles realized that he'd overslept. He woke up with a start and a hard dick. This was bad, because he was distracted by a fantasy that could never be real.

Sitting up and swinging his legs on the side of the sofa, Charles yawned and threw his head back. When he heard Yolanda's bedroom door open, Charles snapped to attention.

"Good morning," he said when he locked eyes with her. She had a look of don't talk to me until I've had coffee on her face.

"That's debatable," she said, then padded toward the kitchen. Charles waited until he heard the coffee bean grinder start up before going into the kitchen.

"We need to talk about last night," he said as Yolanda poured the grounds in the coffee maker's basket.

"No we don't," she said as she reached for two coffee mugs. "I get it. This is a job for you and I need to stop looking at you as more than a blunt object who's here to keep me alive."

"That's harsh."

"But it's true. I won't apologize for being attracted to you, but I will get my hormones under control so that we can find the person who wants me dead."

To say he was surprised by her brutal honesty would've been the understatement of the decade. Her realism should've given him peace, not pause. This is what he wanted and how he needed them to interact. He should've been a lot happier, but he wanted to know more about her attraction to him. Wondered if he should open up about what was giving him pause. Nope, he was going to do his job and they could both move on.

"So, what do you want our next steps to be?" Charles asked.

"I'd love to hold off on anything until my sister's wedding." Yolanda slumped her shoulders. "She deserves to be happy without my black cloud hanging over her."

He wondered if now was the time to tell her how much trouble she was in. Madison made this Danny character seem as if he was someone whom the law didn't apply to.

"I have to go into my shop this morning and wait for some deliveries," Yolanda said, cutting into his thoughts. "Breakfast is going to be bananas and strawberries if you want some."

Oh, he wanted something, but it wasn't what she was offering. "I'll stick with coffee," he said, turning away from her. Yolanda had on a pair of white cotton shorts, a blue tank top, and no shoes. Her small feet looked as if they were made of satin. He was a foot man, and like everything else about Yolanda Richardson, her feet were perfect.

She moved around the kitchen in silence, grabbing the banana and strawberries from the fridge and slicing them into a bowl, then filling their coffee mugs. She slid Charles his coffee and smirked at him.

"What was that for?" he asked, then took a sip of his coffee.

Yolanda plucked a berry from her bowl and shook her head. "How do you do it? Just turn your emotions and feelings on and off."

"I can't afford to let emotions cloud my judgment," he said wistfully. He knew how that turned out and it wasn't pretty. He couldn't allow history to repeat itself. Turning his emotions off would be a wonderful skill, but last night showed him that he couldn't do that, no matter how hard he tried.

Charles wanted to kiss her and that was going to haunt him.

"Okay, then why . . . I get it. You've made that mistake before, someone fell into hero worship with you and then when she was safe, she broke it off with you?"

Charles snorted. "Nope."

"Just so we're clear, I'm not looking for anything other than your body," she said.

He snapped his head up and locked eyes with her. "What?"

"I think I was really clear," Yolanda said, then popped a strawberry into her mouth.

"Yolanda," he said, trying to wrap his mind around what she said.

"What? I've laid it all out on the table. You can take it or leave it."

Before he could reply, Yolanda's cell phone chimed. "My shipment has arrived."

"Let's get dressed and go, then," he said as he rose to his feet. Yolanda sauntered out of the kitchen and looked over her shoulder at him.

"I meant what I said," she cooed. "And you know you want me as much as I want you."

Was he that obvious?

Richmond, Virginia

Danny smiled at his new investor, Vanessa Blades, a writer who had just made the *New York Times* bestseller list and was looking to diversify her portfolio and double the advance she was given for her next book. She was the kind of client who added credibility to his company. And it didn't hurt that she was beautiful.

"You have to forgive me for being unfamiliar with your book," Danny said. "But it is on my list of books to read when I finally get to take a vacation."

"I can forgive you for that. At least you have a copy," she said with a smile.

"And, I understand what a feat it is to make it on the bestseller list."

She nodded and was about to reply when Danny's throwaway phone rang. He cursed inwardly as he reached into his desk to silence the phone. As much as he hoped this was the call he'd been waiting for, that Yolanda was dead, he couldn't pull out that flip phone in front of Vanessa. And if he rushed her out of the office, he wasn't going to be able to ask her out to dinner. Well, dinner would be the excuse; he wanted her on her knees with a mouthful of his dick. Her lips looked like they would cuddle him until he unloaded down her throat.

Danny shifted in his seat. He needed to focus on two things right now: getting her to sign the papers and what the phone call was about. He slid the papers to Vanessa, focusing on her lips as she read over the investment agreement. She read each page of the five-page agreement. While this type of behavior nearly always sent him over the edge, this was just what he needed. Now he could pull the phone out and find out what was happening in Charlotte.

The text message he read didn't bring him joy.

We got a problem. Package has a guard.

"Is everything all right?" Vanessa asked, reminding Danny she was still in the room.

"Yes, just a bit of a family matter. Have you signed?"

"I want to have my husband look over this first. I'll be back tomorrow," she said as she rose to her feet. Danny nearly shooed her out of the office. He needed to call Chase and find out what his fucking problem was with wrapping this bitch in a dirt nap.

Closing the door behind Vanessa, Danny stalked over to his desk and grabbed the burner from his desk.

"Chase, what in the fuck is going on?" Danny howled when his hit man said hello.

"I can't kill that woman when I'm being watched. You made this a lot more difficult than it needs to be."

"What you need to do is take care of this bitch," Danny growled.

"No, I need to find out who this guy is and how to get rid of him."

"With a fucking bullet. I don't have time for this. It's only a matter of time before she has a crisis of conscience and decides to go to the police. I'm not going to jail behind Bobby G.'s stupid ass."

"You brought this on yourself. Why did you go off on Bobby G. so damn publicly? That was stupid."

"I want people to know I'm not playing games with them anymore. When I say I want my money, give it to me or die. Pay what you owe."

"Thought you were supposed to keep your hands clean? That's why I work with you. You're supposed to be doing something important and you fooled all the right people—now you want to fuck that up?"

"People need to know that I'm not to be played with and that's the message I was sending with Bobby G. You have to have skin in the game if you plan to win."

Chase sighed into the phone. "What's the plan for the bodyguard or whoever? If I have to stop two hearts, then the price goes up."

"Do what you have to do. I'm good for it." Danny hung up the phone and shoved it back into his desk drawer with a loud thud. He needed to do something to make sure he wasn't linked to this murder. It would bring down everything he had built and that bitch wasn't going to cause that collapse to happen.

Chapter 13

Two days later in Charlotte, Yolanda, Alex, and Nina were in her showroom trying on dresses. It was hard to believe how many weeks had passed since Nina's accident. She'd healed like Wolverine from the X-Men, it seemed like, as she tossed dresses into a pile.

"Who picked out these dresses?" Nina asked as she held up a princess-styled gown against her body.

Yolanda tilted her head toward Alex.

Alex rolled her eyes. "Whatever. I was trying to help you find something classic for your wedding."

Nina shook her head. "I don't do classic. I want something that embodies my style."

"But no sneakers!" Yolanda and Alex said in unison.

Nina rolled her eyes and glanced over at Chuck, who was watching them with a slight smirk on his lips. "Excuse me," she said. "Do I look like a princess gown type of woman?"

"I have no comment," he said.

Yolanda rolled her eyes and wished her sisters had the sense to ignore him, as she'd been doing all day. Chuck was Nina's fault. Though she couldn't blame her sister for wanting to have sexy times with him. But if Nina had kept her lovely mouth shut, she wouldn't be in this situation. Just looking into Chuck's eyes made her panties wet. And she was dripping right now. Yolanda walked away from her sisters and headed to the storage room, where she kept wine. She hadn't decided if she wanted to share yet. Glancing at her watch, she realized that it was just five minutes before noon. Was it too early to drown her desire in wine?

Nope. Yolanda popped the cork on a chilled bottle of Chardonnay and poured herself a big glass.

"You all right back here?" Chuck's voice made her jump and spill some of the wine.

"Yeah—yeah. Just getting some wine for us. Bored yet?" she asked as she turned around to face him.

Chuck raised his right eyebrow when he saw the glass in her hand. "It's a little . . ."

"Don't judge me. I mean, you're stressing me out right now."

"I'm stressing you out," he parroted. "Not the fact that someone wants you dead, just me?"

Yolanda threw her head back and groaned. "Yes, because you just won't . . ." She set her glass and the bottle of wine on the edge of a bunch of boxes. Then she flung herself into his arms and kissed him. Chuck didn't have time to push her away; their lips melded together and he stroked her bottom as their tongues danced together. Soft moans escaped her throat, and if she thought no one but Chuck heard her, she was wrong.

Alex burst through the door and exclaimed, "What in the hell is going on?"

Seconds later, Nina walked in as Yolanda and Chuck

stared at Alex with guilt and surprise etched across their faces. Nina couldn't hide her grin. "It's pretty obvious," she quipped.

Chuck cleared his throat. "I'm going to check the perimeter." He brushed past the sisters and Yolanda reached for her wine.

"Let's get back to these dresses," Yolanda said. Alex reached out and took the glass from her hand.

"Yolanda, what in the hell is going on with you and the bodyguard? And why do you need one in the first place?"

Yolanda glared at Nina. "See what you and your mouth did?"

"Am I supposed to feel bad?" Nina snapped.

Alex groaned. "Will someone tell me what's going on?"

Yolanda reached for the wineglass Alex held, but Alex lifted it above her head. "Somebody better start talking."

"I got into some trouble in Richmond and told the wrong person about it," Yolanda said, nodding toward Nina. "So, when she blabbed to Dad, he got Chuck to protect me."

"Protect you?" Alex asked, looking from Yolanda to Nina. "What kind of trouble are you in now?"

Nina shifted her weight from left to right as if she was waiting for Yolanda to tell the whole story. Yolanda simply shook her head. "Give me my glass, Alex."

"Tell me what's going on."

Yolanda crossed over to the shelf where she had other wineglasses, grabbed another one, and filled it with the Chardonnay. "Are we going to find Nina a dress or nah?" she asked after taking a sip.

Alex drank the wine in the glass she held, then stomped

out of the room. Nina shook her head at Yolanda. "Why don't you just tell her what's going on?"

"Do me a favor, mind your business." Yolanda blew past Nina and headed into the showroom. Alex was standing by the discarded dresses, picking them up and putting them on hangers.

Alex glanced at Yolanda and the look on her face screamed annoyance. Yolanda didn't want to fight with her older sister and she didn't want to tell her the entire truth.

"You don't have to do that," Yolanda said quietly.

"It's okay. I'm used to cleaning up after you."

Yolanda rolled her eyes. "This is why I don't like dealing with you. Everything is a judgment. You think you are so perfect and you're not!"

"You are so childish! And here you are in trouble again—enough trouble to have a bodyguard, but I'm wrong for being concerned?"

Yolanda snorted as she picked up another discarded dress. "You're not concerned. You just want to . . . I'm not doing this."

"Good, because at this point, I don't even care anymore." Alex dropped the dress she'd been placing on a hanger and tore out of the shop. Nina walked up to Yolanda and placed her hand on her shoulder.

"You really should tell her the truth."

"Nina, I don't want to talk to you right now. If you would've kept your mouth shut, this wouldn't be happening."

"And you could be dead! I'm not going to apologize for telling Daddy."

Before Yolanda could reply, Chuck walked in and gave

Yolanda a cold glance. She threw her hands up. "So, is everybody in the building mad at me?"

Charles wasn't mad at Yolanda, but he was pissed with himself. Why did he kiss her? And why did it feel so damn good? Yolanda was trouble. First, she'd awakened something inside him that he thought had died with Hillary. Then she kissed like a dream. The same dream he'd had last night, only better. Now he had to forget it and focus on the job. Losing focus would mean losing Yolanda.

Prepare her then, he thought. What if Yolanda knew how to protect herself from danger and he stopped seeing her as a helpless victim? He could teach her how to shoot and what to look out for. Charles stroked his face and considered what he was thinking. If he was honest, this might have been the worst idea he'd ever had. As feisty as Yolanda was, giving her a gun might put her in more danger than he needed to have her in. Was he doing it because he wanted a green light to make love to her?

Stop it, he thought. *Do your job and keep your pants zipped.*

Charles turned around and saw Nina walking toward him. "What's going on with you and my sister?" she asked once they were standing face-to-face. "You know you're supposed to protect her from a killer and not whatever else is going on here."

"Nina, right?" Charles asked, even though he knew.

"Yes. Are you going to answer my question?"

"There is nothing going on with me and your sister. I'm doing my job."

"I hope that's all you're doing. I need my sister to . . ."

"Nina!" Yolanda exclaimed. "Are you really doing this?"

Charles threw up his hands and shook his head. "Ladies, this isn't helping anything right now. Yolanda, can we talk in private?"

She raised her right eyebrow at him. "About what? Because I'm not going to apologize for what I . . ."

He touched her elbow. "That's not what I want to talk about."

"Fine," she said, then shot Nina a nasty look. "We can go into my office."

Nina shook her head and turned to the other dresses that she hadn't tried on. "I guess I'll amuse myself and pick out my own damned wedding dress."

Charles tried not to smile, but these women were funny. He'd never seen people love each other that much and be so loud about it. And he thought he had it bad with his sisters.

Once they made it into Yolanda's office, she sat on the edge of the desk and looked up at him. Beauty didn't come close to describing her. Even when she was being indignant.

"I have a plan," he said. "And I think it's important for your safety going forward."

"What's that?"

"You need to learn how to shoot. I want you to be able to—as a last resort—defend yourself. We don't know where this threat is coming from and I don't want to ever be caught off guard."

She leaned into him. "Absolutely not."

"Excuse me?"

"I don't want to play around with guns. I want to . . . Can we talk about the kiss?"

"No, because it's not happening again. Yolanda, you at some point are going to have to get serious about this. Do you know who Danny Branch is?"

He could tell she was familiar because her body nearly went limp. "H-how do you know about him?"

"I had a friend do some investigating for me. This guy is bad news and the police seem to be on his side. Someone could be here right now waiting to take you out and no one would even connect it to him."

"If the police are on his side, why do you want me to actually go to Richmond and make a statement? Thought you were supposed to keep me alive, not lead me to the slaughter."

"As long as you're with me, you're going to stay alive. And that's why I want you to know how to defend yourself as well."

Yolanda rose to her feet and paced the small office space three times before stopping in front of him. "You know what? Maybe you're right."

"About?"

"Being able to take care of myself. Then when I can do that, you can go home."

Charles gave her a half smile. "You keep trying to fire me and I don't work for you."

"I'm sure when my sisters tell my daddy that you grabbed my booty he'll fire you. And then . . ."

"Stop it."

She inched closer to him. "Are you married? Spoken for or otherwise entangled? I'll respect your relationship."

Charles should've pushed her away, but the heat of her

body was hard to resist. His hands wanted to touch her and he was powerless to stop pulling her in. "There is no relationship to respect, but I have to be honest with you, this is dangerous."

"More dangerous than people trying to kill me?" she mimicked.

"Yolanda, be serious."

"I seriously want to fu—"

Before she could finish, the door opened and Nina walked in. Now Charles had to let her go. "You know what," Nina said as she walked in. "I don't know who you two think you're fooling, but I know there is something going on and . . ."

Yolanda shook her head. "Nina, can you just go sit your ass down somewhere?"

"Think about what I said," Charles said. "Where is your other sister?"

"Who cares," Yolanda snorted. Charles shook his head.

"There could be people out . . . I'm going to look for her. Stay here."

Yolanda wasn't the kind of woman who listened to what someone told her. But when Chuck said, "Stay here," she didn't move. Well, until Nina pinched her on the shoulder.

"What the hell?" Yolanda snapped.

"You got some explaining to do," Nina said. "What are you and the bodyguard doing?"

"Nothing!" Yolanda called out.

"You're lying. Please tell me that you're taking this whole thing seriously," Nina said as tears welled up in her eyes.

"Nina, please don't start crying. I'm not ready to do this right now. I'm scared and if I want . . . This is your fault."

"My fault? Because I wanted to keep my sister alive? Stop trying to make me feel guilty and stop distracting your bodyguard with your boobs!"

Yolanda laughed. "That man can't be distracted. First night we were here he saw me naked."

"Oh my God!" Nina exclaimed. The door opened and Alex walked in with a white bag of food.

"What's going on now?" she asked as she dropped the bag on Yolanda's desk.

"N-nothing," Nina said. "What's in the bag?"

"Sushi. And who sent Charles to find me?"

Yolanda rolled her eyes. "I'm sure you just happened to run into him as you went to get us lunch."

Alex shook her head. "I got lunch for me and Nina. I'm sure you'd rather put something else in your mouth."

Nina brought her hand to her mouth and failed to hide her laughter.

"This is why I can't stand you," Yolanda snapped.

"Calm down, hot thing, I was just kidding," Alex said. "Geez, I don't even like sushi."

Yolanda hugged her sister and smiled. "You know what, I'm tripping and I'm sorry."

"Can you please tell me what's going on?" Alex asked. "I want to know the whole story."

Yolanda closed her eyes for a second and considered telling Alex what happened. But what could she do? She couldn't change anything. And after what Chuck told her, she didn't want her family to know how much danger she was really in.

"Can we just eat first?" Yolanda asked. "The wine in my belly is lonely."

Alex rolled her eyes. "So, you drink like a fish and you have a bodyguard. But everything is fine." She reached into the bag and pulled out the sushi rolls and a carton of shrimp fried rice for herself.

"Everything is fine," Yolanda said as she opened one of the containers. "Ooh, California rolls? Good job, Alex."

"Don't be greedy over there," Nina said. Yolanda held the box out to her sister.

"Please put something in your mouth so you can be quiet," Yolanda sniped. Nina rolled her eyes and snatched the box from her sister. Then she turned to Alex and smiled. "Please tell me you have soy sauce."

Chuck walked into the room and cleared his throat. "Ms. Richardson . . ."

"Yes?" the three women said, then broke out laughing. He held up another white paper bag.

"You left this in the restaurant," he said. Nina took the bag from his hand even though she knew he had been talking to Alex.

"Thanks for bringing that," Alex said. "And just for the record, everyone in this room is *Miss Richardson*."

"Not for much longer," Nina sang as she pulled out the different sauces. Yolanda crossed over to her sister and shook her head.

"For someone who asked for soy sauce, why are you hoarding all the spicy mayo?"

Alex sucked her teeth and looked up at Chuck. "Would you like some sushi or rice? It seems my sisters lost their manners."

"Thanks, but I'm not hungry. Besides, I have some work to do." He crossed over to Yolanda. "When you're done we need to talk about the security cameras and the alarm system."

She nodded and popped a sushi roll in her mouth. And though her sisters watched, neither of them said a word when Chuck gave her elbow a fleeting touch and Yolanda visibly shivered.

They ate in silence and Yolanda kept watching Chuck as he passed the door to her office every few minutes.

Alex turned to Nina. "Are you going to ask or do I have to be the bad guy again?"

"Ask what?" Nina said as she twirled her chopsticks.

"If either of you were trying to whisper, you failed," Yolanda said. "Anyway, I'm going to meet with Ch-Charles. I'm sure you two will take care of this mess?"

Before they could reply, Yolanda was out of the office and heading to the storage room, where Chuck had taken their lunch hour to turn it into a surveillance room.

"What the? You did all of this in an hour?" she asked as she looked at the four wall-mounted monitors, a computer system sitting on a black metal table, and a chair. "What happened to my stuff?"

He pointed to a stack of plastic storage containers. "This is what I wanted to talk to you about. How do you want to organize them and everything back here?"

She slapped her hand on her hip and realized that her storage room had never been more in order. And there was more room with everything in those storage boxes. Space to hide, space to wrap her body around Chuck

Morris and come until she felt as if her knees were made of rubber. And speaking of knees. She could . . . *Stop it.*

"Um, just stack the boxes on the shelves, I guess."

He chuckled. "I'm not trying to be funny but those shelves are pretty high and . . ."

"Call me short and I'm going to fight you. Besides, that's what stepladders are for."

"All right. Are you going to label the boxes at least?"

She closed the door behind her and speared him with a questioning look. "Can we talk about the other boxes in the room?"

Chuck shook his head. "We made a mistake and shared an amazing kiss. We're facing something serious here and we should put the focus there."

Yolanda inched closer to where he was sitting. She placed her hand on his knee. "It's hard to focus when all I really want to do is this." She leaned in and kissed him slow and deep. Chuck responded just the way she'd hoped he would, with fire. He pulled her onto his lap as the kiss deepened. She felt his erection through his jeans and quaked with a lustful need. She wanted to strip her clothes off and ride him until they both screamed.

Screaming wasn't an option. Her sisters were still there. Nosey sisters who would run to the door and demand to know what was going on. Chuck broke the kiss and pushed the stool back some more. But he didn't let Yolanda go. And when she looked into his eyes, she knew they both wanted the same thing.

"Yolanda," he said, his voice husky with desire. "We can't do this here."

"But we are going to do this?"

He shifted on the stool and she moaned quietly. If he felt like this encased in jeans, she couldn't wait to have him inside her. "I'll make a deal with you."

Yolanda groaned; all he had to do was say yes. "What is it?"

"Learn to shoot. Take the fact that people want to kill you a lot more seriously and it's a one-and-done thing."

Yolanda hopped off his lap and tilted her head to the side. "One and done?"

"Am I attracted to you? Yes. But I have to focus on the reason I'm here."

"Things change all the time. And it's going to be so good, you're not going to be able to keep your one-and-done promise. But I'll accept your offer. However, I choose the time when it happens."

"All right. But your first lesson at the range starts tomorrow morning," he said.

Yolanda shrugged and wondered what in the hell she had gotten herself into. When she opened the door, Yolanda wasn't surprised to find Alex and Nina pretending to look around the shop but standing really close to the door.

"Real subtle," Yolanda muttered as she looked up at the clock on the wall.

A few seconds later, Chuck walked out of the storage room. "Ladies, how much longer are you going to be here?"

Nina grinned. "Do you need time alone with Yolanda?"

Alex nudged her and Yolanda actually blushed.

Chuck, with his face stoic, simply said, "I have to go pick up a few things and I want to make sure I know your location. If you're going to stay here, that's fine—there are alerts on the doors. But if you plan to head back to the town house, I can escort you there."

"And all of this security is needed for what reason?" Alex asked, looking directly at Yolanda.

"I think we're done here," Yolanda said.

"But I haven't picked out my dress yet," Nina said.

"And we have another shipment coming in tomorrow. No one said you'd buy a wedding dress in one day," Yolanda said.

"She has a point," Alex said. "And I'm a little tired of being in here."

"All right then, let's go," Chuck said as he led the Richardson ladies out of the shop. Nina slowed down to look at the Charlotte skyline.

"I'm going to miss this place, at some point," Nina said. "But I'm getting used to ocean breezes again. And Clinton's arms."

"And you hurry up and get married, because I'm tired of you," Alex said with a laugh. "Clinton is just as love-sick."

Lovesick. Yolanda shot a quick glance at Chuck. Had he ever been in love? He probably broke hearts because his work was so dangerous. Maybe the love of his life left him because he couldn't give up his superhero work. It started making sense as to why he made up rules for engagement.

Did he think she believed sex and love were the same thing? Yolanda wanted an orgasm, not a long-term commitment. Those things never worked out. Her dad lost her mom and he was never the same.

Her sister Robin thought she'd met Prince Charming and now she and Dr. Logan Baptiste were on their way to divorce court. She wasn't going to put her heart at risk. And Chuck was a risk that she couldn't fully take—right?

What the hell am I doing?

Chapter 14

By the time Yolanda and her sisters arrived at the house, Yolanda felt conflicted about being alone with them knowing there was a killer out there hunting her. Chuck may not have believed that she was taking this seriously, but knowing that she may bring harm to her sisters—even Alex—scared her.

"You made some big changes here," Nina said as she looked around her former home. She pointed at the downstairs bedroom. "You sleep down here?"

Yolanda nodded. "Your old room is the perfect design studio."

Nina clasped her hands together and jumped up and down. "Does that mean you're going to start your fashion line?"

Alex rolled her eyes. "Can you explain how you keep coming up with these business ideas but you . . . Is Daddy going to finance your fashion line?"

Yolanda ran a frustrated hand across her face. "This is why I . . . Alex, you have such a low opinion of me and what I've done. I moved here without Dad's help. The business is in my name. And if I want to design clothes, then I'm going to do it. I'm going to live my dreams while you stay buried under yours!"

"Guys, can we not fight?" Nina exclaimed. "I'm sorry I said anything."

Alex stormed toward the door, but Yolanda grabbed her arm. A picture in her head showed an unseen gunman shooting her sister. "Wait, sis," Yolanda said calmly. "I'm sorry."

Alex took a step back, surprise contorting her face. "What the hell is going on?"

Even Nina was shocked by Yolanda's complete one-eighty. This was usually the part where Alex left the room and Yolanda started cursing. "We had a pretty good afternoon, let's not mess it up. Alex, I get that you don't understand fashion as a business, but one thing I have learned from you is to have a business plan. I have a few. That's why I was able to pay Dad back for his investment."

"I don't understand the move to Charlotte," Alex said. For a change her tone was calm.

"How about I get us some snacks and we talk about it?" Yolanda said.

"The truth about it?" Alex said as she started to sit on the sofa.

"Ah, don't sit there, that's Chuck's bed."

Nina burst out laughing. "You make that big man sleep on this tiny sofa? Is that why you sleep down here?"

Before she could answer, the front door opened and Chuck walked in carrying two black bags.

"Charles," Alex began, "I'm so sorry that my sister acts as if she doesn't know how to make a guest comfortable. The sofa?"

Yolanda sucked her teeth and sat on the love seat near the sliding glass door.

"Well, ma'am, it makes more sense for me to be down here for security precautions, and I have to say, Yolanda has been quite hospitable."

"I bet," Nina muttered and Yolanda shot her an evil look.

"So, when is anyone going to tell me about why my sister needs a live-in bodyguard?" Alex asked.

"That's not my place," Chuck said. "I'm going to put these things up in your studio and we need to go over what I have."

Yolanda nodded, then said, "Wait. Um, don't go up there yet." The last thing she wanted was for him to see any more of her sketches of him. The last one she did, it was a nude.

"What's in the bags anyway?" Nina asked.

Charles thought his sisters were nosey and hard to deal with. The Richardson sisters made the Morris girls look tame. He did understand why Yolanda was being hesitant about telling her sisters the whole story, but how much longer would she be able to keep them in the dark? Well, keep Alex in the dark. Nina seemed to know part of the story and was the one who went to their father.

"You write for *Sports Illustrated,* right?" Charles said.

"Um-huh. So, what's in the bags?" Nina replied.

"Stuff for me and your sister," he replied. When he heard Yolanda call his name, Charles wanted to run up the stairs to get away from Nina and her questions. But he kept his cool and headed up to Yolanda's studio.

"You brought guns in here?" she asked as he walked into the room. She nodded toward the black bag she'd opened. "What in the hell were you thinking?"

"We have a plan," he said. "I didn't think you and your sisters would be sitting there talking about whatever you were talking about."

"I didn't tell them that you were bringing guns into the house." Yolanda's eyes stretched to the size of quarters as she glanced at the bags. "How many guns are in here? Are we planning to shoot it out with whoever is out there?"

"No. First of all, we're not planning a war," he said with a chuckle. Charles reached into the bag and pulled out a revolver. "And you only need a handgun."

"Why don't I get to have a rifle?" she teased as he returned the revolver to the bag.

"Because I said so." He winked at her and pulled out a .380 semiautomatic handgun. "This is small and powerful, but with a semiautomatic, you have to consider the possibility of it jamming."

"That doesn't sound safe."

He reached into the bag and pulled out another gun, this one a shortbarrel .357 revolver. "I would recommend the revolver. It's a gun that is a lot more reliable. But when we go to the range in the morning, shoot both and see which one you're more comfortable with."

"This is . . ." Yolanda looked at the guns, and for the first time, he saw real fear. He saw that she had actually turned down the sex, the attitude, and the bravado. "Someone is out there who wants to kill me and I don't want my family to suffer. Chuck, I didn't do anything. I was simply at my shop and . . ." Tears sprang into her eyes and he pulled her into his arms.

This wasn't a seduction, wasn't Yolanda trying to hide her emotions behind her swagger. He felt her tears wet his chest and Charles knew that he was going to do everything he needed to do to protect her.

"Yolanda," he whispered. "I'm here for you and I'm going to do whatever I have to do to protect you and everyone you love."

She lifted her head and looked up at him. When her lips trembled, he wanted to kiss her. He needed to kiss her.

Stop it, he thought as he turned away from her. *You have to stay focused. Despite that stupid deal you made with her.*

"I'm sorry," she said. "I'm so sorry to be this basket case. Being around my sisters today has me shaken. I don't want this Danny person to try to get me, miss, and one of them pays."

"Even though y'all fight a lot, you ladies are close."

"Yes. We are. And I'd never forgive myself if something I did hurt them."

"Just remember you didn't do anything wrong."

Yolanda nodded. He cupped her chin and forced her to face him. "Yolanda," he said. "You didn't do anything wrong."

"You're right. Thank you." She fingered the .357. "And this is the more reliable option?"

"It can be," he said. "Like I said, we'll try both of them tomorrow morning. What time are you and your sisters going to the shop? I think we need about two hours in the range so that you can ease into your comfort level with the guns."

She closed her eyes and sighed. "That means I'm going to have to get up early and cook breakfast before we head out," Yolanda said as she eased out of his embrace.

Had he really been holding her that long? Was it really feeling that good to have her heat against him? *One and done. What the hell were you thinking?*

"Um, knock-knock," a voice said from behind them.

"What is it, Alex?" Yolanda groaned.

"Are we cooking dinner or is there going to be a delivery or something? Personally, I was hoping for shrimp and grits. And your sister said Clinton taught her a recipe, so please stop her."

"Oh hell no," Yolanda exclaimed as she started down the stairs. "Nina, you'd better not be in the kitchen."

Charles tried to cover the guns, but Alex saw them and didn't pull any punches. "You're about to arm my sister? Look, Charles, I know you're trying to pretend that you're working for Yolanda and you don't have to answer to anyone but her and my father. Let's be clear, I've been making sure you get your paycheck. Now what in the hell is going on?"

He sighed and closed his eyes for a quick second. "Alex," he said quietly. "Yolanda is in trouble."

"Well, that's obvious."

"Your father knows what's going on and you need to speak to him about it. I need your sister to trust me and I can't violate what we have by doing the one thing she asked me not to do."

Alex shook her head. "Yolanda is always in trouble.

Just do what you have to do to keep her out of trouble and . . . How serious is it?"

"Please, speak with your father. But know that I have your sister's best interests at heart and I'm going to do everything in my power to keep her safe."

Alex gave him a nod of approval. "Please do. Yolanda means more to me than she even knows," she said, then left the room.

Charles laughed as he heard the women in the kitchen arguing about grits and how to make the shrimp. They really loved each other, and now he knew there was more to why Yolanda wanted to hide from her family how much danger she was in.

Chapter 15

Dinner was interesting, at least for Yolanda. She actually allowed Nina to cook the shrimp because she kept talking about how Clinton had taught her how to pan fry shrimp with bacon grease. Neither Yolanda nor Alex would let her touch the grits.

"If this is trash, I'm blaming you," Alex whispered to Yolanda as Nina prepared the shrimp.

"She hasn't set off the fire alarm yet, so . . ."

"I hope you heffas know that I can hear you," Nina snapped. "The shrimp is almost done."

Alex crossed over to her baby sister. "No the hell it isn't! Are you going to cut the tails off? If this is how Clinton is . . ."

"You make the shrimp and I'll get the grits going," Nina said.

"No!" Alex and Yolanda exclaimed.

"Put some pepper on that shrimp," Yolanda said.

"And a pinch of salt," Alex added.

Nina sucked her teeth. "What the hell is a pinch?"

"Just go sit down," Alex said. "We'll take it from here."

Nina shrugged. "Fine. I was tired of cooking anyway."

She headed for the dining room and Yolanda checked the shrimp. She had to admit, Nina's skills had improved. Clinton was more than just a marketing genius, he was a miracle worker.

"Taste this," Yolanda said as she held a piece of shrimp out to Alex on a fork. "Nina has changed."

"Harumph," Alex said before taking a bite. "Oh my goodness. This is good. I still don't trust her with grits."

"I can hear y'all," Nina called out from the dining room.

"We know," Yolanda shot back.

"Technically, this is still my house and I can kick you out," Nina said.

"The shrimp is good, though," Alex said as she stirred the grits. "Yolanda. How much trouble are you in?"

"A lot and I don't want to get you involved," Yolanda said.

"But you had no problem getting Daddy mixed up in . . . whatever you have going on."

"Thank Nina for that—my plan was to handle this by myself."

Alex raised her right eyebrow. "But if you need a bodyguard then this must be . . . Yolanda, are you going to tell me what's going on?"

"No, because that defeats the purpose of telling you that I don't want you involved. I know you, Alex. All you can do in this situation is make things worse."

Alex crossed over to Yolanda and gave her a tight hug. "Why are you so damned hardheaded?"

"Because I had a great teacher?"

Alex pinched her on the shoulder. "You're not funny." As the sisters broke their embrace, tears welled up in

Yolanda's eyes. She hadn't realized how much she needed a hug from her bossy big sister.

"Will Charles be joining us for dinner?" Alex asked as she wiped moisture from her eyes. Yolanda could tell that she was worried about her and she wished that she could tell her everything. But she knew Alex would leap into action, want to take her to the police station in Richmond and force her to make a report. And didn't Chuck tell her they were dealing with someone very dangerous?

"Yolanda," Alex snapped.

"What?"

"Are you feeding the bodyguard or not?"

"I'm sure Chuck will eat something later."

Alex shook her head as she checked the grits. "Why do you call that man *Chuck*?"

Yolanda giggled. "Because his last name is Morris."

Alex nearly dropped her spoon. "His mama played a joke on him. Does he know karate?"

"I do. And several other forms of martial arts," he said as he appeared out of what seemed to be thin air. Yolanda still didn't know how a big man like that moved in such silence.

"Well, *Chuck Morris*," Alex said, "will you be joining us for dinner? Shrimp and cheese grits."

"Who made the grits?" he asked as Nina walked into the kitchen.

"Seriously? You tell everybody about the one mishap I had with cooking grits," Nina said, flashing an accusatory glance at Yolanda.

"That wasn't a mishap, that was an embarrassment,"

Alex said. "But you've almost redeemed yourself with these shrimp."

"Thank Clinton by giving him the day off Friday."

Yolanda laughed. "That's not going to happen."

Chuck watched the women as they moved around the kitchen, joking, fighting, and laughing. Yolanda caught his eye as she crossed over to the freezer and pulled out two plastic containers of collard greens.

"Why didn't you tell me you had collards?" Alex exclaimed. "We could've had fried chicken and macaroni and cheese."

Nina shook her head. "Um, Robin isn't here and neither of you can fry chicken like Robin."

Yolanda and Alex rolled their eyes at her. "Oh, that child has a nerve," Alex quipped.

"Where's the wine, Yolanda?" Nina asked, then stuck her tongue out at Alex.

"How about we have cranberry juice tonight," Yolanda said as she set the collards on the counter and crossed over to the refrigerator and pulled out a bottle of juice.

Alex and Nina exchanged questioning looks. "That's good for you," Nina said. "But where's the wine?"

"At the store."

Alex sighed. "Fine, I'll go and . . ."

"No," Chuck said, holding up his hand. "I'll pick up a bottle of wine for dinner."

"Two," Nina called out to his retreating figure. "Because Yolanda is going to have a glass as well. *Juice*. Yeah, right."

"Nina," Alex said, shaking her head.

When Chuck left and Alex headed into the living room to check in on the bed-and-breakfast, Nina leaned against the counter while Yolanda heated the collards in a pan.

"Tell the truth and shame the devil, you and Chuck have fu—"

"We have not but we're going to, and you don't get to ask any more questions about him since you're the reason he's here."

"Did you tell Alex what's going on?"

Yolanda shook her head. "Can you guys just let me figure this out? After your wedding, Chuck and I have a plan. But I'm not doing anything to ruin your day after all you've been through." Yolanda closed her eyes and remembered watching her sister battle for her life after that horrific accident in Charlotte. When she'd heard about Nina's accident, she thought it was the people after her trying to stop her from talking and not just an accident because she and Clinton had had an argument. Turning around to face her, Yolanda pointed her fork at Nina. "If you bought another Mustang, we're going to fight."

Nina furrowed her eyebrows. "Where did that come from?"

"Nowhere," she said. "But what are you driving these days?"

"Clinton's car," Nina said, then started out of the kitchen.

"But doesn't he have a . . .Y'all make me sick. You need a Buick."

Nina turned around and shook her head. She was about to say something when the front door opened and Chuck walked in. "Saved by the bodyguard," Nina whispered as he headed for the kitchen.

Chapter 16

Chase was getting bored with this stupid assignment. How many people did this woman have in and out of her life? She had a house full of people and that man was still there. Chase was sure that he'd seen the green-eyed giant spot him in the tree line where he was hiding. That woman knew someone was after her and this was going to make eliminating her that much harder. *Dumb-ass Danny,* he thought as he moved from his spot once the man entered the town house. Since North Carolina was an open-carry state, he calmly walked to his car with his rifle on his back. Just as he'd secured it in the trunk a police cruiser slowly drove through the neighborhood. He had seen him. Shit! Chase climbed into the car and called Danny.

"Is it done? Finally?" he asked when he answered.

"No, you goddamn idiot. Her bodyguard saw me and now the police are riding through the neighborhood."

"No one told you to take this long to handle the situation."

"And no one told you to create such a fucked-up situation. What were you thinking, Danny?"

"Do your fucking job."

"Fuck you." Chase ended the call and tossed his phone in the glove box. He watched from the car as the man walked out of the town house and talked to the patrol officer. He groaned, knowing that he'd been seen. This didn't happen. Who in the hell was this man?

"Thanks for coming out. And you didn't see anything?" Charles asked the cop.

"No. And you said you saw her stalker in the woods?" she asked as she stared at Charles and not the area where he'd seen the white man.

"Yeah," he said, turning toward the woods. "Right over there."

"Yes, yes," she said as if she'd fallen back into the reason why she was on the scene. "I'll check it out, and if I find anything I'll let you know. Do you know if she has reported that she has a stalker?"

Charles folded his arms across his chest and shook his head. "If she thought the police could handle it, then I wouldn't be here."

"Well, how do we know what to be on the lookout for?" she said as if she was offended.

Charles snorted. "I just told you." He turned back toward the entrance of the town house and saw Yolanda standing at the door.

"What was that all about?" she asked as he walked inside.

"Thought I saw something outside," he said truthfully.

"Something, or *someone* trying to . . ."

Charles pressed her against his chest. "You're safe, all

right? Where's that dinner you and your sisters invited me to?"

Yolanda pushed away from him and glared at him. "Was my killer out there? Are we in danger?"

"No. At this moment, no one is out there."

He watched her shiver in fear. "But he's here?"

"Let's eat."

"Don't do this." Her voice was low and filled with fear.

"Yolanda, no harm is going to come to you while I'm here. I got you," he said.

She dropped her head in her hands. "But my sisters are here and . . ."

"This is why we have to go to the police. Yolanda, I know you're afraid, but . . ."

Alex walked into the living room. "Hey, are we going to eat or what?" She looked from Yolanda to Charles. "What's going on?"

"Everything's fine, ma'am." Charles knew Alex didn't believe him by the scowl on her face.

"Sure it is," Alex said. "The food is getting cold."

"Thanks, Alex," Yolanda said. "We'll be right there."

Alex turned on her heels and headed for the dining room.

"This, this is what I've been afraid of. I don't want my family hurt because . . ."

"Yolanda," he said softly. "We have to fix this. Right now we have a Band-Aid on the situation. Let's just eat."

She sighed and walked toward the dining room. Nina and Alex were seated at the dining room table with the shrimp and grits and collard greens in the middle of table. "It's about time," Nina said. "I'd be eating right now if Alex wasn't Alex."

"Am I the only one in this family who has manners?" Alex asked as Yolanda and Charles took their seats. Yolanda rolled her eyes as they started passing the bowls of food. "You eat once everyone is at the table. Daddy would be so disappointed in y'all."

Nina piled her plate with collard greens. "Daddy also says no fighting at the dinner table, but there you go starting."

Normally, this would be the moment when Yolanda and Nina would tag team Alex, but all Yolanda could think about was how close to death they had been. And how much Chuck wasn't telling her.

Everything just clicked as to how serious everything really was.

"Yolanda? You all right over there?" Nina asked.

"Yeah, I'm good. Just not as hungry as I thought I was." She rose to her feet and gave her sisters a nod before heading upstairs. Chuck grabbed his plate and followed her into the studio.

She turned around and shook her head at him. "I said I wasn't hungry."

"I know, the food is for me," he said as he set the plate on an empty spot on her desk. "What made it click today?"

"They're here and because of . . . I know this isn't my fault because I was at work, doing what I loved. Those men invaded my peace and robbed me of being safe." Tears poured down her cheeks and Chuck drew her into his arms.

"You know what you have to do to stop this," he said calmly. "And I know you don't want to go to the police, but you have to. I have someone working on finding an officer we can trust. That's the only way to get your peace and safety back."

She held on to him tightly. "I just can't keep you around forever?" she quipped.

"It doesn't work like that. And you'd get tired of me. To hear you tell it, you're already tired of me."

Yolanda looked up at him and the gleam in his eyes ignited something in her chest. What was this all about? She needed to focus on staying alive and not the wanton need she had for this man.

"That deal we made," she said. "Let's just call it off."

Chuck smiled. "But you're still learning to shoot, right?"

"Yes, but I'm not going to the police until Nina's married, like I said before. And now that you know what kind of people we're dealing with, maybe you can stop judging me for the decision I made."

Chuck nodded and stroked her arm before letting her go. "You should eat. This is pretty good and your sisters are concerned about you." He reached for his plate and took a big bite of the collard greens. There he was again showing those dimples and an appreciation for her food. She'd made the greens and she knew they were amazing.

"At least you know good food," she said. "But I don't allow food in my studio."

"Is that your not-so-subtle way of telling me to get out?"

"Are you sure you haven't missed your calling as a comedian?" Yolanda quipped. Though she wanted him to stay, she needed a minute to put her mental armor on and pretend she wasn't scared out of her mind.

The next morning, Yolanda woke up with a start, then smelled sausage. Alex must have been up cooking. She glanced at her phone and it was early, even for Alexandria Richardson standards. "What in the hell?" She hopped out of bed and headed for the kitchen. When she saw Chuck standing at the stove—wearing gray sweatpants and shirtless—she had to stop herself from whistling at him.

"Good morning," she said.

Chuck turned around. "Good morning. I was trying not to wake you," he said.

"You didn't; the smell of your breakfast did."

"Hmm, you don't usually smell it," he said with a smile, then returned to the pan. Yolanda crossed over to the stove and wondered what she wanted to taste more, his egg, cheese, and sausage scramble or his sexy mouth. "I guess I wasn't sleeping as deeply as I normally do or this is what happens when you skip dinner? You do this every morning?"

He nodded as he turned the heat down on the pan. "Right after my workout."

"My God, when do you sleep?"

"When I'm tired. You want some?" Chuck asked.

Oh, she wanted something, but she was supposed to act as if she didn't. What was he thinking cooking half naked? "I'll just have a banana."

"You're going to need your energy at the range. The first time you hear gunshots it might be jarring."

Yolanda shivered. The first time she'd heard gunshots

had been jarring, like bombs going off in her ears. "Yeah, it is. But at least I'll be ready for it this time," she said.

"At least let me make you some toast and honey to go with the banana."

"You got coffee?"

"That's what I don't make this time of morning because I know the coffee will wake you up."

She glanced at the steaming mug next to him. "What's that?"

"Promise not to laugh?"

Yolanda shook her head no.

"Then I'm not telling."

She crossed over to him and picked up the mug. It looked like coffee. And it smelled like coffee. "Is that instant coffee?"

"It is. Now, if you want to wake up this time of morning every day, I'll brew a pot for both of us every day. And instant coffee isn't as bad as you think. Taste it."

She looked down at his mug, thinking that sipping his trash coffee was probably the only way she'd taste his lips, then took a sip. And. It. Was. Trash. She coughed as she poured the swill down the drain.

"Hey, I was going to drink that," Chuck said behind his laugh.

"I can't allow you to do that," she said as she began prepping the coffee maker. "I may have been giving you a hard time, but that coffee is torture."

Once the coffee started percolating, it didn't take long for Alex to come downstairs. She and Nina had decided that Yolanda's studio was the best guest room ever and slept there.

"Why are you two up so early?" Alex asked as she walked into the kitchen.

"Oh," Yolanda said. "Now you know how it feels. But isn't it obvious that we're having breakfast?"

"This is even early for me. But the smell of the coffee made me think of home and how Nina and I need to get moving. I know our sister will sleep until ten, but I want to get into the office before noon today."

"I'll bet you're wondering how the bed-and-breakfast made it twenty-four hours without you being there," Yolanda said as she poured the coffee.

"I'm not doing this with you this early in the morning," Alex said as she rubbed her eyes. "As a matter of fact, I'm going back to bed and y'all can do whatever you were doing before I came down here."

"See!" Yolanda hissed. "We were just having breakfast before we go to the . . . gym. Yeah, the gym."

"Um-huh," Alex said as she waved her hand and headed toward the stairs.

"We should take her to the range with us," Chuck said when Alex was out of earshot.

"Absolutely not," Yolanda said as she passed him a mug of good coffee. His fingers briefly danced across hers, and she imagined that it was around nine in the morning and he was making breakfast after making love to her thoroughly the night before. They were alone in the town house and he'd decided to make her his breakfast on the marble counter. She wondered if he would use his fingers first or dive right in with those lips and his marvelous tongue.

"Yolanda," Chuck called out. She snapped back to

reality and saw that she was a couple of pours away from overfilling her mug. "Are you all right?"

"Yeah, yeah, I'm good. Just thinking about the range." Yolanda gulped her black coffee and decided that she needed a shower. A cold one.

"What time are we leaving?" Yolanda asked.

"I thought six-thirty would be good. I talked to the owner of the gun range we're going to and we're going to have the place to ourselves."

"Okay, I'm going to take a shower."

"And I'm saving you some of my scramble. That banana just isn't going to do it."

Yolanda dashed out of the kitchen and ran into the bathroom. She spent about fifteen minutes standing under the cold spray trying to get the image of that man out of her head.

She shut the water off after realizing it wasn't working. Yolanda dried off and put a robe on before heading into her bedroom to get dressed.

What do you wear to a gun range? she thought as she stood in front of the closet.

Charles made two plates for him and Yolanda. Then he downed another coffee before washing the dishes. When he heard footsteps, he expected to turn around and see Yolanda, but Nina was standing there.

"You all sure get up early," she said through a yawn.

"I really wasn't trying to wake you guys up," he said. "Coffee?"

"No, because that means I will officially have to be

awake. I've got a question for you," she said as she slapped her hand on her hip.

"All right."

"How are you going to keep my sister alive if you are sleeping with her? That's what this breakfast is about, isn't it?"

Charles shook his head. "I'm not sleeping with your sister and this breakfast is for our training this morning."

"Training?"

Charles nodded. "I'm going to help Yolanda protect herself."

"Thought that was your job."

"It is, but I'm a personal protection agent and part of my job is teaching my clients how to react if they have to."

"What's going on with you and my sister?"

"I'm here to protect your sister, that's it."

Nina tilted her head to the side. "Are you sure?"

"Yes. Why do you think something . . . Nina, I'm doing my job and that's it."

"What are you doing up so early?" Yolanda asked her sister as she walked into the kitchen.

"I smelled coffee." Nina gave Yolanda a slow once-over. "Why are you dressed like Catwoman?"

Charles drank in Yolanda's image: form-fitting black jumpsuit, black and white sneakers, and a black ball cap. Catwoman was a fitting description.

"Because I'm going to start my . . . What's going on in here?"

"Nothing," Charles said. "Your sister said your coffee woke her up."

Nina nodded. "Coffee is the alarm clock," she said.

"But I'm going back to bed so you two can get ready for your training or whatever. Knowing Alex, she's going to be up in fifteen minutes."

Once Charles and Yolanda were alone in the kitchen, he smiled. "Your sisters are something else."

"Like yours?"

"Nah. My sisters leave me alone these days."

"Did you make this for us?" she said as she nodded toward the plates.

"I told you that a banana wasn't going to be enough for the range," he said. "And after you saved me from instant coffee, I can't let you go out like that."

"You're too sweet," she replied with a smile.

Charles handed her a fork and Yolanda took it from his hand. "I hope you like it."

She closed her eyes for a brief second and then stroked the back of his hand. "I'm sure I will. It smells great."

Charles moved his hand from hers and watched her as she dug into the scramble. When Yolanda moaned as she ate, he wondered what she would sound like if they had kept their original plan. Would she make those sounds when he was deep inside her?

Wait! What? Why was he having these thoughts when he'd just told her sister that there was nothing going on between him and Yolanda?

"You're a dangerous man, Chuck Morris," she said after swallowing another bite of the scramble. "There is no way you should look this good and be able to cook."

"This is the by-product of growing up in a house full of women. Everyone pulls his or her weight. Since I woke up earlier than most, breakfast was my assignment."

"Wow," she said. "That's some childhood."

"I enjoyed it. Making my mother smile meant a lot to me."

"Were you close to your dad?"

"He died before we had a chance to become best friends."

"I'm sorry," Yolanda said. Charles could almost see her thoughts about her own father.

"He was a hero, so it's sad, but it framed my life. My father was in the marines and that's why I joined the service. He fought in the first Gulf War and I continued his mission until I couldn't."

"What happened?" she asked.

"That's a story for another day. Eat so we can go."

"All right," she replied, then finished off her breakfast. "I'm ready when you are."

"Let's go."

As they headed for the door, Charles asked, "What are you shooting, the revolver or the semi?"

"Why not both?" she asked with a shrug. "That's what you suggested, right?"

"So, you do listen?"

"Oh, whatever," she snapped.

Chapter 17

After two hours at the gun range, Yolanda realized that she didn't like guns. She wanted nothing to do with the loud things, though she also realized how much she needed one to keep the killer off her heels. But if she knew how to shoot, did that mean less time spent with Chuck around her? Those thoughts made her cringe as they walked to his car.

"Somehow, I thought this was going to be a lot more fun," Yolanda said as they got in the car and Chuck started for her house.

"Guns aren't toys, I don't get why you thought it would be fun."

She shrugged. "Maybe because I watch too much TV." Yolanda looked down at the scratch on the back of her hand from where the .380 had dug into her skin. Chuck had called it a Beretta burn. That's when she'd decided that that revolver was going to be her weapon of choice.

"Does it hurt?" he asked as he noticed her rubbing her hand.

"It stings a bit."

"That's because you have small, delicate hands. It's my hope that you won't have to ever use that gun."

She looked at the paper target at her side. Granted, she wasn't a professional, but most of her shots had landed center mass, as Chuck called it. Yolanda chuckled inwardly when she thought about how she'd closed her eyes the first two times she'd fired the gun. Chuck had walked up behind her and wrapped his arms around her waist.

"You can't shoot what you can't see. The gun is only going to fire if you pull the trigger." The heat from his breath against her ear had made her shiver. Then when he'd placed his hand on her midsection to help her with her form, Yolanda had wanted to press him against the wall and let him do everything she'd ever dreamed about. After all, they were alone in the gun range. But that hadn't been why they were there.

She was supposed to be learning to protect herself and possibly her family. Why was it that every time she was alone with that man she wanted to get in his pants?

Glancing over at him and those damn gray sweatpants, she knew why. He was sexy. He was fierce like a jaguar and she had no doubt that he'd make her body tingle. He'd done it with his kisses and . . .

"Yolanda?"

"H-huh?" she stammered.

"What's going on over there?"

"Nothing, I was just thinking about my sisters, wondering if they'd left yet."

"You think they would leave without locking up the house first?" Chuck furrowed his brows as if he was thinking that they'd leave the doors wide open or something.

"Nina has keys to her old place," she said.

Chuck nodded. "That makes sense. You think they'd leave without saying good-bye? It's still pretty early."

Yolanda looked at her watch. "Yeah, but this is when Alex would be organizing her meetings and whatnot. She is . . ."

"Your sister doesn't play," Chuck said with a laugh. "You all are something else."

"What do you mean?" Yolanda had heard this all before. People marveled at the Richardson sisters' relationship. While they fought internally, you didn't want to mess with them—in most circumstances. There was no way her sisters could help her stop a killer, but there were quite a few people in Charleston County who knew better than to go up against a Richardson.

"You're very protective of each other. It's refreshing to see sisters get along like that."

"Yeah, don't tell Alex I said this, but last night, I really needed a hug from my sister and I was so glad she was there."

"Why wouldn't you want her to know that?"

"Because she'll use it against me in the next argument," Yolanda said with a laugh. "And with Alex there is always a next argument."

Once they arrived at the house, Yolanda wasn't surprised to see Alex loading the car with her bags.

"Leaving so soon?" Yolanda asked as she crossed over to her sister.

Alex gave Yolanda a slow glance. "What in the hell do you have on?"

"Training clothes," she said, then struck a karate pose.

"Oo-Kay Kung Fu Panda," Alex quipped. "I'm glad

y'all made it back before we left. I have three meetings I need to prepare for."

Yolanda shot Chuck a knowing look. "Did you guys eat something?"

Alex nodded. "I actually put my life at risk and ate your sister's grits."

Yolanda brought her hand to her mouth and gasped. "Are you all right?"

"Let's just say she has improved, but I'll never do that again." Alex laughed. "This time I was able to use a fork."

Chuck shook his head, then proceeded to check the perimeter around the town house. A few seconds later, Nina walked outside carrying her backpack and computer case. Yolanda could tell her sister would've enjoyed at least another hour of sleep.

"Heard your grits have been upgraded," Yolanda said.

"Oh, hush. I can't believe how early you people get moving around here." Nina yawned. "At least I can spend some time with my fiancé."

"Your fiancé better be working," Alex said.

"Ugh, let's go," Nina said, then turned to Yolanda. "Where's Charles? And do me a favor, sis, don't make Chuck's job harder. Or him, for that matter."

"You little . . ." Yolanda stopped speaking when she saw Chuck heading their way. Did he find something in the woods again? "Y'all should get going before traffic gets too bad."

"You do have a point," Nina said. "Let's hit the road. Chuck, please take care of my sister."

"Will do," he said with a mock salute. Yolanda closed her eyes for a second and wondered what life would be like if he wasn't her bodyguard but more. And if there wasn't a crazy man trying to kill her.

Stop daydreaming and get your life right. You spent the morning learning to shoot a gun and you think someone is hiding behind every shadow.

"Are you going into your shop today?" Chuck asked as they watched Nina and Alex pull away.

"Yes, around noon, I want to work on some sketches for a while. I've been up so early I feel like half the day is gone."

"That just means you have more time to get stuff done. I'm going to make some calls and we'll be ready to go at twelve."

Yolanda nodded. "Thanks for this morning."

"No problem."

Charles watched Yolanda as she walked into the house. Once she closed the door, he pulled out his phone and called Madison.

"Hey, Chuck," she said when she answered. "Hope your package is still breathing."

"For now. Got a question about Danny. Since you say he has his reputation to uphold, how does he keep his hands clean? I know someone is watching Yolanda."

"That sounds like his MO. I know in Richmond he's been known to use the gang connections from the kids he's supposed to be helping. How he plans to reach your girl, I have no idea. He probably has a professional on her."

Charles frowned. "That's what I'm afraid of. Do me a favor, find out if Danny has ties to the underworld in

Charlotte and Charleston. I need to know exactly what we're facing."

"All right, I'll see what I can find out, but you be careful—in all ways."

"What are you trying to say?"

"Nothing, just be safe. What else could I be saying? Charles, I know you're trying to act like you don't have emotions, but that can be just as dangerous as showing them. I'll call you when I know something."

After hanging up the phone, he took another walk around the perimeter of the house and then headed inside to check on Yolanda. When she wasn't downstairs, he headed up to her studio expecting to find her engrossed in her sketching, but she was stretched out on the futon napping. She looked like a little angel as she slept. He wanted to wrap her in his arms and make sure no harm ever came to her.

It wasn't about losing Hillary anymore. Yolanda Richardson was carving a place in his heart and there was nothing he could do to stop it. He was about to walk out of the studio when he heard her whisper his name. Not Chuck, but "Charles." Low and breathy. Was she dreaming about him? That was becoming a nightly routine for him. Even though he knew she was safe, Charles crossed over to her and stroked her cheek. Her eyes fluttered open.

"What? What time is it?"

"It's a few minutes before ten. I thought you were working," he said.

Yolanda placed her hand on his cheek. "Chuck."

"I like the way you sound when you say Charles."

She sat up. "We'd better stop playing with fire."

"Yeah, you're right. We need to get some things in motion. Your sister's wedding is Christmas, right?"

She nodded.

"I think it's a good idea for you to go to Charleston for a while."

"Absolutely not!" Yolanda exclaimed. "I can have a target on my back but I will not put my family at risk."

"That's why we wouldn't stay at the bed-and-breakfast. You can stay with me until the wedding; then we're going to go to Richmond and put an end to all of this. Whoever is after you, the person Danny clearly hired, doesn't know who I am, and trust me, no one is getting near my place without me knowing about it."

Yolanda nibbled on her bottom lip. "What about my business?"

"Launch it in the new year."

"Ch-Charles, it's not even Thanksgiving yet. That's more than a month of me living in your house. What am I going to tell my family?"

"Your father hired me to protect you and this is the best way until you report the murder. And I hate to say it, but this isn't a suggestion. You're going home with me."

"Well damn," she muttered. "When are we leaving?"

"Let me make a few calls. I'll let you know." Charles walked out of the studio wondering if he had put his heart in danger to save Yolanda's life.

Yolanda sat in her studio dumbfounded. Flabbergasted even. She had agreed to move in with Charles Morris for a month. Actually more than a month. Thanksgiving was still a week away.

Living with him would be different from their current situation. She was on her own turf. She could close her bedroom door, she could lock herself away in the comfort of her studio, and she could dream about him without . . . wait. What did he mean when he said he liked the way she sounded when she called him *Charles*?

"Damn it. This man is driving me crazy," she said as she rose to her feet and paced back and forth. She couldn't live in his house, but there was no way she'd take her drama to the Richardson Bed and Breakfast. Her father was there. Alex. Nina. Clinton. Guests. Anything could happen and cause a tragedy of epic proportions. She wished she had a time machine. She'd go back to that summer night and leave early, as she had planned. The shooting of Bobby G. would just be another news story she knew nothing about. She'd be sleeping through the night and she wouldn't have Beretta burns on the back of her hand.

Her shop would still be thriving and she'd be marking down dresses for a Black Friday sale. She stopped mid-stride and looked out of the window. Was he out there watching her, waiting for her to be alone so he could strike? Maybe Chuck was right; she needed to get away from Charlotte and the dangers that lurked in the shadows. But wasn't being too close to him another danger?

Yolanda walked downstairs, her thoughts pounding in her brain like drumbeats. Safety, desire, and fear collided at the same time as she walked. She entered the kitchen, where Chuck was having a whispered conversation on the phone. Though she wanted to grab a bottle of wine and gulp down a glass or two, she opted for a bottle of water.

"Sounds good. I'll call you back when we're ready," he said into the phone as he and Yolanda locked eyes.

"What was that all about?"

"Our trip," Chuck said. "We're going to leave a little after midnight."

"This is insane." She closed her eyes before taking a big sip of her water. "I'm tired of running."

"It's going to be over soon," he said. "But keep in mind, it was your idea to wait until after your sister's wedding to go to the police. We don't have a choice right now."

When Yolanda opened her eyes, Chuck was standing in front of her. She inhaled and his woodsy scent filled her nostrils. Did his entire home smell like this? Would she be able to move without gushing like a river if she had to smell him everywhere?

Chuck lifted her chin, forcing her to look into those emerald eyes. "You're going to be fine. I've got you."

She expelled a breath and wished he would take her, have her any and every way he wanted. *Stop it.* Was she tripping or was he bringing his lips to hers? Yep. He sure was. The kiss started soft and tender. A type of comforting kiss. But Yolanda's hunger made her deepen the kiss, her tongue parting his lips and coaxing his into her mouth. Chuck pulled her closer and her body vibrated with desire. There would be no stopping this time. No thinking of consequences. Chuck's hands roamed her body and she wanted to explode.

Breaking the kiss, she looked up at him and saw the flicker of need and passion in his eyes. Nodding, she gave him the silent permission to take her. Chuck lifted her up on the marble counter and peeled her catsuit off. His fingers set her aflame as he explored her body. When he slipped his hand between her thighs, Yolanda moaned. Then when he brushed his thumb against her throbbing clitoris, she threw her head back and moaned again. More like a guttural cry that shook her soul.

Yolanda couldn't remember the last time she craved a man like this. Needed him more than she needed air in her lungs. His tongue replaced the touch of his finger, lapping her sweet juices as she thrust herself into his mouth—wanting him to swallow her whole. He sucked her like an oyster, slowly slurping, and she exploded, showering his face with her sticky sweetness. Chuck pulled back from her and licked his lips.

"You're delicious."

She opened her mouth as if she could form words. He lifted her from the counter and carried her into her bedroom. Her body hummed and she brought her lips to his and kissed him slow. She must have been doing something right because he stumbled, damn near dropped her before making it to the bed.

"You know that would've killed the mood," she quipped.

"I'm not going to let you fall," he said. "But you can't kiss me like that and expect me not to be affected." He laid her on the bed then stripped off his sweatpants and T-shirt.

Good God, his body was amazing. From his toned abs to those thick thighs and that dick. If there was a prototype for a sex toy, Chuck had to be the mold. Long and mouthwatering. "Damn," she muttered as she eased to the edge of the bed. Yolanda reached for him, giving his cock a long stroke. Then she brought her lips down on his erection. Giving him the same kind of tongue lashing she'd received in the kitchen. Deep in her mouth, she sucked slow. Then she danced her tongue across the tip of his dick. Chuck moaned as he buried his hands in her hair. Every time he tried to pull back, she sucked him in deeper, nearly bringing him to climax when she cupped his balls and licked them while stroking him up and down.

"Stop, stop," he breathed. "You're killing me."

"Don't say that."

"I mean it." Chuck climbed in the bed and pulled Yolanda on top of him. "I get the feeling that this is your favorite position."

"We can start here," she said as she straddled him. "But this is one of my favorite positions."

He leaned against the headboard and she raised her eyebrow at him. "Do you have protection?"

Chuck groaned. Yolanda laughed. "It's a good thing I do, because you weren't thinking about it."

"I'd be lying if I said I was," he replied as she reached into her nightstand drawer and handed him a condom. If she'd expected him to ask her questions or pretend that he was shocked that she had her own protection, she was wrong, because he didn't. That made her wetter. Could it be that he was a man who understood a woman had needs and desires that went beyond vibrators and boyfriends?

What are you doing? Yolanda thought as she watched him roll the condom in place. *It's just a one time thing.*

He pulled her against his erection, but didn't fully dive into her wetness. With the head of his penis, he sought out her clit and rubbed against her wet bud until she screamed. And she thought she was going to be the one in control. Twice, she'd come. And she hadn't even had all of him inside her yet.

"Ride me," he commanded as he plunged inside. Yolanda followed his edict, riding him slow, then fast. Chuck gripped her hips as if he was trying to catch her rhythm. And the moment they found the same beat, it was like a concert—both of them swaying to the beat of the same drum, grinding to the same notes from a saxophone. Yolanda matched his thrusts, took him deeper inside her valley until she came again. Seconds later, he groaned and squeezed her ass as he reached his own climax. Sweat covered their bodies as they snuggled up together. Yolanda placed her hand on his chest. "Whoa," she said breathlessly. "That was . . . Charles, thanks."

"Um, thanks?"

"That was the icebreaker we needed before going to your place," she said, and immediately hated herself. Why was she trying to act like what happened didn't matter? That she didn't love every second of it?

"Yeah, now we can focus on what matters."

She raised her eyebrow for a second, then realized she'd started this. Yolanda eased out of his embrace, but he wrapped his arm around her. "If you get up, we have to go back to the real world. Let's have this moment." He brushed his lips across the back of her neck. She smiled and pressed her bottom against him.

"I knew you were a smart man," she said as she turned to face him.

"Be a smart lady and kiss me."

He didn't have to ask her twice.

Chapter 18

Yolanda woke up in an empty bed and was convinced that the morning and early afternoon had been a dream. But the soreness in her thighs told her that she hadn't been dreaming at all. But where was Chuck and what time was it? She looked at her alarm clock and saw it was five after two. Had they been in bed that long?

She sat up at the moment that Chuck walked in the room with a tray of food. "I see that only the smell of sausage and coffee wakes you up," he said with a smile.

Dimples.

"You know my weaknesses. What's this?"

"Lunch. Chicken, rice, and broccoli."

"So, you like cooking?" she asked as he set the tray on the nightstand.

He shrugged. "I have to eat and it gives me time to think."

"And what do you think about when you're cooking other than not scorching the rice?"

Chuck smiled. "I'm from Charleston, I never scorch the rice."

"You're from Charleston, yet we never met before.

That's just sad," she said as she picked up her bowl of food.

"Guess we ran in different circles. Where did you go to high school?"

Yolanda smiled. "I went to a private high school. And hated every minute of it. There was no football team, I couldn't be a cheerleader, and everybody was scared of my father."

"Shaped your whole life, huh?" Chuck laughed.

"Is that judgment?"

He shook his head and grinned. "But I know some private school women. They're the most creative and passionate."

She rested her chin on her fist. "Do I want to know where I rank?"

"Top three."

Yolanda scoffed. "It only means something if I'm number one."

"You are at the top of the list, trust and believe," he said with a smile. "How's the food?"

She took another bite and smiled. "Great. You know, if you need a second career, a chef might work for you."

"I'm good with that. I told you, I grew up in a house of women who cut me no slack. I would never open myself to that kind of criticism again."

"Is your family still in Charleston?"

Chuck shook his head no as he took a bite of his food. "My sisters moved out west after my mom passed."

"Oh," she said quietly. "I'm sorry."

"Mom lived a great life and we had a good time with her," he said.

Yolanda tried not to cry, but anytime she thought about how she never got to have that time with her mother that other people had it made her sad. While she shouldn't begrudge people who got to know their mothers as adults, she did.

Chuck seemed to notice her emotion and set his bowl to the side. "What's wrong?" he asked. His eyes were filled with concern. She shook her head and wiped the moisture from her eyes.

"I lost my mother when I was young and . . . I hate to say it but sometimes I get . . ."

He pulled her into his arms. "It's all right," Chuck cooed as he hugged her. "You've been through a lot, huh?"

"That's why all of this is so scary to me. I can't lose anyone else that I love," she said. The last thing Yolanda wanted was to be blubbering in Chuck's arms, but here she was doing just that. His warm arms felt so comforting and safe. Was this what a bodyguard did? Made all the nightmares go away? Yolanda patted him on his arm as she pulled away from him and wiped her eyes.

"I-I, um, I'm going to take a shower."

"Why don't you finish eating and I'll run you a bath?"

"Wow," she said with a bright smile. "I should've cried on your shoulder the day we met." Yolanda wiped her eyes, again. "Thanks, Charles."

He looked back at her as he headed for the bathroom. "Just so you know, I don't have a tub at my place, so you'd better enjoy this."

Charles walked into Yolanda's bathroom and noticed how small it was, for him. But it seemed just right for her. The round garden tub, the jasmine oils, and the pink rose wallpaper. Well, maybe the wallpaper was her sister's style. But the aroma in that bathroom was all Yolanda. She'd been more than he'd cooked up in his dreams. But he was going to have to tuck this day away in his memory banks. Yolanda seemed willing to do the same. Was he okay with that? Maybe it made sense that they got their needs taken care of and now they could focus on stopping a killer. But he knew he'd never be satisfied with just one taste of Yolanda. And if he was going to keep her alive, then he needed to separate what he was feeling for her and realize that he was doing his job.

At midnight, he'd be focused. Because that's when he was taking her back to Charleston. To his home, where she'd be safe and he'd have to keep his hands to himself. Right now, he was just going to run her a bath and marvel at that amazing body.

Ten minutes later, he was leading Yolanda into the bathroom. He'd lit the candles that she had in the bathroom and turned the overhead lights off.

"Wow," she said as she took in the scene. "This is awesome. Thanks."

"Well, you seem like you do this a lot."

Yolanda nodded as she dropped her robe and stepped into the tub. "You even got the temperature right."

"I just set it on hell," he said. "I'm going to leave you to soak."

"Or you could join me," she said with a slick smile.

"Somehow, I don't think we're going to fit in there together."

"You never know until you try," she said with a wink.

"Do we have to get back to the real world right this second?"

Looking at her standing in the tub, the warm water causing her body to sparkle with sweat, Charles didn't want to go back to the real world, the fake world, or a world without Yolanda Richardson in it. This was a problem. He'd hoped to keep things professional. Find the people trying to kill her and move on with his life. But that taste of her sweetness and being inside her had awakened something that he couldn't put back to sleep if he tried.

Though he wasn't going to try today, he was going to have to forget how good she made him feel.

"All right," he said as he removed his clothes and climbed into the tub. Water sloshed over the side as they eased into a seated position. Yolanda's back rested against his chest. She was so soft. Charles ran his hand down her stomach, slipped it between her thighs, and stroked her until she melted against him.

"How are we supposed to get clean when you're playing dirty?" she asked as she placed her hand on top of his.

"That's what you're calling it?" Charles slipped his finger inside her. Yolanda moaned as he toyed with her clit.

"Um. Yes. Yes. Yes!"

With two fingers inside her, Charles drew circles making her scream as she reached her climax. The sated look on her face gave him as much pleasure as he'd given her. He needed to stop. Because he couldn't get addicted to her feel or her taste. He needed to focus on the job. They soaked in the water until it went cold. "We probably should get packed and head down to Charleston."

"The real world is back," she said with a sigh. When Yolanda stood up, Charles wanted to forget that they had to leave. Wanted to pretend that this was the beginning of something beautiful. But like she said, the real world was back.

The couple dried off and Yolanda packed a couple of bags while Charles cleaned the kitchen. He decided to set timers on the lights to make it seem as if someone was still living in the town house. That way if the killer who was stalking her was still watching, maybe he'd make a mistake and get caught by the police. Charles wondered if he could use Yolanda's mannequins to throw things off. He dried his hands then dashed upstairs.

"What are you doing?" Yolanda asked when she saw Charles coming downstairs with a couple of her mannequins.

"Setting a scene. When we leave, if someone is watching this place, they need to think we're—you're—still here. This will give us at least a couple of hours to get away before they've figured out we've given them the slip."

Charles placed the two mannequins around the front room. And Yolanda shook her head. "This is crazy," she muttered. "If we're being watched, won't they see us walk out the front door carrying bags?"

"That's not how we're going to leave," he said once he was done staging the scene. Charles noticed that Yolanda was wearing another catsuit. She looked good in them. This one was gray and black. It was as if she was trying to be a shadow. *Cute,* he thought. *But she needs to stop watching superhero movies.*

"What?" Yolanda asked when their eyes locked.

"Are you a DC or Marvel woman?" he asked.

She tilted her head to the side. "I'm both, and Catwoman is misunderstood, unless we're talking about the Halle Berry version. I'm hard-core Selina Kyle."

Charles threw his hands up and didn't say a word about how she would look amazing in Halle's Catwoman costume. "Those boxes in your studio, do you need them?"

She shook her head. "I've been meaning to take them out for recycling."

"That's how you get your bags out. But I'm sure we're not being watched at the moment."

"Does that mean I can get one last kiss before you return to being Chuck Morris?" She crossed over to him and pressed her body against his. Leaning down, he brushed his lips across hers. She flicked her tongue across his bottom lip. He captured her mouth and kissed her deep and hard. They were supposed to stop this. He knew that kissing her was something he wasn't going to stop doing. Not when she felt so good in his arms.

Pulling back, she looked up at him and smiled. How was he going to live with her for a month and not fall hard for her?

Chapter 19

It was after midnight before Yolanda and Chuck left the town house. Instead of taking the highway to Charleston, they headed down the back roads and added about another forty-five minutes to their trip. He told her that driving down the two-lane highways would allow him to see if someone was following them or not. So far, they were the only car on the roads. Yolanda felt weird when she saw Charleston come into view. Usually, she'd be heading to the bed-and-breakfast, ready to drive Alex crazy, hang out in her dad's office, and talk about his choice of suits.

Not tonight. She was heading for the Morris residence, where she was going to hide out for a month? How was she going to come up with a story to cover why she wasn't in Charlotte to help Nina with her wedding dress search?

"You know," she said as Chuck turned down a neighborhood road, "we didn't think this out. I still have to help Nina prepare for her wedding. I'm sure my sisters are going to want to know why I'm not in the shop."

"We'll figure it out later today."

Yolanda sighed. And as she watched the houses that they passed, she realized where they were. "Ashley Hall, huh?" she said. "I don't know why I figured you had a house on the beach."

Chuck laughed. "Is that why you keep drawing pictures of me in swimming trunks?"

"Stop looking at my sketches, okay? And now that I've seen the real thing, I might need you to model those trunks for me if I ever get them made."

He shook his head as he turned onto the driveway of a ranch-style home. Yolanda was happy that it wasn't a town house. They would have enough space to avoid each other if need be, and maybe he could spare an extra room for her to work in. Well, she was making assumptions about the inside of this man's house. When he drove into the garage, the workout equipment didn't surprise her.

"So that's how you do it," she said as he placed the car in park.

"Do what?"

"Keep your body tight." She nodded toward the weight bench.

"It releases stress when I can't get to the gym." Chuck hopped out of the car and crossed over to the passenger side to open Yolanda's door.

"Do you have pets?" she asked as he took her hand and escorted her out of the car.

"No, I'd be the most irresponsible pet owner ever. I'm rarely here."

She nodded. "I guess you feel the same way about relationships, too?"

"Woman, it's late and we need sleep. I'll get some blankets for the bed in the guest room."

Guest room?

Charles was tired and trying to remember the dumb promise he'd made himself about not getting too caught up with Yolanda. He noticed the scowl that darkened her face when he said *guest room*. He should just take her straight to his bedroom and go to sleep. They hadn't been followed; they could unpack and get sleeping arrangements settled later today. *You know, if she is going to be in your bed tonight, you'll never let her leave,* he thought as they walked into the house through the garage door. He pressed the code to disarm the alarm system and then turned the lights on.

"Welcome to my home," he said.

Yolanda seemed to drink in her surroundings. Charles's kitchen was right off the garage, filled with stainless steel appliances that shone against the earth-tone walls. He had a marble island in the center that he used more for work than dining or preparing complex meals. One of his laptops rested on the middle of the countertop. He had a couple of file folders stacked next to a bowl of fruit.

"Where's the coffeemaker?" Yolanda asked as she looked around.

"I know you're not trying to . . . I have a K machine," he said and nodded to the black machine next to the stove.

Yolanda snorted. "You drink one cup of coffee a day, don't you?"

"Yeah, and sometimes it's decaf."

She grabbed her chest and pretended she was having a heart attack like on the old *Sanford and Son* shows. "Who hurt you?" she quipped.

"Let me show you to your room and you can talk about my coffee choices later." He led her to the room next to his master bedroom. The bathroom was across the hall from the bedrooms. He pushed the door open to the guest room and nodded toward the queen-sized bed.

"I hope you'll be comfortable," he said.

She walked into the room and smiled. It was another earth-tone palette with a bit of red and gold. "Do you need more blankets?" he asked as she plopped down on the bed.

"This should be fine. Thanks."

"You want me to bring your bags in or . . ."

"I'm just going to go to sleep," she said and Charles could've sworn he heard a bit of disappointment in her tone.

He nodded and started to head out of the room. "Chuck."

"Yeah?"

"Um, good night. Or is it good morning?"

"See you soon."

"Better not be with no decaf coffee," she quipped as he walked out the door.

Yolanda closed her eyes as Chuck left the room. Was she tripping because they had sex and she thought it meant more than just the two of them getting pleasure? Was she really acting like one of those women who confused her heart and vagina?

This wasn't who she was. Sinking into the bedding, she closed her eyes and sighed. How was she going to make it for the next thirty days in this house without losing her mind? And how in the hell did he turn his feelings on and off? Chuck Morris was back and her sweet, passionate Charles seemed to still be in Charlotte.

The man said he is doing his job, so let him do it.

Richmond, Virginia

Danny looked at the report his social media maven, Brittany, had given him. She had found out more about Yolanda Richardson than he'd expected. And now he knew he had a big problem on his hands. When that woman came up missing, she'd be noticed. Knowing more about Yolanda made having her death look like an accident more imperative.

Danny was certain that it wouldn't be long before she decided to tell the police what she saw.

"Hey, Danny," Brittany said. "I'm going to head out. What did you think of my report?"

"It was great. You have that SEO magic," he said with a smile. "If you keep this up, you're going to be in a marketing department before you're a freshman in college."

"Thank you," she replied. Danny reached into his pocket and pulled out his wallet. He gave her two one hundred–dollar bills.

"Have a nice weekend on me," he said, then walked her out of the office. After she left, he pulled out his burner phone and called Chase.

"What?" he snapped when he answered.

"We have to change things up. Unless you've taken her out already."

"She's missing," Chase said. "That man who was with her had to be a personal security guard. They disappeared and made it look as if there was someone in the house. He has the police doing more patrols in the neighborhood. Who the hell is this woman?"

Danny sighed. "A bigger problem than I initially thought."

"You made this a bigger problem with your handling of Bobby G. when . . . What's the next move?"

"Clearly, you have to find her first," Danny snapped. "And remember what I said, that it needs to look like an accident."

"This is absolute nonsense. Now I have to find her again and hope I can create some fucking story of an accident."

"You will if you want to get paid."

"This is some bullshit. How in the hell am I supposed to know where she is?"

"There's a bed-and-breakfast in Charleston, South Carolina, that you should check out. Do whatever you have to do to make her disappear. I'll make it worth your while."

Charleston, South Carolina

Yolanda woke up and almost screamed. Where in the hell was she? She blinked and calmed her heart rate. She was in Charleston. In Chuck's home and in his guest room because he didn't want her in his bed. Sitting up in the bed, she swung her legs over the side and sighed. It was a little after ten and super quiet.

She didn't like the silence. Did Chuck leave her alone in the house . . . with decaf coffee? Yolanda groaned and rose to her feet. She hated being this close to the bed-and-breakfast, yet unable to enjoy a cup of coffee and a big, juicy blueberry muffin.

"Yolanda, are you up?" Chuck said from the other side of the door before knocking.

"Yeah, come in," she said.

"How did you sleep?" he asked as he walked into the room.

She shrugged. "The bed is comfortable." *I wonder what yours feels like.*

"I started to fix breakfast, but I wasn't sure if you were hungry or not."

"I really need some coffee and my sketch pad," she said.

Chuck smiled. "Your things are in the living room. And I do have some coffee with caffeine in it just for you."

"Look at you being all hospitable."

"Come on, lady, let's get some food. How do you feel about banana pancakes?"

She raised her right eyebrow. "You've been hiding the fact that you can make banana pancakes?"

"I don't think you had the right kind of bananas at your place for me to make them. You can take a shower and I'll cook."

"Chuck," she said, "I have to let my family know that I'm here."

"Kind of defeats the purpose of being here if you do that. Take a shower, have some coffee, and we can talk about everything."

She wanted to kiss him, wanted to feel his arms around

her. But Chuck walked out of the room without a word. Fine, she could play his game too.

After a quick shower, Yolanda wrapped up in a towel and headed into the living room, where Chuck had placed her things. As she pulled out a pair of leggings and a T-shirt, she watched him move in the kitchen. She tried to tell herself that he was just cooking because he had to eat and that she needed to forget about what had happened in Charlotte. One and done was the play and they had more things to consider.

She dashed to her room and dressed before joining Chuck in the kitchen, where he had finished the pancakes and was starting on eggs and sausage.

"This is chicken apple sausage," he said when she walked in. "I hope that won't be a problem."

"Beggars can't be choosers," she replied. "Can we talk about . . . Why are you so distant?"

"What do you mean?" He turned back to the stove to check the eggs.

"Will you at least look at me?"

"Yolanda, this is why we should've never crossed that line. This is when mistakes happen and I'm trying to avoid that. I want to make sure that . . ." He moved the pan of eggs from the burner and turned the stove off. "I have to keep you safe and protect you from everything that can bring you harm and that even includes me."

She raised a skeptical eyebrow at him. "That doesn't even make sense."

"Trust me, it does. Yolanda, I know what it's like to get too close to someone and lose focus. I don't want that to happen with you."

"Then . . . all right, fine." She had no idea what he

was talking about and she really didn't want to hear his lame-ass excuses. Wait, why was she so worked up? She had been the one who put it out there that she just wanted a physical thing with him. But she also had the right to change the rules if she wanted to. "One day, I guess you'll open your heart to me. Hopefully, I'll still want to listen," she said. "I'm going to get my sketch pad."

Chapter 20

Charles knew he'd messed up. Knew this was the moment he should've been real with her, told her how he was afraid because he'd lost Hillary. But he couldn't, more like he wouldn't. *Maybe it is time to come clean,* he thought as he fixed their plates and started a pot of coffee for Yolanda.

"Food's ready," he said as he walked into the living room. Yolanda was sitting on the edge of the sofa drawing in her sketch pad with strokes that seemed to broadcast her anger.

"I'm not hungry. I need to get this done," she said.

"You need to eat something," he said as he set the plates on the coffee table.

She looked up at him and speared him with an annoyed look. "I'll eat when I'm done." She returned to the drawing and Chuck wondered if she was designing something or creating a picture of him to burn later. A couple of seconds passed before she looked up at him. "Are you just going to stand here and watch me? That's annoying."

"Don't want to annoy you," he said.

"But that's what you're doing," Yolanda said. She closed her sketchbook and stared at him. "I didn't expect to come here and play house with you. But you're acting as if last night didn't happen."

Charles cleared his throat. "That's not what I'm doing. You have to realize that my major responsibility is to keep you alive. And being distracted by feelings could be a problem."

"Okay then," she said, then picked up her plate. "You don't have to worry about me ever distracting you ever again."

"But I don't want us to go back to being . . . Yolanda, this is the best thing for both of us. We wanted each other and we've had each other—now we can move forward."

She didn't answer; she simply shoveled a forkful of eggs in her mouth. A few beats passed before she acknowledged him. "Chuck, we never have to have this conversation ever again. I got my answer as to where things stand and I'm fine with it. By the way, this food is delicious."

Though he wanted to smile, Charles figured it was starting an argument if he did. "Do you still want coffee? I made a cup for you."

"I'd like that," she said. "But if you don't mind I'll fix it myself."

Charles nodded and watched her walk into the kitchen. Yeah, he'd messed up royally.

Yolanda didn't like being an asshole, but that's where she was. And for her own sanity, that's where she'd have to stay. *He hurt my feelings and I have the right to act out,* she thought as she poured her coffee. But she needed to get over herself, sooner rather than later, because she wanted to talk to him about seeing her family safely. Since her father knew the basics of what was going on, she wanted him to know everything now.

"Chuck," she called out. "Can you come in here for a second?"

He walked into the kitchen with his empty plate. "What's up? Coffee too hot?"

"Funny," she said, then rolled her eyes. "I know we're here because Danny Branch found me, but I want my father to know what's going on."

He nodded. "I can understand that. I'll call Mr. Richardson and have him meet us here. Though I don't think we were followed from Charlotte, I don't want to take the chance of leading the wrong people to your family."

She nodded. That was her biggest fear and she'd never forgive herself if she was the cause of one of her people getting hurt.

"And you were right. We need to stop distracting each other. I guess I just thought things would be easier since we . . . I'm clear as to where everything stands and you don't have to worry about me acting like a brat anymore today."

Chuck released a low laugh. "But I might be in trouble tomorrow is what you're saying?"

She shrugged. "Depends on what you make for breakfast. The least I can do is cook dinner to make up for my bad attitude this morning. I'm really not like this. I do understand that sex doesn't have to lead to some kind of commitment or declaration of love. I get it. But, I'm scared. And I don't know how to process all of this."

Chuck set his plate on the kitchen table and crossed

over to her. He pulled her into his arms and held her for just a moment. It was the salve that Yolanda needed. And when she closed her eyes, she felt safe in his arms. *Don't get comfortable,* she thought as she broke the embrace. "Thanks," she said as she wiped the moisture pooling in her eyes. "Um, do you have a place here where I can work? I don't want to put you out, but I need some natural light to draw. Since I won't be launching my shop in Charlotte for a while, I figure I can get my line together."

"My sunroom is available. Why don't I give you the tour of the place and you can figure out what works for you?"

"That sounds like a plan. Let me finish my breakfast first. I can't let that goodness go to waste. Seems like you've figured out how to calm me down."

"Banana pancakes?"

She nodded, then headed back to the living room. Even cold, the food was great and she ate every bit. When she walked back into the kitchen she wasn't surprised to see Chuck engrossed in work on his laptop. The kitchen was spotless and whatever he was cooking for lunch was resting in a plastic bowl next to the sink. She washed her plate and set it on the drying pad next to the sink.

"I would've taken care of that for you," he said. Yolanda turned around and wondered how long he'd been looking at her. Probably not long at all since he didn't want to be distracted.

"Well, I try to clean up my own messes," she said with a smile.

"Cute," he muttered as he rose to his feet. Yolanda wasn't sure if he was talking to her or the computer.

"Are you ready for your tour?" he asked.

"Yes. And am I allowed to leave this place?"

"I'll take you anywhere you need to go."

"Good, because I need some material."

"What are you making and can't you order material online?"

"Not until I touch and feel what I need."

Chuck threw his hands up. "Whatever you say."

"It's important to know how the fabric feels and works for a specific design. Some of the stuff online arrives feeling like a tablecloth."

"I bow to your expertise," he said.

"Good, because I need you to be my model," she said.

"Didn't agree to that. I just said I would take you where you needed to go."

"Chuck, now is the perfect time for me to make those swim trunks. And you have the perfect body for them."

"No."

"Please," Yolanda cooed. "According to you I have to be in your house for a month. I need something to do or I'm going to go crazy."

"That doesn't mean that I get to be your personal Barbie doll."

"No, you'd be my model. Wouldn't that just be so cool?"

"I'll give you one day and then I'm done."

"Good thing for you I only need one day. Thanks, Chuck. Now let's do this tour," she said as she clasped her hands together.

His smirk made her wet and she wanted to punch herself when they had just talked about this. No more sex. But she couldn't turn off her attraction. How could he do it so easily?

She followed him out of the kitchen as he gave her the tour of his house. She liked ranch-style houses; they were simple and beautiful. Chuck's was as well. The hardwood floors were her favorite part. She couldn't tell if it was cherrywood or something else. When she got the chance to go home, she was going to redo Nina's carpeted floors. Would she ever be able to go home? Yolanda sighed and Chuck turned around and looked at her. "What's wrong?" he asked.

"I was just thinking about . . . Will it ever be safe enough for me to go home? When we go to Richmond, what if that's where . . ."

"Yolanda, I'm working on that. I want you to feel safe again and live your life. When Danny Branch goes to jail, you're not going to have to look over your shoulder."

"But if he's the monster that you say he is, then how can I be sure? You're not going to be with me forever."

Chuck didn't reply; he just led her into his sunroom. It was amazing. Floor-to-ceiling windows that looked out on a rose garden. A leather love seat and an oak coffee table.

"There's a remote to close the curtains," he said, nodding toward the blackout curtains. The remote was in a holder against the wall.

"Why would you ever close these curtains?" she asked as she spun around in the room. "This is just a beautiful room."

"Glad you like it. Come on," he said as he reached his hand out to her. Yolanda looked down at his hand and took it. Why was he acting like this now? She didn't want to hold his hand and walk down the hall with him. She didn't want to confuse what she was feeling. Once they walked out of the room, she dropped his hand.

"Do you grow the roses yourself?" she asked.

"It's a memorial garden for my mother. She loved roses and I wanted to make sure I'd have a space where I could think of her."

Yolanda nodded. Her cooking was how she thought of her mother. Even though she hadn't been old enough to cook in the kitchen with Nora Richardson like Robin and Alex, she would watch her mother's joy as she prepared dinner. She always added something new to her meals and never used a recipe.

And she was always smiling when she cooked. Her mother had the most amazing smile.

"You all right over there?" Chuck asked when they stood at his door to his office.

"Yeah, yeah. I was just thinking about your garden and how I wish I had more memories with my mother."

"I'm sorry," he said and paused for a second as if he wanted to give her a hug or something. Yolanda knew she wouldn't be able to handle it and would probably burst into tears.

"It's not your fault," she said, fanning her hand. "What's behind the door?" She tilted her head toward his office.

"This is the one place that I need you to stay out of. I have a lot of sensitive information in here as well as my security camera feeds."

Yolanda shrugged. "All right. So, I can have the sunroom?"

"It's yours. When do you want to go get this all-important material?"

"After you call my father and set up this meeting." Yolanda folded her arms across her chest.

"When you dig your heels in, you mean it, huh?"

"When it comes to my family, I sure do."

"Let me finish a report, then I'll call your father."

"I'll be in the sunroom," she said.

Charles had to rein this thing in with Yolanda. But as he watched her glide down the hall, he knew he was a goner. He needed to focus all of his energy on keeping her safe and not falling in love with this vibrant woman.

Who was he fooling? He was halfway there, even though he knew the consequences of it all. He returned to the kitchen and sat down at the counter where he'd set up his computer. Madison had sent him information on Daniel Branch: official accounts of his work in Richmond, a background report on his life and his alleged crimes. This man was dangerous. But Charles was happy to see that he didn't have any business in Charleston. Maybe he didn't know about Yolanda's family. But he knew it wouldn't be long before he found out. From what he'd seen in Madison's investigations, Danny was a smart guy. And Yolanda was proud of her family's name. She didn't hide who she was and where she was from. He noticed that on her social media and company website.

He wanted her in Charleston because he had a network here where he could offer her another layer of protection. Sighing, he pulled out his cell phone and called Sheldon Richardson.

"This is Sheldon," the man said when he answered.

"Mr. Richardson, it's Chuck Morris."

"Chuck, did something happen?" Sheldon's voice wavered.

"No, sir. Everything is as fine as it can be in this situation. I wanted to call you because Yolanda and I are in Charleston. She wants to meet with you and I want to go over the details as to why we're back."

"Meet with me? Why doesn't she just come to the bed-and-breakfast?"

"It's a complicated issue and a matter of safety," Charles said. "I'm going to text you my address, sir. When is a good time for you to come by?"

"As soon as I get the text, I'll be on my way."

"Mr. Richardson, I know how close you and your daughters are, but I need you not to tell them that we're here right now," Charles said.

"I don't like what I'm hearing right now," Sheldon said.

"I'll explain everything when you get here, but please don't tell your girls that Yolanda is here."

"All right, I'll see you soon."

Charles ended the call with Sheldon and sent him the text with his address. He rose from the stool and headed to the sunroom. Standing at the door, he watched Yolanda as she worked on her sketch. Her strokes were a lot less angry than before. He smiled at the look of peace on her face. The last time he saw her look like that was in . . . *Stop it*. Those were memories he needed to tuck away. Her safety was the top priority.

"You're staring again," she said without looking up.

"Sorry, it's just interesting to see how your face changes when you sketch. It's almost as if you're the work of art."

This time she did look up. "I don't know if that was cute or corny. Corny cute? Is that a thing?"

"Whatever. I wanted to let you know that your father is on his way."

Yolanda set her pencil on the table and smiled at him. "Thank you for doing that."

"I asked your father not to tell your sisters that you're here."

"Good thinking. Alex thinks she is in control of all of Dad's affairs."

Charles shook his head. "I find it hard to believe that your father answers to anyone."

Yolanda snorted. "You've met Alex. She thinks everyone answers to her."

"You can't fault her for looking out for her family. I guess that's why you haven't told her the real deal about what's going on."

She folded her arms across her chest and he couldn't take his eyes off her amazing breasts. Less than twenty-four hours ago, he was . . . *Stop it*.

"Had I known Nina was going pull this number on me, I should've just called a family meeting." Yolanda stood up and wiped her palms on her thighs. He was glad she had on leggings and those thighs were covered from his wanton glance. Was he fooling himself thinking one taste of Yolanda Richardson was going to be enough? From the way his dick jumped in his pants, he was.

"Your dad a coffee or tea guy?"

"Water. But I'll take some more coffee. And no offense, but you should let me make it."

He laughed as they headed for his kitchen. "I can't tell, you drank it all."

"That's because I was trying not be rude. It wasn't bad, if you like hot water."

Charles grabbed his chest. "You just broke my heart."

She sucked her teeth and rolled her eyes. "I'm sure a man like you has never had his heart broken."

He went still and watched her prepare the coffee. "You'd be surprised," he said quietly. Yolanda either didn't hear him or decided to ignore his comment. No one took coffee that seriously.

As the brew percolated, she looked around the kitchen. "This is a pretty big kitchen for a guy who lives alone."

"What would I look like with a closet for a kitchen? Anyway, you know I love to cook."

She nodded toward the marble island. "What do you make with the laptop?" she quipped.

"Work. I don't eat in my office, so I do a lot of work out here."

Yolanda nodded. "Cute. You're one of a kind, Chuck Morris."

"I don't get Charles anymore?"

She rolled her eyes and hid her grin. "Charles stayed in Charlotte," Yolanda replied. "Hey, do you make banana bread?"

"I can't get it right."

Yolanda clasped her hands together. "We're having banana bread for breakfast."

"You make it?"

"No, but there are always cookies and banana bread at the bed-and-breakfast."

Charles dropped his head. "You know we're here for you to lay low, right?"

"We have to go out and get material and I know a back entrance into the kitchen. You can't expect me to be this close to my family and not get my favorites from the B&B."

Before Charles could reply, the doorbell rang. "I'll be right back," he said. Looking at his watch, he knew it had to be Sheldon at the door. When Charles opened the front door he was right.

Sheldon Richardson offered him a smile and held up a brown Richardson Bed and Breakfast bag. "Knowing Yolanda, she was planning to come by and get banana bread and cookies. I threw in some coffee, too, because you don't want to deal with my daughter if she doesn't have coffee in the morning or the middle of the night."

"Well, hello to you too, Daddy," Yolanda said from behind Charles. Sheldon side-stepped Charles and gave Yolanda a tight hug.

"I've been very concerned about you," he said once he released her. Then he turned to Charles. "So, what's going on?"

"Let's sit down and talk about it," he said as he ushered Sheldon into the living room. The older man took a seat on the leather recliner near the sofa. Yolanda took a deep breath and sat on the end of the sofa closest to her father.

"Mr. Richardson," Charles said as he took a seat on the other end of the sofa. "There's a really nasty guy after your daughter and he had someone watching her in Charlotte. I haven't been able to identify him yet, but I have some people working on it for me. I wanted to bring her here because I don't know if the man who wants her dead has put two and two together yet and knows about her roots being here."

"Why haven't you all gone to the authorities about that man yet?"

Charles gave Yolanda a quick glance. She cleared her throat and said, "That's my fault. Daddy, as soon as this man finds out that I reported what I saw, we're going to be in even more danger. And with Nina's wedding coming up, I don't want to be responsible for something happening to anyone else."

"You're not responsible for what happened to begin with," Sheldon said. "How did you know a murder was going to happen outside of your shop?"

Yolanda dropped her head. "I didn't, but I know now if I say something I'll be responsible for something happening to the family."

"And I'm just supposed to sit back and let something happen to you?" Sheldon boomed.

"Mr. Richardson, I'm not going to let anything happen to Yolanda," Charles said. "And we're going to the Richmond police after Nina's wedding."

Sheldon nodded. "I wish you would go sooner," he said.

"I'm not going to ruin Nina's wedding."

"Do you think I want to have a wedding and then a funeral?" Sheldon snapped.

"Mr. Richardson, this is why Yolanda's going to stay here with me until the wedding. We need to keep our story straight about why she's not going to be able to be in touch with her sisters," Charles said.

"Whatever I need to do to keep my daughter safe. But how dangerous is this guy?"

"Very."

Yolanda wasn't ready to hear the full Danny Branch story. She'd heard of him a few times in Richmond. He was supposed to be a community jewel. She hadn't recognized him in May because he didn't look anything like the smiling guy who showed up on the news or on the cover of monthly magazines. And the fact that he was so connected made her wonder if it was even worth it to try to report him. He was a big donor to the Police Athletic League. He worked with inner-city kids, teaching them life and business skills.

As Chuck told her father about why they hadn't gone to the police, Yolanda shivered. This was worse than she thought.

"This is a lot to take in," Sheldon said as he rose to his feet.

"I don't want to scare you guys but this is serious and I have to do whatever it takes to make sure Yolanda isn't hurt," Chuck said.

Her heart seemed to swell. She wanted to believe that he wanted to keep her safe for reasons other than just doing his job, but she knew better.

"I'm going to get some coffee, Daddy. You want some?" she asked.

"No, baby girl. I'm going to have a hard enough time sleeping tonight as it is," he said, then stood up and crossed over to her. He pulled Yolanda into his arms. "Listen to what Chuck tells you. I'm not going to lose you."

She held on to her dad and cried silently. "I'm sorry, Daddy."

He stepped back from Yolanda and lifted her chin up. "You didn't do anything wrong. And I'm actually glad you didn't go running to the police, because they could've found you. I'm going to tell your sisters that you're skipping Thanksgiving, but you'll be here for Nina's wedding. I sent you to Milan."

"You know Alex is going to flip her lid."

"Um, last time I checked, I was still the daddy. If I want to send you to Milan, I'm sending you to Milan. I'm an investor in your company, remember."

Yolanda smiled through her tears. "I love you, Daddy."

Sheldon kissed her on the forehead. "Love you too. And don't try to sneak into the kitchen for food."

"Yes, sir," she said. Though she knew at some point she was going to creep to the bed-and-breakfast to get other things that she wanted.

"Chuck, walk me outside," Sheldon said. Yolanda knew that was his way of telling her to stay inside. But he didn't tell her not to follow them to the door. She leaned against the door to hear what they were talking about.

"What do I have to do to help you keep my daughter safe?" Sheldon asked, with his arms folded across his chest.

"There's not much we can do right now. I'm pretty sure that whoever was watching her didn't follow us to Charleston last night. But I'm not willing to wait forever to turn this guy in. I have a source in Richmond who has been working with me to figure out who we can trust to nail this guy."

"Yeah, he needs to be nailed because if any harm comes to my daughter I'll kill him with my bare hands."

"Mr. Richardson, I wish this was a lot simpler than it is. Because the last thing that I want is for something to happen to Yolanda."

"Good to know that we're on the same page. Now, I

love my daughter but she can be a handful. Are you sure it's a good idea for the two of you to be hidden away in your home for the next month?"

"There's really not another option for us right now. We're going to make it work."

"I'm holding you to that, Chuck." Sheldon shook Chuck's hand then headed to his car. Yolanda dashed into the kitchen so that Chuck wouldn't know she had been eavesdropping. Now, she was sure all she was to this man was another job and she didn't like how that made her feel.

Chapter 21

Charles walked into the house, and when he saw Yolanda in the kitchen, he was pretty sure she'd been listening to his conversation with Sheldon.

"Are you okay over there?" he asked as he crossed over to her.

"Yes, I'm fine. Why wouldn't I be?"

"I was born at night, but not last night. I'm pretty sure you heard my discussion with your dad."

Yolanda shrugged. "Maybe I did. Chuck, how are we going to do this for the next month? I know my dad is going to tell my sisters he sent me to Milan. But what about us?"

"What do you mean?"

She turned and faced him. "You're too smart to play dumb. Just tell me what's going on between us. If I don't mean anything to you other than a job just let me know. But you can't keep looking at me like there's something more here and expect me not to respond."

"Then I'll stop staring, because we have to remain focused on what's important."

"And what's important to you?"

"What I just told your father, keeping you alive."

"Are you alive?"

"What do you mean?"

She tilted her head to the side. "Life is about much more than solving cases, protecting people, and putting the bad guy away. You need to live."

Charles sighed. "I have work to do."

"All work and occasional play, that isn't living." Yolanda dumped two teaspoons of sugar in her coffee mug and headed out of the kitchen.

Why did her words sting like a swarm of bees?

Yolanda wasn't in the mood to draw anymore. She felt stupid for trying to make something happen between her and Chuck. It was clear that he was doing his job and she just needed to accept that. But she couldn't.

Now she was making everything uncomfortable and pretending that she was some kind of free spirit who was all about living life and being happy. When really all she wanted was to have another day like they had in Charlotte.

Oh, what the hell am I doing, she thought. *I'm not this desperate. And just because that man gave me multiple orgasms does not mean he owes me anything else.*

Yolanda tossed her sketch pad across the room and tucked her legs underneath her. She had gone ahead and put her foot in her mouth and she still needed him to take her to get some material and she wanted him to pose for her boxers. Now he was going to think that she was trying to use this design to get in his pants. Okay, so that was the plan to begin with, but now she had to readjust.

Days like this she wished she could just reach out to her sister Robin and talk to her. She rose to her feet and headed to the living room to see if she could find her cell phone. It had just hit her that she hadn't seen her phone since she'd arrived at Chuck's place. Yolanda dumped the contents of her purse on the floor and looked for her phone. It wasn't there. Okay, this was strange. She knew that she kept her phone in her purse at all times.

"Um, hey, Chuck?"

He walked into the living room and she gave him a slow glance. "What's up?"

"Have you seen my phone?"

"Your phone is in Charlotte. I wasn't sure if you have been bugged or geotagged so I thought it was best that your phone stay behind."

"I can't believe you did that shit! I need my phone. What if I need to . . ."

"I have a landline and you can use it whenever you need to. But I don't think you understand how you can be tracked through your electronic devices, so, believe me, I did it for you."

Yolanda stood in front of him and folded her arms across her chest. "You don't get to make those kinds of decisions for me, because if I need my family, I need to get in touch with them and nobody is going to answer a number they don't know."

"Your family is about to think that you're in Milan. So, calling them from a Charleston area code is going to make them believe that, right?"

She dropped her hands to her sides. "Oh, shut up."

"Do you want to go pick up your material now or are you still in the middle of your temper tantrum?"

"What you're not going to do is patronize me. But let me grab my shoes, then we can go." Yolanda dashed down the hall to the sunroom and grabbed her sneakers. Why was she allowing this man to drive her crazy every five minutes? Because Yolanda had to admit something to herself: She really liked Chuck. And she had not felt this way about a man in years. It wasn't fair that they were brought together only because somebody wanted to kill her.

When Yolanda left the living room Charles was still smirking. He now knew who the troublemaker was in the Richardson family. He could only imagine the trouble that Yolanda got into as a kid. He was definitely intrigued, but he knew he couldn't act on what he was feeling even if he wanted to.

"All right, let's go," she said when she returned to the living room.

"Where exactly are we going?" Charles asked as he stood up.

"There's this fabulous shop in Mount Pleasant."

"Is this where you normally shop?" he asked with a raised eyebrow.

"Yeah, like three or four years ago. You do realize I haven't lived here for years. There's nothing routine that I do here other than go visit my family."

"No old flame that you hook up with occasionally?" Now, why in the hell did he ask her that?

"Not that it's any of your business, but no. Can we go now?" She rolled her eyes as she picked up her purse. "You didn't take anything else out of here, did you?"

"Let's be perfectly clear: I never went in your purse. I removed your phone from the charger when you were sleeping. I grew up in a house full of Black women; I know better than to open the purse—with or without permission."

That made Yolanda smile. "Seems like you are as smart as you look."

They headed to his car. Charles opened the passenger door for Yolanda and their hands brushed against each other as she entered the car. Charles felt as if his body had caught fire and his need for Yolanda was like an ember that was going to burn him to a crisp.

"You know, you don't have be a gentleman every time we get in and out of the car. I can open the door for myself."

"Excuse me for acting like the man my mama raised me to be," he said with a wink.

"My apologies to your mom," she said as he climbed into the driver's seat.

"I'll accept your apology on her behalf." Charles started the car and headed toward the interstate.

When they arrived at the shop, Yolanda hopped out of the car like a kid heading into a toy store. He hadn't expected to be in the store for three hours. Yolanda seemed to touch every piece of fabric in the store, asked questions about production of the cotton and where the silk came from and if there could be special orders for jersey material.

Charles felt as if he learned more about fabric today than he had ever wanted to know or care about. Who knew all of this went into making clothes? But what sent him over the edge was the fact that after three hours, Yolanda left the shop with two yards of fabric.

"What?" she asked as they got into the car.

"All that time and this is all you got?"

"I placed an order for some other things," Yolanda said. "Stop being so judgmental. This is a process and not a sprint."

"Yes, ma'am," he said, then started the car. "I know you said you were going to cook dinner, but since we're out, do you want to pick up something?"

Yolanda shrugged. "It doesn't matter to me. To be honest with you, I was going to eat banana bread and sketch."

"That's cold blooded. I was all ready for whatever delights you were going to make in the kitchen."

Is he serious? Yolanda thought. She remembered the last time they had been in the kitchen together, and cooking was the last thing that she'd done. He had jokes and she didn't like it. Well, she was just wanting to feel him tasting her again and making her explode. But they weren't doing that anymore, right?

"I can still cook. How about some fried green tomatoes, salmon, and rice?"

Chuck gave her a slow glance. "Seriously?"

"Yes. What?"

"I haven't had fried green tomatoes in years."

"Then I'm sure we need to stop at the farmer's market and get some."

"My mother made the best fried green tomatoes ever. You've got a lot to live up to," he quipped.

"You will not compare my food to that of your mama's. That is an unfair fight that no woman can win," she replied with a laugh.

"True. And it isn't a competition," he said. "There's a farmer's market not too far from here and the Mount Pleasant Seafood Market is close by too."

"You know, this would be so much easier if we could go to the bed-and-breakfast and get whatever Roberta has on the menu for dinner tonight."

Chuck turned off the interstate. "I'm not even going to get into that with you again today."

Yolanda smiled as he drove to the parking lot of the market. When she and Chuck got out of the car, Yolanda wanted to pretend that she was with a regular man who'd earned a nice meal for spending all of that time with her in the fabric store. She wanted to live in a world where she was just a regular girl with a handsome man by her side because he wanted to be there and not because he was doing a job.

"Why are you so quiet all of a sudden?" he asked. "I just knew you were going to tell me the history of silk and why it's not good to make boxers out of them."

"Funny," she replied as they walked over to a farmer's stand. They spoke to the young woman running the stand and she smiled at them as they looked at the fruits and vegetables.

"Are you two looking for anything in particular?" she asked.

"I'm making fried green tomatoes and I need the perfect tomatoes," Yolanda said, then nodded toward Chuck. "He told me that I can't make them as well as his mom did."

"My husband used to say the same thing to me. How long have you two been married?"

"Um, uh, we're not married," Yolanda stammered. "This is just . . ."

"I cooked breakfast for her and she's returning the favor with dinner. We're really good friends," Chuck said.

"Really? I see something special here," the woman said. "My grandma said I was born with a veil over my face. I can see things that other people can't. I see a wedding here."

Yolanda stroked her throat. "Um, only because my sister is getting married soon. Like he said, we're just friends."

The woman shrugged and picked out some tomatoes for Yolanda. "You need onions too?"

"Yes, and celery."

Chuck nodded. "I see that you might know what you're doing."

"Excuse me?" Yolanda said with a hip bump. "I thought you already knew."

The woman put the vegetables in a brown bag and offered Chuck and Yolanda a huge smile. "Let me give you two a bit of advice. If you follow your heart, nothing can stop you. And the danger isn't as big as you think it is."

Yolanda froze in place. Maybe there was something to this woman's claim that she saw things that other people didn't see. Or maybe she was a part of Danny's attack? *It isn't as if he knew you were coming to Mount Pleasant.*

"Trust me," she said. "And enjoy the meal."

"Thanks," Chuck said as he placed his hand on the small of Yolanda's back. Once they were out of earshot of the woman, he turned toward her. "You seemed a little shook."

"It seemed like she knew that we were—that was a weird interaction."

"You know how some Gullah women are. They see

a man and woman smiling together and they think it's something magical."

"That's not what I'm talking about, *Charles.*"

"Ooh, I get to be Charles again. What did I do to deserve that?"

Yolanda rolled her eyes. "Can we go to the seafood market please?"

Chapter 22

After they had picked up the food and arrived back at Chuck's place, Yolanda was ready to get cooking. Chuck grabbed the groceries and Yolanda took her material into the sunroom. She knew she wanted to make a dress and possibly a pair of pants with the material that she'd gotten. Now she wished that she had gotten more. She made a mental note to order another few yards from the shop's website.

But before she got started on anything, she headed to the kitchen to start the dinner she'd promised Chuck. He was sitting at the counter working on his computer and seemed engrossed in what he was doing.

"Hey, where are your sharpest knives?" she asked.

"That's actually a scary question," Chuck said with a smile. "The ones in the knife block are the best ones."

"I'm not going to disturb you with my cooking, am I?" she asked.

"No. I'm done anyway. What can I do to help?"

Yolanda shrugged. "Stay out of my way but point out where I can find all the things that I need to cook this meal with."

He shook his head. "Got it."

About an hour later, Yolanda and Chuck were gathered around the dining room table about to sit down to dinner.

"This looks good," he said.

"Thanks. I hope you like it, but if you don't keep it to yourself."

Chuck laughed, then cut into the fried green tomato. He moaned and Yolanda's stomach clinched. That was the same sound he made when . . . *Let the man eat*, she thought.

"I need to know your secret because this is the one dish I can't get right," he said after he swallowed.

"I'll never tell you," she said with a wink. They ate in a comfortable silence. She stole glances at him and wondered if he knew how sexy he was when he enjoyed a dish. Hell, he was sexy all the time. Especially in his glasses. And she hadn't seen him wear them in a minute.

"Why have you stopped wearing your glasses?" she asked.

He chuckled. "I only wear them when I'm in a new place and need to know where I'm going without looking like a tourist."

"I knew it! Those *were* Google glasses, right?"

"Something different, but similar."

She cut into her food. "They look good on you, though. Very Clark Kent–like. I've always liked him better than Superman."

"What?"

"Clark got to change his clothes. Superman flew around in his Underoos. It's not as if the suit gave him powers."

"You've really put some thought into this."

She shrugged then laughed.

Chuck took his empty plate to the sink and Yolanda was glad that she'd already washed the pots and pans that she'd cooked dinner in. One thing she could tell about him was that he liked order and cleanliness.

"Do you mind if I go sit in your rose garden?" she asked as she walked over to the sink.

"No, not at all. There's a security light out there if you want to take your sketch pad."

She looked at him and smiled. "I'd like to take you," she said.

"Yolanda . . ."

"Just to talk and maybe I want to draw you, too," she replied.

"Fine. Give me about fifteen minutes to check my e-mails and I'll be right out."

Richmond, Virginia

Danny was surprised to see two police officers at his door. Had that bitch gotten the balls to talk? He was going to kill Chase with his bare hands if she had. "Gentlemen," he said as he opened the door to his quarter-million-dollar penthouse in downtown.

"Mr. Branch, I'm Detective Tabor and this is Officer Edwards. May we come in?"

Danny stepped aside. "What brings you two by?"

"My boss wanted me to talk to you. Actually, alert you to a problem."

Relief flooded Danny. It was good to have the right friends in the right places. Richmond PD was a good place for him. It also helped that a bunch of officials at the department liked to gamble.

"And your boss is?"

"Deputy Chief Paul Putney," Tabor said. "It seems that some questions have come up about the disappearance of your ex-wife, Simone Branch."

"I have no clue where she is, and if I can be blunt here, I really don't care. We had a very ugly divorce and she left with a substantial amount of my money."

Edwards cleared his throat and said, "Mr. Branch, I work with some of the police youth groups you fund and that's why I'm here. We don't have any reason to believe that you did something to your wife, but we're worried about the optics. So, we need to get an official statement from you that we could share with the press about your *concern* for your ex."

Danny shook his head. "I'd rather not. I mean, we had an acrimonious divorce that played out in the media and is probably why I keep fielding questions about where she may or may not be."

"What if," Tabor interjected, "we just say that you're giving us your full cooperation and keep your statement on file just in case the PI who's digging around files a public information request?"

"That's fine, I guess." Danny walked over to his wet bar and pulled out a bottle of scotch. "Care for a drink?"

Edwards nodded, but Tabor stopped him. "We're still on duty," Tabor said. "But thanks for the offer."

"When do you want me to make the statement?" Danny asked.

"Let's set up some time to meet in the morning," Tabor

said. "And you can bring that bottle of scotch as a thank-you."

Danny gave him a mock salute. "Will do." He walked the officers to the door and thanked them for their visit. Once they were gone, Danny groaned. This was a wrinkle he couldn't afford. Why would anyone be looking for that Simone? He'd thought that part of his life was dead and buried. And he knew she'd been taken out. Now a private investigator was on the case? Why? The way his life was unraveling was giving him pause. Too many problems were popping that could bring him down.

At least that Richardson bitch had sense enough to keep her mouth shut, but for how long?

She was probably thinking about turning him in now. Wherever she was. Chase had failed him, and he was going to pay for it. That woman should be dead. Fucking Bobby G.

Even in the ground he was causing him more problems than he was worth. Danny walked over to his bar and downed the scotch he'd poured. Then he headed to his bedroom, where she was. Some random chick who was there for his pleasure. Danny hoped she liked pain, because he was going to pound his anger out inside her.

Charleston, South Carolina

Charles didn't know what was more uncomfortable, sitting still while Yolanda drew or trying to hide his erection. It was clear—both were hard. How could she be this sexy while doing something as simple as putting a pencil between her lips? Lips that he'd tasted. Lips that had tasted him. He was coming undone as she looked at him.

"Can you hold your head up a little?" she asked.

Charles jerked his head up. "How much longer?"

"Just sit there, how hard can it be?"

Oh, she had no clue. Ten minutes later, she was finished, and Charles stood up and stretched. "Why did you want me to model for you in the rose garden?"

"Because I think it's sweet that you have this place for your mom and I just wanted to capture you in it." Yolanda closed her sketchbook.

"You're not going to let me see it?" Charles asked as she stood up.

"Not until it's ready."

"And when will that be?"

She shrugged as she turned to sniff one of the yellow roses beside her. "Nina would love it out here. I don't think anyone loves roses as much as she does."

"And you don't like roses?"

He could've sworn he saw her shudder. "Let's just say I never want to pick up a bouquet of roses that has been delivered to me ever again. This is nice, the garden setting. Don't have to worry about threatening notes."

Charles didn't understand where the anger came from, but for a woman's love of roses to be ruined, that was foul. "Whoever did that to you deserves to have their ass kicked."

"And thrown into a prison cell," she muttered. "That's how I knew they were watching me. It came in a nice bouquet."

Charles drew her into his arms and gave her a tight hug. When she leaned her head against his chest, Charles felt her tears and his heart ached for her. He brushed his lips across her forehead. "You've been through a lot," he whispered.

"And it's still not over," she said.

"It will be soon." Charles knew he should've let her go and taken a step back from her. But her heat kept him holding on. He needed to comfort her as much as she needed to be comforted. The way she held him let him know that the feeling was mutual. Charles knew the next move he was about to make would blur the lines between them even more. But he couldn't help it. He leaned in and kissed her. It was a slow and tender kiss—at first. Then she coaxed his tongue into her mouth. Fire exploded between them and Charles decided at that moment that he wasn't going to play by the rules. He wasn't going to live in the past; he was going to get what he needed. And that was Yolanda Richardson.

He scooped her up in his arms and carried her inside. "Yolanda," he intoned when they broke the kiss.

"I thought we weren't going to . . ."

"Do you want to stop?"

She shook her head. "I want you."

"I need you," he replied as he took her into his bedroom. He laid her in the center of his king-sized bed and smiled. She looked as if she belonged right there. Yolanda wiggled out of her leggings and Charles dove between her legs face-first. He sucked and licked her as if she were a delicious piece of chocolate. Yolanda pressed her hips against his face as he made circles inside her with his tongue.

"Yesss!" she cried. "Don't stop."

And he didn't. He deepened his kiss, sucking her

clitoris until she came, drenching him like a summer rain. Charles looked into her hooded eyes and smiled. He loved seeing her satisfied, happy, and safe.

He needed to make sure that he kept her safe no matter how much he wanted her. He needed to make sure he didn't fall down on the job again. But in this moment, he wanted to make sure that Yolanda was satisfied. Charles rose from the bed and stripped off his clothes. There was something about the way that she looked at his naked body that made him want to do nothing but live up to her salacious thoughts.

Yolanda pulled her T-shirt above her head and tossed it toward the end of the bed. Charles loved her taste in underwear. She was a silk and lace girl. And as much as he wanted to nibble on her nipples, he wanted to make love to her while she kept that bra on. Black looked amazing against her skin.

"I've got to protect us," he said as he scanned her body. As hard as his dick was, he was tempted to throw caution to the wind.

Yolanda nodded. "Okay."

He grabbed a condom from his dresser drawer and crossed over to the bed just as Yolanda was about to unhook her bra. "Wait," he said. "Don't take it off yet."

"Why?"

"Because you look beautiful in it," he said as he rolled the condom into place. Charles joined her on the bed and wrapped his arm around her. She was about to mount him, but he pressed his hand against her chest. "Let me please you," he said as he brought her leg around his waist. Charles dove into her wetness and nearly lost his mind as she tightened herself around him. Their bodies danced to the beats of their hearts, slow and tender. Their eyes locked and Charles ran his tongue across her full bottom lip as his climax attacked his senses. Yolanda screamed his name and clutched his back as she came. Seconds later, they held each other in a sweet silence. It was as if they were sharing the same breath.

"I-I thought we weren't going to do this again," Yolanda said after a beat.

"You and I know that we were going to end up right here, again."

"And what does this mean?"

Charles shrugged. "It means that we need to be a lot more careful."

Yolanda narrowed her eyes at him. "Is there a remorse switch stuck up your ass?" she snapped.

"Yolanda."

"Don't *Yolanda* me! Be real with me. Why do you do this?"

Charles sighed. "Because I've been here before and I don't want to lose you."

"Lose me?" She raised her eyebrow at him. "What are you talking about?"

"A few years ago, I fell in love with a woman and I feel as if my love for her got her killed. I refuse to let that happen again."

Her silence seemed to speak volumes. Charles wished he'd kept his mouth shut.

Chapter 23

Yolanda tried to find the right words to say. She brought her hand to his cheek and sighed. "I'm sorry."

"Losing Hillary made me change my life and . . ."

"You really loved her."

Chuck nodded. "Haven't loved anyone else since."

Yolanda nearly bristled when he said that. Would he ever love anyone else? Was she just a placeholder for a dead woman? *Stop it,* she thought as she stared at him.

"I didn't want to tell you about this. I just . . ."

"No, I'm glad you told me," Yolanda said as she eased out of his embrace. "It makes things clearer."

"Yolanda, I don't want you to think that things are different now because . . ."

"I understand more about you," she said.

"I'm still going to protect you."

She swung her legs over the side of the bed. "I don't doubt it. I'm going to take a shower."

"Let me join you," he said.

Yolanda rose to her feet and smiled at him. "I just

need a few moments alone, if you're okay with that. Five minutes?"

"Sure."

Yolanda walked across the hall and started the shower. She took a seat on the toilet and cried. She wanted to believe that there was a future with her and Chuck, that after her nightmare ended she could really give him her heart.

Not now. Not when her competition was a ghost. She unhooked her bra and stepped in the shower. Sure, she had been crying for over five minutes, but as the water beat down on her, she wondered if Chuck had changed his mind about joining her.

Charles knew he'd made a mistake telling her about Hillary. Did that mean they weren't going to be able to move forward? And he wondered if he actually wanted to walk down those shaky halls again. He loved and lost Hillary. Would falling for Yolanda be another heartbreak?

He headed for the bathroom, not sure how much time had passed. The steam covering the mirror and coming from behind the curtain let him know that more than five minutes had passed.

"Yolanda," he called out. "How hot do you have the water?"

"It's just an illusion because you have it so cold in here." She pulled the curtain back. "Come on in, the water's fine."

Charles smiled at her before he stepped in. Her wet body made his dick hard. Made him want to spend another twenty years with her in bed. Made him want to tell her that he was falling for her like a bag of bricks.

"That's the best invitation that I've had in a long time,"

he said. Charles wrapped his arms around her. She smelt fresh. He realized that his soap had never smelled this good on his skin. She made it sparkle. Made Irish Spring seem like a French perfume that belonged on Hollywood actresses. "You smell good."

"You feel better," she replied as she stroked his hip. "A lot better."

"Yolanda," he said as she stroked his penis.

"We're naked in a shower, what am I supposed to do with my hands?" She gripped his dick and gave him a soft squeeze.

"Not that," he moaned.

She dropped her hands. "Fine, I'll stop."

"You are such a tease. I don't know what I'm going to do with you."

Yolanda stepped back from him and smiled. "I have a few ideas, but I'm going to keep them to myself for now."

Charles closed the space between them and captured her mouth. Her kisses were his weakness. If anyone had a magical mouth, it was Yolanda Richardson. She'd convinced him that he could love again.

"If you kiss me like that again," she said, "we're not going to get clean in this shower."

"Is that a promise?" He stroked her backside. "I could do this all . . ." An alarm blared and Charles hopped out of the shower, grabbed a towel, and wrapped it around his waist. Yolanda couldn't tell where the gun came from or how he moved as fast as he did without slipping on the damp floor.

Charles rushed into his office and checked the camera and the alarm site. He set his gun on the desk when he saw two cats tussling near the garage. Taking a deep breath, he headed back for the bathroom. Yolanda had closed the door and locked it. He tapped on the door. "Yolanda, everything is okay. Just some frisky cats on the motion detector alarm."

"Are you sure?"

"Yes. Open the door, please."

She opened the door and Charles gave her a hug and a peck on the cheek. "I'm sorry if I scared you."

"You did that, sir. How in the hell did you jet out of here basically naked with a gun and not slip once?"

"I've had to do this a time or two before. But are you all right?"

She placed her hand to her chest. "I think my heart rate has returned to normal."

Charles scooped her up into his arms. "Come on, let me take you to bed."

"First, you need to get me some cookies," she said. Charles smiled at her and realized that he was in big trouble.

"I'm going to tuck you in and then bring you the cookies."

"A warrior and a gentleman," she quipped.

Charles walked into his bedroom and gently laid naked Yolanda in the center of his bed. "Be right back," he said. He headed for the kitchen and grabbed a bag of the cookies Sheldon had brought over that day. The chocolate chip cookies were huge, soft and smelled delicious. No wonder Yolanda was trying to sneak into the bed-and-breakfast to get them.

"These cookies are legendary, huh?" Charles said as he entered the bedroom.

"You mean you didn't take a bite of one before you made it in the room?"

Charles shook his head. "Thought that might be considered rude," he replied with a wink.

Yolanda took the bag of cookies from his hand. "Normally, yes." She pulled out a cookie and broke it in half. Then she brushed a piece against his lips. Charles bit into the cookie and realized that as sweet as the cookie was, it had nothing on how good Yolanda tasted.

"And you grew up on these?"

She nodded as she chewed on the cookie. "People love the bed-and-breakfast because of these cookies. I believe they're my mother's recipe."

"Really?"

Yolanda nodded and polished off her cookie. "One thing I can't do is bake these things. And it's probably a good thing."

"Why's that?"

"Because I'd never be able to fit into my designs. I'd eat these cookies every day."

Charles thought about what he'd like to eat every day and glanced down at her thighs. "Well, I'd better take these and put them aside for another special occasion," he said.

"You mean the next time the cats start fighting?"

He leaned in and kissed her on the cheek. "I'm going to move the monitor and talk to Mrs. Dena about keeping those animals in the house."

"I'd better get some clothes," she said.

"Or, you could sleep in one of my T-shirts, if you want to sleep in here with me tonight."

Yolanda smiled. "I thought you'd never ask."

Chapter 24

Over the next month, Yolanda got good at pretending that she was taking trans-Atlantic flights and was bringing Nina dresses from Paris and Milan. She'd designed the dress her sister had chosen for her wedding reception, only she couldn't tell her. The sisters were in Charlotte at Yolanda's shop doing a final fitting before the wedding. Though Charles was keeping his distance from the sisters, Yolanda felt his presence. She even missed his touch.

"Why are you so quiet?" Robin asked as they sat outside the dressing room. "Jet lag?"

"No. Just thinking about everything that's going on with you and Logan."

"Don't do this."

"Why don't you tell me what's going on with you and Logan and when I can kick his ass?"

"Stop it," Robin said.

Alex walked over to them with a bottle of wine and three glasses. "I figured you would've brought some French wine back with you," she said.

"I've been traveling light."

"I'm sure Dad appreciates that. Why is he bankrolling your . . ."

"Are we going to do this now?" Yolanda snapped. "Dad knows that I'm going to launch my own line and he's supporting me. Why do you have a problem with it?"

Alex set the wine on the floor and handed each of her sisters a glass. "I'm just wondering when you're going to start supporting your own dreams."

"Alex," Robin said. "Don't do this."

Yolanda folded her arms across her chest and thought about telling her sister the truth, but Alex was so damn judgmental. "Nah," Yolanda said. "Let her get it out because I'm sick of her shit."

"And I'm sick of you acting like Dad owes you the world. Hell, Nina's more responsible than you are and . . ."

Nina walked out of the dressing room in a formfitting Simone Carvalli wedding dress. "This is the one," she said as she spun around. Her entrance couldn't have been timed any better. The argument that was brewing stopped in its tracks as the sisters fawned over Nina. Alex even pulled up a photo of their mother to show Nina how much she looked like her. And of course, Nina started to cry.

"Nope," Yolanda said. "No teardrops on the dress."

"Just beautiful," Robin said.

Yolanda figured now was the time to break out some champagne instead of the Chardonnay that Alex had chosen. "Let's celebrate," she said. "I'm going to grab a bottle of champagne." She ducked into the storage room and ran chest first into Chuck. "Whoa."

"Y'all all right out there?" he asked.

"It's a Richardson thing," she said with a shrug. "Have my stalkers found out that we're here?"

"Not that I can tell."

She eased past him and headed for the refrigerator and grabbed a bottle of champagne. "At least Nina found her dress."

"I'm sure you helped, right?" Chuck smiled at her.

Yolanda held her bottle up and smiled. "That's what I do."

"How much longer are you guys going to be here?"

"Um, I think Alex has one more argument in her, then we can leave. We're probably going to get something to eat."

"Have it delivered. I don't like you out in the open like this."

She offered him a mock salute. "I know I haven't said it lately but thank you."

"I think this is the first time that you've ever said it at all."

She pinched his forearm. "Whatever." God, she wanted to kiss him. "All right, let me take this out here before they come looking for me."

"Good idea. But you should go a little easier on Alex."

She shot him a cold look. "Don't defend her."

"I'm not, but you're the one who decided that you didn't want your family—meaning your older sisters—to know what was going on."

"Don't." She shook her head. "Because this was your idea. You said I needed to . . ."

"Yolanda, did you have to make the champagne?" Nina called out.

She rolled her eyes at Chuck then headed back into

the showroom. "I had to make sure I had the good stuff," Yolanda said with a forced smile. She couldn't believe Chuck was really on Alex's side when he said this lie was necessary. And she knew that Alex always felt some kind of way about their father investing in her business. It didn't matter to Alex that Yolanda had paid Sheldon back and had shared her profits with her father from the store. Maybe she didn't know, but it pissed Yolanda off to no end that her sister treated her as if she were a freeloader. Yolanda popped the bottle open and filled her sisters' glasses. "Here's to Nina and Clinton, may this wedding be the first step to a lifetime of happily ever after," Yolanda said. As she and her sisters clinked their glasses together, Yolanda glanced at the storage room. She wondered if she and Chuck . . . No! She couldn't let Nina's wedding make her think that everyone was going to fall in love now. At least Robin was forcing a smile with her marriage being in shambles. Robin and her husband, Dr. Logan Baptiste, were in the midst of a divorce battle after a nurse at the hospital where he worked said that he'd fathered her son. Robin had been heartbroken and moved out of their Richmond home. While Robin tried to keep a brave face in front of her sisters, Yolanda knew she was hurt and that made Yolanda want to hurt Logan for breaking her sister's heart. And Alex was just being Alex. By the time they'd finished the bottle of champagne, it had gotten dark outside and a small shiver of fear had attacked Yolanda's spine. What if Chuck had missed the mystery killer and one of her sisters got taken out as they left the building?

Chuck walked out of the storage room. "Are you ladies ready to go?" he asked.

"Where did you come from?" Nina asked.

"I've been here. And I ordered dinner for you all. Sushi, shrimp fried rice, and spring rolls."

"Wow," Robin said. "You really know us. Please tell me you have some veggie fried rice on that order. I'm a vegetarian."

"I do," he said. "Let me just do one last security check and then we can leave."

Alex and Robin exchanged a look. "Security check?" Alex asked.

He didn't reply as he headed out the door. Yolanda turned the lights off in the shop and checked the locks on the back doors. She couldn't wait until she would be able to have the grand opening in her shop and make Charlotte her home. This life she was living, lying to her sisters, falling for a man who seemed to flip his feelings on and off like a light switch, and hiding from the world, was driving her crazy. Today would've been perfect if Alex wasn't being an asshole.

"Has Dad been paying you and Charles to roam around Europe?" Alex asked as they waited at the front door.

"Shut up, Alex," Yolanda snapped. "Why are you even like this?"

"Because you're taking advantage of our father, and if no one else is going to acknowledge it, I will."

"Guys," Nina interjected. "We're not doing this."

Robin nodded in agreement. "Alex, whatever Dad is doing for Yolanda, that's between them."

Alex folded her arms across her chest and shook her head. "Whatever."

Yolanda closed her eyes and took a deep breath.

Maybe she should've told them all the truth. Nina wasn't in on the latest plan, but she knew why Chuck was with her. And since the last thing she wanted Nina thinking about before her wedding was this situation, she didn't tell her what was going on. Besides, if she had Nina would've just blabbed to her sisters and that would've defeated the whole purpose of the ruse.

It killed her not to be able to talk to Nina about her current situation, since she was the one whom she'd talked to the most. Tears welled up in her eyes and she wanted to just tell them everything. She didn't want to fight with Alex; she wanted her sisters to rally around her and tell her that everything was going to be all right.

Chuck walked back into the shop. "Let's go, ladies."

The air was crisp, and it was quiet outside. Yolanda glanced at her watch and realized that Uptown Charlotte didn't get bumping until the clubs and bars opened. Most people in the city were shopping in SouthPark or Northlake right now. Yolanda knew when she got into her shop full-time she was going to have to make her place the go-to spot for shoppers.

But she couldn't do anything until the threat against her life was eliminated. *But what if Danny has given up because I haven't gone to the police yet?*

"Yolanda," Nina called out when she noticed that her sister hadn't crossed the street. "Are you okay?"

"Yeah, I'm coming," Yolanda said. She rushed over to Nina.

"Is everything all right? I know you haven't told Robin and Alex everything. But can you be honest with me?"

"Everything is fine. All that matters right now is that you get down the aisle with Clinton."

"I'd like to think that my sister being alive is also important. Yolanda, what's going on? Are you really just hanging out in Milan and Paris to hide from the people who want you dead?"

"It's complicated. And we can talk about this later."

Nina shrugged. "If that's what you want."

"And by later, I mean not around Alex and Robin."

Nina shot her a thumbs-up sign. "That sounds like we're going to be having cookies in bed tonight."

"Maybe not," Yolanda said with a smile.

"You're sleeping with your bodyguard?"

Yolanda started to say no. She wanted to pretend that she was doing the right thing and allowing Chuck to do his job. But over the last month, waking up in his arms and kissing him whenever she wanted to do so made her think that they had moved beyond being just an assignment.

Even knowing that she was going to go to the police in Richmond was going to change things. She wondered what would happen once she and Chuck weren't bound by his need to protect her. Would he move on to the next damsel in distress and forget about her?

Stop it, she thought as she and Nina climbed into her car. She listened to her baby sister talk about her wedding and her fiancé. Yolanda was so happy that Nina was still around to talk to her. Part of her would always feel guilt that she thought Nina's accident was her fault. Remembering the sight of her sister in that hospital bed and thinking that she was the reason why she'd been there, she now listened happily.

"So, what's going on with you and Charles Morris?"

Nina asked when they pulled into the parking garage across from the town house.

"What are you talking about?"

"Don't try to play me. I know that you have a lot of wine and champagne in your shop and it doesn't take you that long to get a bottle. So, what is the deal and why haven't those people after you been found?"

"It's complicated," Yolanda said. "But Chuck is making sure they aren't still out here stalking me."

"Is that why Daddy sent you to Europe?"

"Don't be little Alex."

"I'm just asking because I care. And I can't wait to see you start your own line. Any samples you want to send me, I'm down."

As soon as they arrived at the house, Yolanda wanted to run inside and shield her sisters from the people who wanted her dead. Of course, if she made that kind of scene, she would have a lot of explaining to do.

Chuck opened the front door for the women and nodded toward Yolanda as she entered the house. She rolled her eyes at him, still a bit miffed that he had the nerve to take Alex's side earlier.

"Where's the food?" Nina called out.

"Three minutes away," Chuck said, then grabbed Yolanda's arm. "You all right?"

She glanced down at his hand. "I'm fine," she replied tersely. "I need to talk to my sisters."

He dropped his hand and shook his head as if he didn't understand her attitude. When she walked into the kitchen, Robin was whispering into her phone and Alex was flipping through her e-mails on her smartphone.

Robin ended her call and turned to her sisters. "I have

to go back to Richmond. That asshole won't sign the divorce papers."

"What are you going to be able to do tonight?" Nina asked.

"I want to end this and I'm tired of this shit," Robin snapped. "All he has to do is sign the papers, and if I have to take them to him and serve him myself, then I will."

"Don't leave like this," Yolanda said, images of Nina after her accident popping into her head. Seeing Robin show this much anger scared Yolanda. Her attorney sister was the epitome of calm, cool, and collected. But this outburst made her wonder what was really going on between Robin and Logan.

"I'll go with you," Alex said. Yolanda and Nina exchanged wary looks.

"Alex, I know what you're trying to do, but I'm going to do this alone."

"I'm trying to make sure you don't run off the road because you're angry. Now, if you insist on leaving tonight, I'm going with you."

Robin sighed, "Fine. Let's go." Robin left the kitchen to grab her overnight bag. Alex turned to her younger sisters.

"We're going to Charleston because I don't think Robin needs to see Logan like this."

"How are you going to make that happen?" Yolanda asked.

Alex shrugged. "I'll figure it out. When we get to the bed-and-breakfast, I'll give you guys a call."

"Good idea," Nina said, then gave Alex a tight hug.

"And you two stay out of trouble," Alex quipped. Chuck walked into the kitchen with the takeout order.

"Is everything all right?" he asked.

"For the most part," Alex replied. "Sorry you ordered all of this food, but Robin and I are leaving. Family emergency."

Chuck raised his eyebrow. "Is Mr. Richardson all right?"

"Please, if this was about Daddy, we'd all be leaving," Nina said as she reached for the food. "But, since you look like you can fight, why don't . . ."

Robin walked into the kitchen and Nina stopped talking. "All right, Alex, let's go."

"Don't rush me. Charles, why don't you hand us the shrimp fried rice and the veggie fried rice so that we won't have to stop for food."

"Isn't it a little late to . . ."

"Alex!" Robin bellowed. "Can we go?"

"I guess we will be stopping." Alex and Robin bolted out of the town house and Chuck followed them to the car. Yolanda held her breath until she heard him return. No gunshots. Her sisters were going to make it home safely. That is, if Alex was able to pull off the miracle of talking Robin out of going to Richmond.

"So," Nina said. "What's Milan like? And what have you learned about fashion while you've been there?"

Yolanda shrugged and opened one of the bags of sushi. "A lot," she said before stuffing a California roll in her mouth.

"I don't believe you."

Yolanda nearly choked. "What?"

"You haven't been in Milan; you've been in hiding. At some point you're going to have to tell Robin and Alex what's really going on."

"I don't have to do anything I don't want to do. Nina, I'm trying to focus on your wedding and all the happiness you deserve. Once you and Clinton are on your honeymoon, we're going to go to the police. Just let it go," she said.

Nina rolled her eyes and grabbed a roll of her own. "What's with the chill between you and Chuck all of a sudden, though?"

"Go interview somebody else. I'm trying to eat."

"You can act like you aren't into him, but I know you. I see how you look at him. The last time I saw you act like this was . . . never."

"Shut up, Nina!"

Chuck walked into the kitchen. "Y'all good?"

"We are," Nina said. "Are you good? Have you been good to my sister in *Milan*?"

"Ask your sister."

"Nina," Yolanda said. "Why are you being such a brat?"

"So, you're saying I should sit here and eat my food?"

Chuck laughed and Yolanda wanted to punch him and Nina. She grabbed the rest of the California rolls and several packets of soy sauce. "I'm going to my studio. Try not to talk about me too much while I'm gone."

"Oh, she's big mad," Yolanda heard Nina say as she climbed the stairs.

Walking into her studio, she thought about how much had changed since she was here last. How Chuck made sure the house looked lived in and whisked her away to his home to be safe. But why did she get so mad at him for no reason?

Yolanda didn't want to admit it, but she had fallen in love with him and she did not like the feeling. Maybe it was because she didn't know how he felt about her. He was still doing his job and trying to protect her from the killers who were stalking her in the shadows. As much as she wanted to make sure her sister got married and had a wonderful wedding, Yolanda knew this thing wasn't going to be over anytime soon.

"Are you up here sulking?" Chuck asked from the doorway.

"Why aren't you downstairs eating? I wanted to be alone. I'm sure you and Nina had some things to laugh about."

"Yolanda, what's your problem? You've been acting strange since we left your shop and I'd like to know why."

"Because you really sat there and pretended that I'm the cause of the arguments between me and Alex. You're the one who created this lie."

"I'm doing what I have to do to keep you safe. You're the one who decided not to tell your sisters the truth about what happened. It's been a month and I still don't know where the threat is. So, if you have to pretend that you're traipsing around Europe then you're going to do it."

"Well, if I'm going to do it then you could at least be on my side."

Chuck smiled as he crossed over to her. "Listen, I'm always on your side. But you have to admit, starting an argument with your sister is not the way to keep the charade going."

"Is that all this is—a charade? Chuck, what happens

when we go to the police or this guy gets arrested and the danger is gone? Are you just going to disappear?"

"I don't know."

Yolanda took a deep breath and closed her eyes. "What the hell do you mean you don't know? So, this past month has still been just a job to you?"

"Yolanda, we don't need to do this now. You know, when this is over who says that you're still going to want anything to do with me? You can't let me protecting you be confused with anything else."

"Oh, that's how you feel? I've got it. Why don't you go run a security check or something? I still want to be alone." She turned her back to him because she didn't want him to see the tears welling up in her eyes. Had she been that much of a fool to think there was something more between them because they shared orgasms every now and then? Well, not just every now and then. She could have sworn they were connecting on a deeper level. When had this become more than sex to her and why did she allow it to happen? When she turned around Chuck was gone, and she realized she had been a fucking fool.

Charles knew he had messed up again. He didn't understand why he couldn't just tell Yolanda the truth about how he felt for her. Maybe he was haunted by Hillary more than he cared to admit. Every time he wanted to tell her that he was falling for her, something stupid came out of his mouth. But he didn't know that a disagreement about how she was dealing with her sisters would cause all of this. Yes, he had created the ruse to hide her away, but it was for her safety. Whatever she and Alex had going on he had no idea that it was that serious. But he knew the way he felt for her was serious and that scared him. It made him think that he could lose her, and he couldn't go through that again. So maybe he did do things to push her away. And if he kept doing it, he was going to lose her after all. He looked up toward the studio and thought about going inside and kissing her senseless, but that would only reinforce what she was thinking, that he was just using her for sex. And that couldn't be further from the truth. Spending this last month with her and falling into a routine together made him happy. Happier than he had allowed himself to be in a long time. Yolanda had to know that she meant more to him than just a piece of booty.

He couldn't tell her now. Not until the danger had passed. There was no way he could make the same mistake twice and lose another woman he loved to a bullet. Why was it so hard for him to make that clear to her? Easy—he didn't want Yolanda to think that she was taking Hillary's place or competing with a ghost.

Charles returned to the kitchen and wasn't surprised to see Nina there waiting for him.

"So, did you calm her down?" Nina asked.

"Your sister is eating and designing," he said. "And I'm pretty sure you know that she likes to be alone when she draws."

"Seems like the two of you have gotten a lot closer over these last few weeks. I told you to take care of my sister, not to sleep with her."

"I don't understand what you're talking about. I have taken care of your sister—she's still breathing, isn't she?"

"I'm not blind and I know there's something going on with you two. But tell me this, Chuck Morris, do you know who's trying to kill my sister?"

Chapter 25

Yolanda was almost tempted to let Nina grill Chuck, but even he didn't deserve full-on reporter Nina mode. "Leave people alone," Yolanda said as she walked into the kitchen.

"Then people ought to answer my questions," Nina said. "And I know you didn't eat all of those California rolls."

"If you want them, they're upstairs, go get them." Yolanda tilted her head toward the stairs. "And stay for a while to enjoy them."

"If you wanted to be alone with him, you should've just said so. I'm taking the spicy tuna, too," Nina said as she snatched the box from the countertop.

"I was eating those, too," Chuck said, trying not to laugh.

"Too bad, too sad," Nina called out as she left the kitchen.

Once they were alone, Yolanda realized that apologizing wasn't her ministry. It wasn't even something she'd done often. And there were plenty of times when she should have.

"You're just going to stand there and stare at me or are you going to speak your mind?"

"I'm sorry," she said. "I'm sorry that I've been a total bitch to you when you haven't done anything to deserve it. Everything about us is new to me. These feelings are new to me and I don't handle change well unless we're talking about wardrobes."

"Why did you say that like it hurt?"

"I'm being serious and pouring my heart out and you want to make jokes?"

He pointed to his face. "Do I look like I'm smiling?"

Yolanda folded her arms across her chest. "This is why I make it a rule to never apologize."

"Let's agree to never do anything that would need an apology again." He pulled out another box of sushi and opened it, revealing spicy tuna rolls.

"Aww, you do care," she said as she grabbed a roll.

Charles did care more than she knew, and he wanted to tell her. Instead, he asked, "When do you want to go back to Charleston?"

She rolled her eyes. "It'll make sense to go when Nina leaves since she is about to be in full-on wedding-planning mode. I have to be there to help her."

"I imagine so. Do you plan on staying at the bed-and-breakfast? Can't keep pretending we're going back and forth to Milan now."

"Should I?"

"I wouldn't recommend it, but I know that would cause more conflict with you and your sisters. I'm just going to have to stay with you and be your shadow. Same rules apply."

She eased closer to him. "And what are those rules?"

"You have to do what I say. Let's not forget that there are still people out there chasing after you who want to put a bullet in you."

"You know we blurred the lines of these rules of yours a month ago."

"And that was my mistake." Charles regretted those words as soon as they left his mouth. Yolanda's face was contorted with anger and disappointment.

"I wish you could teach me this party trick." Her voice was a slight hiss.

"Wait, I . . ."

She shook her head and threw her hands up. "I'm so over this little game with you. One minute you act like you care and then it's ice-cold Chuck. What do you really want from me?"

"My priorities haven't changed; I have to keep you alive. And we made an agreement that after your sister's wedding you would go to the police about Danny and the murder."

"I know what I said. But how do you do it? You act as if nothing that happened between us these last thirty days means anything. That's not how I roll."

"What do you want from me? Yolanda, I have a job to do."

"Great, then do your fucking job and don't you ever touch me again!" She flipped the last three spicy tuna rolls into the trash can and stormed into her bedroom. Charles wanted to follow her, but he knew better than to try to talk to her with both feet in his mouth. He'd gotten too close to her and now he was paying for it. The last thing he'd wanted was to hurt Yolanda. But things had gotten out of hand and he knew where this road led. There was no way he could go there again. Even if it meant losing a chance to love an amazing woman like Yolanda Richardson.

You're just going to let fear run your life forever? He hadn't heard Hillary's voice in a while. But there she was whispering in his ear. He headed toward Yolanda's closed bedroom door, and as he lifted his hand to knock, the door swung open.

There was less anger on her face, but she was wearing a mask of disappointment. "What do you want?"

"Can we talk?"

"I'm tired of talking to you. I've had better conversations with a brick wall."

"I deserve that."

"There are a lot of things you deserve, and my conversation is not one of them."

Charles placed his hands on her shoulders and massaged them gently. "Yolanda, it scares me to think about how I feel for you. And maybe I don't deal with it properly, but you have to understand that this was unexpected."

"You think I wanted this to happen? That I wanted to . . . I think we should keep it professional. I mean, in a few days we're going to be done with each other, right?"

"No."

"Once I turn Danny in this whole shitshow will be over. At least that's what you've been saying all this time, right?" she said as she shrugged his hands from her shoulders. "I don't want to keep reminding you of the ghosts haunting you."

"There are no ghosts," he said. "Yolanda, please understand that . . ."

"What's going on here?" Nina asked from the stairs. "And don't give me that nothing bullshit."

"How about it's none of your business," Yolanda snapped.

"Do you know how scared I've been for you? And if you are letting your hormones put you in danger because you and this guy can't keep your hands off each other, then that is a problem. And don't you dare say that it isn't my business."

"But it isn't," Yolanda said. "And let's not forget that it's your fault he's here."

Nina crossed over to Yolanda and glared at her. "Let that shit go."

"I'm not," she snapped. "You created this whole mess."

Charles shook his head as Nina and Yolanda went back and forth.

"Yeah, 'cause you dying was a much better alternative!" Nina's voice vibrated through the house. Yolanda grabbed her sister and gave her a tight hug.

Nina pointed her index finger at Charles and shook her head once she and Yolanda broke their embrace. "You'd better take care of her."

"That's the plan. If she allows me to do my job."

Yolanda rolled her eyes. "Since there's still shrimp fried rice in the kitchen, we should eat it."

"Maybe you should; I was thinking about going for a walk," Nina said.

"No," Yolanda exclaimed. "Get on the treadmill or something."

"Yolanda, this was my neighborhood before it was yours. It's really safe out there."

"Nina, your sister is right," Charles said. "One of the reasons why we left was because somebody was watching her. And the last thing Yolanda wants is for something to happen to you guys because of this."

"Wait. What? Those people know that you're here now? I thought you were supposed to keep her safe from them finding her!"

Charles threw his hands up. "Unfortunately, Yolanda posted about her new business and I think that's how they found her. It's also another reason why the shop hasn't been opened officially."

Yolanda turned away from them as they spoke about her stalker. Charles wanted to pull her into his arms and tell her everything was going to be okay. But after what she had said to him, he knew that was not a good idea.

"I didn't know all of this was going on, and of course Alex doesn't know either. Yolanda, why do you want to hide everything from us? You know we could help you."

"Because this is my problem and I'm trying to solve it. I get tired of everybody thinking that I'm the flaky one who can't handle herself and I always need Dad's help. You know, if I hadn't been designing my window for summer fashions none of this would have happened. I could have gone on with my life, ran my shop in Richmond, and not be stuck in here with this guy."

Charles bristled at her comment. Now she was stuck with him? "I'm sorry you feel that way," he said. "But that doesn't mean that I'm going anywhere, not while the threat is still out there."

"You've made that painfully obvious," Yolanda said as she turned on her heels and headed for the kitchen.

"This just means she really likes you and you must have done something to piss her off," Nina said, then followed her sister into the kitchen.

Charles felt like now was a good time to go and run a security check.

Yolanda dug into the cold shrimp fried rice and realized that she was being a jerk. More than a jerk, an asshole. And for what reason?

Because you love that man and he clearly doesn't feel the same way.

"I know you're not going to eat all of that rice, and I hope you heated it up," Nina said. "Or do you still eat cold rice when you're mad?"

"Why don't you leave me alone?"

"Because I never listen to what you say, and I want answers. When did you fall in love with Chuck Morris?"

Yolanda slammed the container of rice on the counter. "I'm not in love with that man."

"Sure, you're not, Jan," Nina mocked. "I know one thing. You don't get mad at people that you don't give a shit about. So, what did he do and why are you so upset?"

Yolanda reached for one of the containers of vegetable fried rice and rolled her eyes at her sister. "He thought I was being too hard on Alex at the shop."

"Yep, you like him a whole lot. You actually got mad

at this man because he told you the truth. You haven't been in Milan this past month, have you?"

She didn't see the point in lying anymore. "No."

"Where the hell have y'all been, then?"

"At his place in Charleston."

Nina's mouth dropped wide open. "So, did Daddy know or was . . ."

"Don't tell Alex, but yes. He knew and was on board with it."

"I can't believe he kept this from us. But wait, you and Chuck Morris—"

"Why do you have to say his whole name?" Yolanda interrupted.

Nina shrugged. "Because it's funny. So, you and Charles have been in his home for over a month and I'm supposed to believe nothing is going on? Okay, then."

Yolanda groaned. "Yes, there is something going on and it's crazy because when we're alone together, he's a different person. But when we get in front of people, he acts as if I don't matter at all."

"Or maybe he's just doing his job when y'all are out in public? Is this even ethical? He's supposed to be a bodyguard, not your boyfriend."

Yolanda tossed a packet of soy sauce at her sister. "He is not my boyfriend!"

Nina swatted the package away and laughed. "Whatever you say. But let's get serious for a minute," she said. "Who's after you?"

Yolanda sighed and thought about not telling Nina the whole story. But her sister didn't become a successful journalist because she stopped asking questions.

"It's a lot worse than I thought. The shooter, Danny

Branch, is a legend in Richmond. But Chuck found out that he's a criminal the cops just won't touch."

Nina pulled out her smartphone and Yolanda assumed she was Googling the man.

"So, what are you going to do?" Nina asked. "Hell, he's a civic leader."

Yolanda crossed over to her and took Nina's phone from her hand. "Didn't I tell you this is my problem to solve? All you need to be thinking about is your wedding."

Nina rubbed her hand across her face. "I can multitask."

"Not this time. Your only task is to be a beautiful bride on Christmas Day. Charles and I can handle this."

All Yolanda had to figure out was how to handle her heart.

Charles wasn't sure if he was seeing someone move in the shadows or if the wind was stirring up dead leaves. He followed the rustling and saw a cat. Damned cats were going to give him a heart attack. Maybe not the cats, but worrying about his feelings for Yolanda had him on edge. Things were going to change real soon. Once he found someone in Richmond to arrest Danny, they'd go on about their business.

Then what? he thought as he walked back to the house. *What happens when she no longer needs me? She's going to be in Charlotte and my business is in Charleston. I'd be a fool to think that she won't meet someone else who can give her what she needs. But I need her, and I have to figure out how to make her understand that. But is now the right time for that? I know what happened the last time I put my feelings before a case was done, and I can't let that happen again.*

Charles unlocked the front door and walked into the house. He heard Yolanda and Nina laughing in the kitchen. He admired the Richardson sisters' relationship. Although they could fight with each other like cats and dogs, the love they shared was evident. He almost felt sorry for the man who had broken Robin's heart. If her sisters could get ahold of him, he'd be in big trouble.

But Charles wasn't worried about that too much, although he knew Yolanda would somehow end up going back to Richmond before it was time because that's where Robin lived. Maybe he could talk her out of making that mistake but he highly doubted it. He headed for the kitchen, and when he walked in the laughter stopped.

"Everything all good in here?" he asked.

Nina smiled at him. "Oh, we're fine, and to show you that there are no hard feelings we left you a whole bunch of veggie fried rice."

"I don't think you made a good point there, ma'am," Charles said with a grin.

"You don't eat much anyway so you should be glad we left you anything," Yolanda said.

Charles bit back a comment about how much he had eaten over the last month but now wasn't the time to go there. But when he raised his right eyebrow at Yolanda the blush on her cheeks showed that she had gotten the message.

Maybe Nina felt something in the air because she yawned and then excused herself from the kitchen.

Alone with Yolanda, Charles struggled not to kiss her.

"How are we going to do this?" he asked after the silence in the room became too thick.

"Do what?"

He cleared his throat. "Get ready for your sister's wedding and convince everyone that you've been hanging out in Italy."

"I have to be at the bed-and-breakfast to prepare for Nina's wedding. That can't be avoided."

"Just so we're clear, you're not going back alone. I know you're mad at me right now, but I'm going with you."

Yolanda rolled her eyes. "For me to be mad at you would be assuming that I actually give a damn," she said.

"When you want to have a real conversation about anything else just let me know." Charles grabbed a container of the vegetable fried rice and headed to the microwave to heat it up. He could feel Yolanda watching him, and as much as he wanted to say more to her and explain why everything had changed, he knew she wasn't ready for that kind of conversation. So, he just let it go.

In a perfect world, the week leading up to Christmas with Yolanda would've been a celebration like nothing Charles had experienced since he was six. He tried not to think about the last month they'd spent at his home, waking up together. Him posing for those swim trunks that she was allegedly going to design. But all he could do now, while staying at the Richardson Bed and Breakfast, was stay in contact with Madison and find out what was happening in Richmond.

"I don't understand how you allowed her to change

your rules," Madison said when he told her that they were at the family property and not his house. "Chuck, tell the truth, you care about her, right?"

"I do and I'm trying not to make the same mistake. . . ."

"This isn't Hillary. And I know I'm the last person to tell you to let the past go, but do that."

"Have you?"

"You got closure when that bastard who killed Hillary went to prison. I haven't gotten my justice for my sister, but I will."

"Madison, you can tell me how I need to let go of the past, but you can't do the same."

"That man is still out there and I'm going to find him and put a stop to his reign of terror. I'm getting closer to stopping him."

"What happens if you don't get closure, Madison?"

"Then I guess I'll be a sad sack like you. Chuck, I'm going to make him pay and no one is going to stop me this time."

"Do you know who he is?"

"I have to go," she said, and then the call ended.

Chapter 26

Christmas Eve at the Richardson Bed and Breakfast started out so much differently than Yolanda had expected. The family breakfast had been marred by the appearance of her soon-to-be former brother-in-law, Logan Baptiste. When Robin disappeared with him, Yolanda wanted to follow her sister and ask her what the hell was wrong with her. She'd even grabbed the keys to her father's car and was about to track her down before Chuck stopped her at the door. She tried to push him aside, but he wouldn't move. "Don't do this. I need to find my sister," Yolanda said.

"What are you doing?" he asked. "You find her and do what? What just happened with your sister and her husband has nothing to do with you."

"Will you just get out of the way?" Yolanda snapped.

"Yolanda, you're not going anywhere. You're supposed to be keeping a low profile because this time we don't know if we have been followed here. I've already said that you were going to have to follow my rules if you wanted to be here with your sisters."

"Do you know what he did to her?"

Chuck sighed. "I hate to sound harsh, but that isn't my concern. Give me the keys."

She glared at him for a few seconds before thrusting the keys in his hand. "Fine, I'm going to my room and I'll be in there alone." As she flounced down the hall, she noticed that Alex had seen their exchange. "What?" she snapped at her sister.

"I didn't say a word," Alex replied calmly. "But he's right. Whatever Robin and Logan are doing right now has nothing to do with any of us."

"Are you really going to let her . . ."

Alex held her hand up. "This is one time when we have to follow her lead. Yolanda, they're married, and I'd like to believe that he hasn't done what he's accused of. What would you really help if you got up in their faces adding fuel to the fire they're trying to fight?"

Yolanda was really taken aback by Alex's stance. She figured she'd be the first one telling Robin to dump his trifling ass. After all, DNA tests didn't lie, and according to Robin she saw a test that said Logan was the father of that nurse's baby. How could anyone forgive that? "Well, I guess . . . Fine."

"Want some coffee and muffins?"

Yolanda hitched her eyebrow at her sister. "Why are you being so nice?"

"Because it's Christmas, heffa. And we need to focus on Nina's wedding. Lord knows there is enough drama with you and Robin to derail that girl's day."

Yolanda bit back her sarcastic comment in the spirit of the holiday. "I'll take some coffee if you spike it. Obviously, I won't be leaving this place until Nina and

Clinton are hitched." She looked over her shoulder and saw Chuck was watching her every move.

When Alex and Yolanda headed back to the dining area in the family section of the bed-and-breakfast, they found Sheldon and Nina talking about the upcoming NFL playoffs.

"Just like old times," Yolanda said as she nudged Alex. "She starts talking sports with Daddy and we get the chores."

"Don't remind me," Alex replied with a laugh.

Nina rolled her eyes. "Are you jealous because I'm Dad's favorite?"

"How about we don't start this today. Y'all do want Santa to stop by tonight, right?" Sheldon said with a hearty chuckle. That's how he'd been stopping arguments with his daughters on Christmas Eve for years. He filled a plate with bacon, eggs, raisin toast, and fruit, then rose from his chair.

"Where are you going, Dad?" Yolanda asked.

"I'm not going to let Clinton eat Pop-Tarts when I know he's in his office trying to sneak a peek at his bride," he replied. "Besides, I need to have a heart-to-heart with my future son-in-law."

"Tell him I'm counting down the minutes until I'm Mrs. Clinton Jefferson," Nina said.

Yolanda rolled her eyes and hid her laugh. She knew that her sister and Clinton spent last night together making a lot of noise until eleven-fifty. Meanwhile, she'd tossed and turned all night wishing Chuck would've gotten off the sofa in her room and joined her in the bed.

But she was the one who said they needed to keep it professional.

You did it to yourself and now you simply have to deal with the fallout, she thought as she joined Nina at the table.

Alex took Sheldon's empty seat at the head of the table. She glanced over at Yolanda. "You're really going to be rude and not invite Charles to join us?"

Yolanda rolled her eyes. "He's a grown man and if he's hungry, he can see the food."

Alex shook her head but kept silent. It didn't take long for Chuck to walk into the dining area. After he told Alex and Nina good morning, he took a seat at the table next to Yolanda. She closed her eyes as his masculine scent overpowered the delicious smell of breakfast. How many times had they eaten breakfast at his place? Only, he'd been shirtless, and she'd cooked the shrimp and grits in one of his white T-shirts that hit her right above the knee.

What a difference a month made. Yolanda eased her chair a couple of inches away from him. If Nina or Alex noticed her move, at least they had the good sense not to say anything. As did Chuck. He just ate his breakfast.

"So, are we opening a gift tonight or no?" Nina asked.

"You're going to bed so Santa will still come, and you won't have bags under your eyes tomorrow," Alex said. "I know if you and Yo-Yo stay up, there is going to be a lot of wine missing from the cellar."

"Like it isn't already," Yolanda quipped. "Ooh, you know what, we should have mimosas."

Alex looked down at her watch. "I need to go check the reservation arrivals, but you two have fun."

"Do you even know what that is?" Yolanda asked.

Alex pointed her finger at her sister. "I'm not doing this with you today. Some of us still have to work."

Chuck tapped her knee as if he knew Yolanda was on the edge of an explosion. As much as she didn't want to admit it, he did calm her down.

"Just make sure all of you are around at eight so we can watch *The Wiz*," Nina said, then stood up and mimicked some of Michael Jackson's moves as the Scarecrow.

Alex shook her head. "Only because you're getting married tomorrow."

"How sweet of you, Alex," Nina said sarcastically. "And there'd better be popcorn with lots of butter and sugar."

"You know, you are making a lot of demands for somebody who needs to be resting and relaxing," Yolanda said. "And if you even think about trying to sneak up to the office to see your fiancé, I'm going to take that *Wiz* DVD and throw it in the ocean."

Alex clasped her hands together. "Now that is a good idea. Because you know your sister lacks self-control—a trait that both of you share," she said.

Yolanda decided not to reply to Alex's argument starter. It was Christmas Eve, one day until Nina's wedding, and she hated to admit it, but Alex was right. Yolanda's self-control was being tested right now in ways she had never imagined . . . all because of Chuck Morris.

"All right, I'll see you guys later," Alex said.

Chuck stood up and started clearing the dishes from the table. Nina smiled. "You don't have to do that. It's actually Yolanda's job."

Yolanda rolled her eyes. "Don't you have some kind of spa ritual or something to do? Go away."

"I'm going to watch the NFL pregame show. You two behave."

Alone in the dining room, Chuck and Yolanda silently cleared the table. He looked over at her and said, "Merry Christmas."

"Merry Christmas to you, too. Are you often away from your family on the holidays?"

"We don't really do big celebrations anymore. It's just another day."

Yolanda couldn't imagine holidays without her family. Even after her mother's death, Sheldon tried to give the girls a somewhat normal Christmas and it had been that way ever since. Nina wouldn't say it out loud, but she covered sporting events during the holidays because it was hard for her to hear about memories that she wasn't a part of with their mother.

"What's with the radio silence?" Chuck asked.

"I was just thinking about how today changes a lot for our family. Nina is going to have a Christmas memory that will last forever for her, and she won't have to hide behind her job anymore to avoid the holidays with us."

"Well, why did she do that to begin with? I figured the Richardsons had the most elaborate holiday celebrations of anybody in Charleston County."

Yolanda shrugged. "It used to be like that before Mom passed. And Nina doesn't admit it out loud, but she feels some kind of way about her lack of connection to Mom's memories."

When Chuck drew her into his arms, that was when Yolanda knew she was crying. Okay, so it wasn't just Nina who missed the connection with Nora Richardson.

Pull it together, girl, she thought as she pulled out of Chuck's embrace. "Sorry, I get a little emotional when I think about Christmas and my mom. Didn't mean to pull you into this."

"It's okay," he said, then stroked her cheek. Yolanda shivered and wished she hadn't been this open with him. "Do you want to talk about it?"

"I don't want to talk, but doing what I want to do would make everything we've said recently a lie."

"Yolanda," he said quietly. "We have to focus on what happens when we go to Richmond."

"I know that, but . . ." What was the harm in a Christmas kiss? She stood on her tiptoes and brushed her lips against his. Chuck pulled her closer and deepened the kiss. He ran his hands up and down her back. She nearly lost it when he ran his tongue across her bottom lip. This either had to stop or be moved to her room.

Yolanda pulled back from him. "I thought I saw mistletoe," she quipped.

"You're funny," he replied. "We can't do this again. The last thing that I want is for your father to walk in and catch us."

"Don't tell me that you're one of those men afraid of my dad," she said with a smirk.

"I know how men are about their daughters, so yeah."

Yolanda took a step back from him and expelled a sigh. "You're right. And we don't want that smoke," she said. "Come on, let's go and raid the kitchen."

"I'd love to, but I have to make a call."

She nodded and wondered if he was walking away

from her only because he wanted her just as much as she wanted him.

Charles walked out of the bed-and-breakfast and looked toward the ocean. That woman drove him crazy and he had to make sure he stayed on task. He pulled out his phone and called Madison, since he knew she was the only other person who was working on a holiday.

"What's up, Chuck?" she said when she answered the phone.

"Have you talked to anyone with Richmond PD?"

"Merry Christmas to you, too," Madison said.

"Yeah, yeah," he said. "Come on, I'm being serious. Yolanda's ready to go to the police about Danny and I don't want to lead her to slaughter."

"Got you. Well, something interesting happened over the last month. The police are finally investigating the disappearance of his ex. There was a little blurb about it online. I've been trying to find out who the main detective is and why this case is back on the radar."

"Okay. I know that's important to you and I feel like you're the reason this case is back. But I need details. After her sister's wedding, Yolanda plans to make her statement."

"Jeez, you're acting as if you can't wait to be rid of this woman. What happened?"

"Maybe I fell in love with her," he muttered.

"What? Wait."

"Madison, I need a report as soon as possible."

"Got it. I'll see what I can find out by tomorrow. But here's something else that you may find interesting: The

Feds have a shadow investigation on Danny Branch and his investments."

"Interesting," Charles said. "Sad thing is, he'll probably do more time for messing with money than killing people."

"That's the fucked-up world we live in. Life only matters when people claim they're pro-life. Once a baby is born, it is all about the money."

"Cynical much?"

"Very. Enjoy Christmas Eve with your girlfriend."

"She is not my girlfriend."

"Yet," Madison replied, then ended the call. Charles hated it when she was right.

Chapter 27

It was midafternoon when the Richardson clan got together a small dessert buffet before the kitchen staff went home. It was a Christmas tradition at the bed-and-breakfast. Sheldon would have dessert catered for the staff to thank them for their hard work. It had been Nora's idea to do dessert, since everyone had their family dinners the next day. Dessert always gave everyone a sweet thank-you and a happy holiday.

As the family walked into the dining area, Yolanda was a little perplexed that Chuck had been a ghost since breakfast. Did her kiss shake him up that bad or had something happened?

"Where's your bodyguard?" Alex asked as she reached for an apple tart.

Yolanda shrugged. "Don't take all the apple tarts," she said.

Alex rolled her eyes and handed the tart to Yolanda. "Merry Christmas."

"Oh, you are so gracious," Yolanda quipped. "How did you keep Clinton from joining us and where is Nina?"

"Clinton is actually with the housekeeping staff handing out turkeys and bags of shrimp. Nina'd better be . . ." Before Alex could finish her statement, Sheldon and Nina walked into the kitchen.

"I see I've been watching the wrong sneaky child all my life," Sheldon said with a grin. Nina folded her arms across her chest. "Daddy, you really had the wrong idea here. I-I was just trying to check the score of the game."

"Let me guess, she was trying to hand out turkeys?" Alex laughed.

Yolanda shook her head. "You really need to follow the tradition of staying away from that man until you see him at the altar. We need some more good luck around here these days."

"True," Alex said. "Especially when . . . Where is Robin?"

"Mind your business and help me hand out these bonus checks," Sheldon said as he handed Alex a stack of envelopes.

Nina walked over to Yolanda. "Did you at least save me an apple tart?"

Yolanda bit into her tart and shook her head.

"Just evil," Nina said as she frowned at her sister. "Why is Chuck walking around outside like you don't want him around?"

Yolanda shrugged. "I can't understand that man and I'm going to stop trying. It's exhausting."

"He won't give you none for Christmas?"

"Shut up."

"What happens when your life gets back to normal?

Do you think that you just want him because he's the only option right now?"

Yolanda cleared her throat and swallowed a caustic comment. "Nina, I have never judged you and your questionable dating decisions. Can I get the same respect?"

"Wait, I wasn't judging you. I just don't want you to . . . Never mind. I'm not fighting with you the day before my wedding."

"And I'm not fighting with you. Because there is nothing to fight about. Nina, Chuck is special. I don't know how to explain it but being with him this last month made me feel like love could work."

"Now you're in love with him?" Nina's voice rose and a couple of people at the buffet glanced at the sisters.

"Will you shut up," Yolanda gritted. "But what if I am?"

"I mean, that's all well and good, but how does he feel? What if this is a pattern for him?"

"It isn't. Chuck and I have a lot in common and it's more than him doing his job. He's . . ."

"Good in bed, I get it. But can it be more than that?"

I'd like to think so, Yolanda thought as she grabbed a chocolate cupcake. "This whole watching *The Wiz* thing, do you think Robin's going to be back to watch with us?"

"I like the way you changed the subject there. And here comes Chuck Morris."

Yolanda watched him as he walked toward them. He greeted the workers with smiles. Shook hands with a couple of people who seemed to know who he was. She loved his spirit. She just loved him. And that's why everything felt different. Why she wanted things to mean as much to him as they did to her. But she couldn't account for how he felt and the last thing she could take was finding out that he didn't feel the same way.

"Hey, Yolanda," he said when he made it to where she was standing. "Can we go talk in private for a second?"

She glanced at Nina. "Don't move. And don't go trying to get Clinton to come in here. Matter of fact, hand me your phone."

"What? You don't trust me?"

Yolanda held her hand out and shook her head. "The phone, turkey."

Nina groaned and handed Yolanda her phone. Before she and Chuck had found a quiet spot, Nina's phone chimed with a text message. She didn't have to look to see it was from Clinton.

"What's going on?" she asked Chuck.

"I spoke to my contact and it seems as if some heat is coming down on Danny. We may have the opening to find some cops who are willing to help us get him put away."

"Seriously?"

He nodded. "There are a few things I want to check out before we go to Richmond."

"How soon are you talking about leaving, because you know I'm not going to miss my sister's wedding."

"It's not like we would get anything done on Christmas day, but in a week or so."

She shrugged. "All right. But how do you know the information you have is accurate?"

"I trust Madison. She's been working to make Danny pay for the disappearance of his ex-wife and she's a badass."

Yolanda didn't like the fact that she was jealous. This

Madison person, was she more than a source? Was she the kind of woman he really went for? A badass? Someone who didn't need protection because she could protect herself.

"What's wrong?" he asked when he noticed the scowl on her face.

"Nothing, nothing, I was just thinking about speaking to the police and if it's actually going to make a difference. I remember when his ex went missing. Nobody cared. He was able to spin the story the way he wanted, and it was forgotten."

"Not this time," Chuck said. "He's not going to get away with terrorizing you. Count on that."

She wanted to melt in his arms, because she believed that Chuck was going to make Danny pay.

Charles tried not to think about the last time he'd made a promise like this. *Hillary.*

But things were different this time. This time he had backup. Or at least he hoped the police would take this case more seriously than they had taken Hillary's case. If they didn't, he had to. And that meant, once they got to Richmond, no more blurred lines. No more kisses and no more sleeping in the same bed.

The most important thing was Yolanda's safety and nothing else.

Richmond, Virginia

Christmas Eve had always been Danny's time to shine. He'd go into underserved neighborhoods and pass out Christmas dinners. There were always cameras there to capture his good deeds and write happy stories about him.

This year was going to be different. A story had leaked in the press about his missing ex-wife. Those damned cops were supposed to keep things quiet, but somehow, the media got ahold of his statement and people were talking about *her*. He needed to change the story or allow it to fall out of the headlines. Chase had disappointed him in failing to rid the world of Yolanda Richardson, and now he had to worry about her adding another layer of scrutiny to his life.

This is bullshit, he thought as he walked over to his bar and poured himself a stiff drink. When the doorbell rang, he knew it was his chief operations officer, Will Henson. This year, Will would be handing out dinners and getting his picture taken on behalf of Branch Investments. He crossed over to the door with the drink in his hand but was surprised to see two uniformed police officers standing there.

"Officers, what are you doing here?" Danny asked.

"Mr. Branch, you need to come down to the station with us," the tallest officer said.

"Guys, it's Christmas," he said.

"Well, crime doesn't take a break," the mouthy officer said. "It's a simple formality."

"Then why can't we do this after the holidays?"

"We can't do that," the other officer said. "We have our orders. It's just for a talk."

"And what is this all about?" Danny asked, then took a sip of his drink.

"A body that may be your ex-wife," the mouthy officer

said. "Now, you can come with us or we can come back with a warrant. Your choice."

Danny wanted to toss his drink in Officer Mouth's face, but he knew that it was better to act with decorum. "I'll tell you what, why don't you get your superior officer on the phone right now. I have family coming into town shortly and this is going to put a damper on our holiday celebration."

The other officer gave Danny a sympathetic look. "Mr. Branch, we're not trying to make things difficult for you, but if you come with us now it's just a questioning. You can leave and be back here in less than an hour. But if we have to file warrant paperwork, then it's going to be public and the media is going to be sniffing after you."

He hated to admit it, but this guy had a point. "How do I know you don't have some photographer out here waiting to see me leaving in the back of a police car?"

"Look," Officer Mouth said, "you're making this more difficult than it needs to be. If you just want to be an asshole, we will come back with a warrant."

Danny looked at the man's name tag: Officer D. Bryant. This man had just made his list of people who needed to disappear.

"Do what you have to do. But keep in mind I have a lot of friends at the department and I will let them know of this encounter. Officer Bryant, you're going to find yourself writing tickets on a street corner for jaywalkers."

"Are you threatening me?" Officer Bryant asked with a lot of bravado.

His partner put his hand on his shoulder. "Come on, man, we're not here to start a fight. We can do this later—just don't leave town."

Danny smiled at the other officer and read his name tag: Officer S. Kaiser. It seemed as if he had a little bit of sense. "I'll be happy to come in and answer any questions you all have for me after the holidays. But don't think that you can come and darken my door on Christmas Eve and expect me to go to the police department with you. But hey, if you want to get your warrant and come back then it's a whole other situation. However, I'm not some little punk off the streets. I know my rights and I choose to invoke them and not go anywhere with you."

Danny slammed the door in their faces. Shit had just gotten real.

Charleston, South Carolina

Charles had never seen a group of sisters act like the Richardsons did. One minute they were fighting and the next minute they were jamming to Diana Ross and easing down the road. He knew Yolanda, Robin, and Alex were probably watching this movie just to keep Nina from trying to meet her fiancé before their wedding, but they were having such a good time.

Robin had returned to the bed-and-breakfast and she wouldn't give the details to her sisters about what happened while she was with her husband, but it seemed as if it became a moot point once the movie and the dancing started.

Yolanda's booty was shaking like a bowl of gelatin as she danced, making his dick hard. *Focus*, he thought. They would be in Richmond in a few days, probably looking face-to-face with the man who wanted her dead, and the last thing he needed to be thinking about was how her booty jiggled.

"Hey, Chuck," Nina called out. "You have to come and be the mean old lion."

He threw his hands up and shook his head. "Nah, I'm going to leave this to you guys. I get the feeling you do this every year."

"Unfortunately, we do," Alex said as she wiped sweat from her forehead. "But you would make a great lion."

"I agree," Robin chimed in.

He glanced over at Yolanda and she looked mortified. Maybe the sisters had had a little too much wine.

"Y'all make me sick," Yolanda said, then looked at her watch. "Okay, Nina. This isn't the bachelorette party I would have planned for you, but I was given limitations." She smirked at Alex. "But I do have something special planned for us since we have this amazing day tomorrow. There is a massage therapist in each of your rooms. I wanted to make sure that everyone was relaxed and ready to celebrate the love of my baby sister and her future husband tomorrow."

"Aww, Yolanda," Nina said as she crossed over to her sister and gave her a big hug. "That's so sweet, thank you."

Yolanda shrugged. "This is the least I could do. I want your day to be perfect and I want you to look beautiful. When you walk into your new life, you need to glow. And that's what this massage is going to do, make you radiant."

"Well," Alex began, "this is sweet. And I'm glad you thought of me, too."

Charles bristled, wondering if Yolanda and Alex would

turn this gesture into an argument, but the sisters hugged, and he realized that as much as Yolanda and Alex tried to pretend that they were so different, they were a lot alike. One thing he knew from watching them together was both of them liked to be in charge.

Maybe that had been why she wasn't honest with Alex about what was going on in her life. And that quite possibly was the reason why she had gotten so upset with him in Charlotte. But Charles couldn't say that he was excited about Yolanda going into her room with some man massaging her body. He wanted to be the only person who touched her; he wanted that body to belong to him. *What the hell am I thinking?* he thought.

Yolanda walked over to the TV and turned it off. "So, you guys get going and I'm going to clean up the spilled popcorn."

Nina and Alex exchanged knowing looks. Robin waved goodbye to the group and headed for her room. Charles heard Nina whisper, "Why do I feel like she just did this so she could have some time alone with him?"

"Girl," Alex said, "let's go get massages and they can do whatever they want to do as long as they clean up this area."

"I can hear you," Yolanda said. "Ungrateful heifers. Just go."

Nina and Alex started for the door. But Nina stopped short and turned to her sister. "Um, are you going to give me my phone back tonight or no?"

Yolanda tilted her head to the side and laughed. "FaceTime still qualifies as seeing the groom before the wedding, so no. Go get your massage."

Charles looked around the sitting area where they had watched the movie. There were bowls of half-eaten popcorn, two empty wine bottles, and four dirty glasses. Charles couldn't help but smile. These women knew how to have a good time.

"I guess we'd better get this place cleaned up," Yolanda said as she looked at her watch.

"You're getting a massage too?" he asked.

"No, not unless . . . No, I'm not. But I knew Nina needed to be occupied, Robin deserves to relax, and Alex simply needs to get the stick out of her ass so she can relax. And I'm so sick of watching the damn *Wiz*."

Charles chuckled. "I couldn't tell by the way you were dancing to all of those songs."

"Well, I mean how can you not? I did have a good time with my sisters tonight, even if Robin seemed a little too preoccupied with thinking about that slimy soon-to-be ex of hers. She deserves so much better."

"I thought your dad told you guys to mind your business?"

"Do we look like the kind of people who mind our business when one of us has been hurt? I mean if that was the case you and I would have never met."

"I know you've said it a hundred times, but let me ask you this: When you told Nina about the threats against your life, what did you think she was going to do?"

Yolanda shrugged as she crossed over to the TV and picked up the half-empty bowls of popcorn. "Maybe I thought she'd tell somebody. Maybe I thought she'd keep my secret. I don't know, but I can't say that I thought you and I would end up here together on Christmas."

"Technically it's not Christmas yet."

She grabbed a handful of popcorn from one of the bowls she had picked up and threw it at him. "You know, always correcting somebody is infuriating."

Charles picked up the kernels and tossed them in the trash. "Just imagine how painful it is to always be right," he quipped.

"I can't stand you." But her smile said otherwise. And Charles wanted to wrap his arms around her, take her into her room, and give her a massage that she would never forget—starting from the top of her head down to the bottom of her feet, touching and licking everything in between. But that was out of the question. He had to make sure that they would be able to shut Danny down and then see what happened next.

Yolanda was trying to make her new life in Charlotte and even if she was safe to move back to Richmond, he wasn't going to leave Charleston. And long-distance relationships didn't work for grown-ups. Besides, once Yolanda knew she was safe she might not need him anymore. She might have thought that he could turn his feelings on and off like a switch, but that was the furthest thing from the truth.

"So," Yolanda said. "I make a really mean eggnog. I know you can't drink but I'm not going to deny myself the pleasure of my holiday specialty. Want to join me in the kitchen while I make it?"

"Sure. But don't you think you've had enough to drink for one evening?"

"The night is young and so am I. And you have me trapped on the property, so what else is there to do?"

There were so many things he wanted to do to and for her, but he needed to be vigilant. Madison had sent him a text with some of the headlines that had been surfacing in Richmond about Danny Branch.

What if he was getting desperate and had put the killer back on Yolanda's trail? He wanted this nightmare for her to be over. Even if it meant never having her as a part of his life again.

Chapter 28

It was clear to Charles that Nina's wedding was an event that was just as anticipated as Christmas. So many people came to visit the family and Yolanda was the bartender. She took her eggnog making seriously and it was a hit with the guests who came in and out of the family quarters. Charles was unsettled every time the door opened, not knowing if one of these friendly faces hid sinister intent.

So far, so good. But when this tall dude in a tailored suit and a bright smile walked in and charmed the room, Charles couldn't decipher if he was jealous or if he thought the guy was a threat. For one, he didn't like the way Mr. Slick looked at Yolanda as she served up the eggnog. His eyes lingered on her bottom a little too long. And Yolanda seemed a little too happy to see him. Then again, so did Alex.

You're being ridiculous, he thought as he stayed in the background. Was this guy one of Yolanda's exes looking to make her his Christmas gift? Not while Charles was around. If this clown had a chance with Yolanda back in the day, then he should've taken it then.

Charles felt foolish when he realized that the real reason why Alex and Yolanda had been so happy to see the man was because he was Robin's ex.

He couldn't help but laugh at how the sisters kept pushing Robin and that guy together. For a group of women who complained about each other prying into their personal lives, they were all guilty of it.

"You know," Alex said, breaking into his thoughts, "there's nothing wrong with being a little festive tonight. I'm sure whatever has you here at Yolanda's side can take a break for a couple of hours." She handed him a cup of eggnog.

"Thanks, but I'm not a fan of this stuff."

"Shh," Alex said. "If Yolanda hears that, she is going to lose her mind. This is Christmas in a cup to her."

Charles laughed because it was clear Alex thought the same. "I'll try some later, once everything dies down here."

"How much trouble is my sister in and don't tell me to ask her." She poked him in the chest. "I'm asking you."

"No disrespect, Alex, but I think you're a little tipsy and this might not be the time or place to have this conversation."

She shook her head and pushed a strand of hair behind her ear. "You know why I worry about Yolanda so much?" Alex placed her hand on Charles's shoulder. "Because she is a lot like me. She wants to take over the world and prove she's right all the time. I don't want anything to happen to my sister because I wouldn't survive it."

"I'm not going to let anything happen to Yolanda."

"Because you love her or it's your job?"

"I think you need some coffee, Alex," he said with a nervous laugh. She poked him again and laughed.

"You do. You love my sister. If you hurt her, like Logan did Robin, I'll break your kneecap." She sauntered away and grabbed another cup of eggnog. It didn't take long for Yolanda to approach Charles with questions.

"What was that all about?" she demanded.

"Your sister wants to know what's going on with you. Why haven't you . . ."

"What did you tell her? Chuck, Alex doesn't need to know anything that's going on."

"I kept your confidence, but I think you should have a talk with her."

Yolanda folded her arms across her chest. "You need to stay out of it! What's up with you and your defense of Alexandria Richardson?"

"Darling, you need to calm down. Do you know how much your sister loves you? She . . ."

Alex crossed over to the couple with a tray of eggnog. "What are you two whispering about?"

Yolanda took a cup of eggnog from the tray and watched Charles until he grabbed one as well. Alex gave him an I-told-you-so look. "Is Nina in her room?" Yolanda asked, skirting Alex's question.

"Yes. And since you two keep speaking in circles, I'm going to my room, too," she said, then lifted her cup of eggnog to them. "Charles, whatever you're doing here, just keep doing it."

"No problem," he replied.

"She knows something," Yolanda said once Alex was gone.

"It's kind of hard to miss that something is happening

when your sister has a bodyguard. Yolanda, just relax and think about how this will be over after your sister's wedding."

"Oh," she said. "You're ready to get rid of me?"

"Did I say that?"

"No, but you implied it. I'm going to get a sandwich or something," she said, then turned toward the dining room. Charles started to follow her and explain what he meant, but when he saw Alex sitting at the table, he decided to leave the sisters to their devices.

Yolanda sat across from Alex and gave her a kick underneath the table.

"What in the hell is wrong with you?" Alex snapped.

"Why are you always in Chuck's face asking him about . . ."

Robin walked into the dining room. "What are y'all fighting about now?"

Yolanda shot her a questioning look. "I thought you were flirting with Terell and on the verge of having a rebound affair."

"This is one time I actually agree with your foul-mouthed sister," Alex quipped.

"Clearly hell has frozen over," Robin said as she reached for another eggnog. "Have both of you forgotten that I'm married?"

Yolanda opened her mouth and Alex slapped her hand over it. "I don't know what you were going to say, but don't."

Robin nodded her thanks as she sipped her drink.

"Now," Alex continued. "You have filed for divorce,

so there's nothing wrong with lining up dates for when it's final."

"Please stop," Robin said. "I don't need either of you telling me how to live my life."

"No one is trying to do that," Yolanda said once Alex dropped her hand.

"What if I decide to fight for my marriage?"

Yolanda shook her head. "After what he did to you? What are you fighting for?"

Robin sighed and gave her sisters a thoughtful glance. "Logan said he didn't sleep with her."

"And you believe that?" Alex shook her head. "Robin, what do you expect him to say—to a lawyer?"

She slammed her mug on the table. "I swear, if Nina's wedding wasn't around the corner, I'd leave right now. I love Logan and I don't expect either of you to understand. Just leave me the hell alone."

Alex threw her hands up and walked out of the room. Yolanda started to follow Alex, but she felt a hand on her elbow. Turning around, she glared at Chuck. "What now?" she asked.

"I came for the sandwiches," he said with a smile.

Robin shot them a questioning look then left the dining room to take a phone call.

"Did you? Or were you waiting to talk to Alex?"

"Are we doing this now? You can't possibly think . . ."

"What should I think? Maybe you want to move on to another Richardson once this case is over. Hell, you and Alex have more in common than you and me. Two big old control freaks and . . ."

Chuck captured her mouth and kissed her until she moaned. At that moment, she realized what a fool she had been and that her eggnog may have been stronger than she'd imagined. He broke the kiss and looked at her.

"Here's what we're going to do right now, tonight," he said. "I'm going to stop pretending that you don't mean the world to me."

"What?" she asked as she stared at him. Yolanda's eyes were wider than fifty-cent pieces. She'd been waiting to hear him say something like this and she believed it. He wasn't drunk, he wasn't saying it just because that's what she wanted to hear. Chuck meant what he said.

"You heard me. It took a lot for me to be able to be honest with you. But I can't have you walking around here questioning every move I make."

"I-I don't know what to say," she replied breathlessly. "I mean, can we go talk about this where somebody won't walk in on us?"

"If you mean go back to your room, I'm going to be real with you. When that door closes the last thing I want to do is talk."

"Well damn," she muttered. "I'm not going to argue about that. Let's go." Yolanda wanted to run to her room, but she didn't want anyone to know what was going on. She thought about telling Chuck that she was head over heels for him. That he'd awoken something in her that she had denied existed for years. Part of her felt a little guilty that she was having this awakening when Robin's heart was being torn apart.

As soon as she and Chuck got into her room and he closed the door, thoughts of anyone but the sexy man standing in front of her evaporated.

Yolanda nibbled at the bottom of her lip as he closed the space between them. Chuck stroked her cheek then proceeded to peel her clothes off. First, the black tank top. He cupped her breasts and as he ran his thumbs across her nipples they tightened into diamond-hard buds. Then he ran his right hand down to the waistband of her leggings.

When he slipped his hand inside, Chuck laughed. "I'd been wondering ever since I saw you dancing if you were wearing panties."

She smiled as his fingers found their way inside her wet valley. "And were you right?"

"Trust but verify," he said as he stroked her clitoris. "And I love this kind of hands-on verification."

Yolanda stifled a moan. "So-so do I. But if you do that thing with your finger again, I just might come."

He wiggled his finger inside her, then made circles around her clit with the pad of his index finger. "Which thing?"

She yelped as she came. "That wasn't fair," she said as he slipped his hand out of her leggings. Chuck scooped her up in his arms and laid her on the bed. He pulled her leggings off and spread her legs apart. "Why don't you take your clothes off?" Yolanda asked.

"I will as soon as I do this," he said, then dove between her legs and lapped her sweetness. Yolanda knew the walls in her room were thin and she knew Nina was next door, but when Chuck sucked her clit as if it were a lollipop, she didn't care who heard her scream.

He looked up at her as he licked and sucked her. Yolanda's thighs trembled as she came over and over again. "Now, that was an amazing dessert," Chuck said as he stood up and pulled his clothes off. Yolanda loved looking at him naked. She propped up on her knees in the middle of the bed. "Tell me a story," she said.

"What?"

"The tattoo, what inspired it?"

"That's what you want to hear about right now?" He crossed over to the bed and took her hand in his. Yolanda took her other hand and stroked part of the ink on his shoulder.

"Yes."

"After the war, I wanted to cover up some of the scars that I got in a firefight."

"Oh," she said. "I didn't expect that answer."

Chuck shook his head. "All art doesn't have a romantic story behind it. When I was in Afghanistan, my squad had a battle with a group of insurgents. There were a couple of roadside bombs that went off and I got hit with shrapnel protecting my team. Blew out my knee and lost some vision in my right eye. That's why I occasionally wear glasses."

"But a lot of beauty can come from pain," she said, then leaned in and kissed his shoulder.

He got into the bed and pulled her against his chest. Yolanda wrapped her legs around his waist, and they fell into a slow rhythm, their bodies moving as one. He felt good as he pumped in and out of her. Too good. Flesh to flesh. No protection. She closed her eyes as she felt the heat of his seed inside her.

What had they done? They unfurled their bodies. "That was extremely irresponsible," she said.

"I know and I'm sorry."

"It's not your fault alone," she said with a sigh. "I know I'm healthy and safe."

"As am I."

"But there are other things that could've happened. Like . . ."

He reached out for her and held her against his chest. "We can't see into the future, but know I'm always going to be here no matter what," Chuck said.

"Who said I wanted a kid?"

He tilted his head to the side and smirked. "Why are you assuming that you're pregnant?"

She shrugged. "Because that would just be poetic justice. My sister . . . never mind. Listen, you're a one-of-a-kind man, Charles Morris. I . . . love you."

He kissed her slow and deep. Breaking the kiss, he looked her in the eyes. "I love you too."

Chapter 29

If Yolanda thought she and Chuck were going to spend the days following Nina's wedding basking in the after-glow of being in love, she was wrong. They'd decided to stay in Charleston at the bed-and-breakfast while he waited to hear from his source about the investigations into Danny Branch. Alex continued with her questions until Yolanda blew up at her and told her to mind her fucking business. That went over like a bouquet of lead balloons. Up until the moment that Robin's drama in Richmond with Logan exploded after the woman who had been accusing Logan of being her baby's daddy revealed that she knew about Robin's fertility issues, Alex and Yolanda had gone days without speaking.

When she told Chuck that she was going to Richmond with Alex, he wasn't happy about it. And Yolanda told him where he could put his feelings.

"My sister needs me and I'm going to see her."

"You're walking back into the city where you know Danny wants you dead."

She folded her arms across her chest. "Did I say I was going to throw a parade and announce my location?"

"Yolanda, you're putting yourself in danger, and for what? Whatever your sister and her husband are dealing with, you can't fix it."

"Go to hell. When Alex starts that car in the morning, I'm going to be in it. You can stay here if you want to," she said, then turned to leave the room. Chuck grabbed her arm.

"Why are you so damned stubborn?"

"Are you coming with us tomorrow or no?"

"You know the answer to that. Clearly, you aren't going to be reasonable and stay here."

Yolanda smiled and nodded. "I'm glad you know that. And knowing Alex, we're going to be leaving at the butt crack of dawn."

"I need to make a few phone calls; then I'll join you in bed."

"Maybe you should sleep on the sofa," she said, still low-key pissed off at him.

Chuck rolled his eyes and headed out the door.

Charles didn't want to go to Richmond blind. Maybe Danny had to call off his hit man because of everything that was going on now. But he wasn't sure and he didn't like putting Yolanda at risk. It didn't matter that she was trying to support her sister. She needed to remember that a powerful man wanted her dead. He pulled out his phone and called Madison.

"Hello?" she said in a whisper.

"Madison, is everything all right?"

"Just on a stakeout. I think Branch has finally snapped."

"Can you talk?"

"Not now. Call you later." The call ended and Charles gritted his teeth.

Son of a bitch. What is he up to and how do I keep Yolanda safe? He headed back inside to Yolanda's bedroom and expected to find Yolanda still wrapped up in a funky attitude, but she was sitting on the same sofa she'd ordered him to sleep on holding a cup of cocoa.

"You know what I hate to do more than anything in the world?" she said as she batted her eyelashes at him.

"You're going to have to remind me or do it."

She held up the cup of cocoa to him. "It's an apology in a mug."

Charles shook his head. "Nope, you're going to have to say it." He cupped his hand to his ear.

Yolanda sucked her teeth and rolled her eyes. "I'm sorry, Chuck."

He accepted the cocoa and brushed his lips across her forehead. "I really wish you would reconsider this trip."

"Don't make me take my apology back."

"I should've recorded it. I called Madison and I think she's following Branch," he said.

"Is that a good thing?"

"I don't know and there are too many unknowns for me to feel safe about this trip." He sat down beside her and set the cocoa on the table.

"How about I make a promise to you: I won't make a move without you knowing about it. You can even follow me to the bathroom."

"That's a given."

"And I won't complain about it," she said with a smile.

Then she leaned in and kissed him on the cheek. "Please don't sleep on this sofa. I want to fall asleep in your arms."

"If I was as petty as you are, I'd say something smart and sleep on the sofa. But I like having you sleeping in my arms too much to suffer needlessly." He kissed her softly and then scooped her into his arms. When they got into bed, Yolanda fell asleep effortlessly, but Charles kept waiting for the phone to vibrate. What had Madison found out? Was she still safe?

Richmond, Virginia

Chase realized that Danny had become unhinged and sloppy when he read the story about his ex-wife's case in the paper. It was confirmed when Danny drove into the woods without noticing two cars following him. At least Chase's was one of the cars, but that Chevrolet Cruze belonged to a stranger. And possibly a cop. The Feds would never drive something that practical. He pulled the little Kia he was driving into the woods far enough away from the other vehicle that he would look lost, drunk, or like a hunter. He had a view of the figure in the car, but he had no idea if it was a man or a woman. Maybe he had the wrong idea about the driver. Still, he wasn't trying to let Danny's latest dumb-ass action put him at risk. Grabbing a flashlight from the backseat, he exited the car and headed over to where Danny was . . . digging a hole?

Chase shone the light on him. "Danny, what in the hell are you doing?"

Turning around, Danny held the shovel up as if it were a bat. "What the . . . Chase, what are you doing here?"

"Stopping you from making another stupid-ass mistake! What's out here?"

"Her."

"Her?"

"That bitch."

"You need to stop what you're doing. You're being watched. Danny, you're slipping, you didn't even know I was behind you."

"Who else is here?"

Chase shrugged. "Not sure, but you need to put the shovel down and get the fuck out of here."

"You think I'm going to listen to your dumb ass when you couldn't get one job done?" Danny snarled, then went back to digging. "The police are looking for Simone and I have to find her first."

"You stupid son of a bitch, you brought this on yourself. All you had to do was get rid of your ex in another town."

"Think about this: If they catch me, I'm not going down alone. I'll take you and everyone who has ever taken bread from my plate with me. Jail ain't for me."

"I should've known you'd crack once people caught on to what you really are. But I'll be damned if I'm going down because you got fucking sloppy."

Danny dropped the shovel and rushed toward Chase. His unexpected move allowed him to bowl Chase over. But the skilled killer shook it off and kicked Danny in his midsection, making him roll off him.

Chase pounced on his boss like a cat capturing a mouse. He grabbed his flashlight and bashed Danny across the face. Blood stained Chase's face and his shirt. Danny's body stopped moving and Chase rolled him into the hole Danny had been digging. Why would he be digging up his ex-wife when he still had that Richardson broad to worry about? And now she was all Chase's problem. And he didn't like problems.

Before he could get to Yolanda, he had to find out who was in that car. Chase started walking up the hill toward where the car had been parked, just in time to see the driver speed away.

Charleston, South Carolina

Charles was used to early mornings. But since his nights these days involved holding on to Yolanda, he'd become a five-forty a.m. guy. Alex Richardson wasn't about that life, though. At four-fifteen she was knocking on Yolanda's door.

"Go away," Yolanda moaned as she snuggled closer to Charles.

"Come on, we need to get on the road," Alex said. "I'm not trying to get caught in rush-hour traffic."

"Didn't I tell you," Yolanda said through her yawn. "She's nuts."

"I'm leaving in twenty minutes, with or without y'all," Alex said.

Yolanda yawned again. "Sometimes I just want to give her a high-five to the face."

"Stop it," he said as he brushed his lips across her cheek. "Let's get ready before she leaves us." Charles sat up in the bed and Yolanda buried her face in a pillow.

Charles stroked her back. “How are you going to explain being naked when she comes back, because no one is supposed to know how we spend our nights, right?”

Yolanda sat up. “She has been known to use that master key that she has for the family rooms. Let’s shower and be ready when she comes back on that broom.”

“Broom?” he asked.

“You didn’t know Alex was part witch?” Yolanda quipped.

“That’s mean.”

“But true. You know we could save time if we showered together,” she said with a wink.

Charles started to tell her that the two of them in the shower wouldn’t speed up the getting ready process at all. Then his phone rang, and he saw it was Madison. He held up his finger and answered the phone.

“What’s up, Madison?”

“Danny Branch is dead, and I don’t think that’s the end of your girl’s troubles.”

“How do you know he’s dead?”

“Because I was there, and I saw it happen. And the person who did it is a fucking monster.”

Charles took a deep breath. “All right, Madison, start at the beginning. What do you mean you were there?”

Madison expelled a sigh. “Last night, I followed Branch to a wooded area where I thought he had buried his ex-wife. And clearly, I was right, because he started digging. Then his alleged hit man showed up, and the next thing I know that man was climbing up the hill covered in blood. So, I drove off. Took my rental car back and now I’m trying to figure out what my next move needs to be. But if Chase is tied to Danny’s crimes, he’s going to eliminate anyone that could implicate him. Or anyone he considers a threat. This guy is dangerous and insane."

"What does this Chase person look like?"

"A nondescript white man."

Charles thought about what he had seen in Charlotte. Had that man actually been that close to his woman?

"What's your next move?" he asked.

"I don't know yet. But you need to watch your back and hers."

"Got it. So, I'm guessing that right now wouldn't be the best time to go to the Richmond police about what she knows, huh?"

"Not if you want her to keep breathing. When are you guys coming back to Richmond?"

"Actually, we should be there in a few hours. One of her older sisters lives in Richmond and is going through a really nasty divorce. Something happened earlier and now Yolanda and Alex are heading that way."

"I guess you can't talk her into staying put?" Madison asked.

"You've never met the Richardson sisters. When one is in trouble, the others mount up like a Wild West posse."

"Then why did they need you?"

"Because they aren't about that life," he said. "Look, I'm going to call you when I get in town and we can talk about it."

"How about I give you a call around two. I have to make sure that man doesn't know who I am," she said.

"If you need me, I've got you."

"Your plate is full enough. I can take care of myself."

"I never said you couldn't, but you've been taking care of me for a long time. I'm just trying to return the favor."

"Holding you to that when the need arises."

"You know I'm always here for you," he said as he heard the water start running in the bathroom. "I'll be waiting for your phone call."

"If you don't hear from me in a couple of days, then there is a serious problem." Madison ended the call and Charles wondered if things were going to get a lot worse before they got better.

When he walked into the bathroom, Yolanda was stepping out of the shower and the last thing he wanted to do was go anywhere that required clothes. She caught his glance and shook her head. "You'd better get in the shower and get dressed. Alex is going to be knocking on the door or walking in shortly." She grabbed a towel and wrapped it around her body. "Chop-chop, sir."

"But Alex is the control freak," he quipped. "I think y'all are the same."

Yolanda frowned at him. "Take that back!"

"Nope, I have to shower."

She shook her head as she walked out of the bathroom. Charles hopped in the shower and less than a minute later, he heard Alex and Yolanda arguing. *Well,* he thought, *she knows her sister.*

"Alex, you could've knocked," Yolanda snapped.

"And you could've been ready! Come on. It's not as if you're going to be driving." Alex glanced at an open sketchbook. "Exhibit A, you're going to sit in the backseat and draw."

"With my headphones on because I don't want to

listen to your driving play list or NPR. How long are we staying?" Yolanda took a deep breath. "There are a few things I need to handle in town, and I know how you are."

Alex shrugged. "I have about two days I can spare before I have to come back here and get prepared for the New Year's Day promotions. Yolanda, this is the last time I'm asking. But what kind of trouble are you in? I'm worried."

"Can I get dressed before *he* gets out of the shower?"

Alex scoffed. "I'm supposed to believe he hasn't seen you naked?"

Yolanda stroked her throat. "Bye, Alex."

"Five minutes and I'm leaving," she said as she walked out the door. Yolanda looked down at the towel covering her body. *Really?*

Chuck walked out of the bathroom and Yolanda tried to figure out when he'd taken his clothes inside. He had on black joggers and a white tank top and there she was still in a towel.

"You're going to get left," he said as he crossed over to her.

"Whatever. Maybe you and Alex should stop distracting me." Yolanda dashed over to the closet and grabbed a pair of leggings and an oversized sweatshirt. She dressed quickly, then threw some clothes and toiletries in a tote bag. "There, I'm ready."

Chuck, now wearing a gray and black sweatshirt, matching Nikes and carrying a small bag, looked as if he had been ready for hours. How did people do that?

"Don't forget that," he said as he nodded toward her sketch pad.

Yolanda grabbed it and a couple of charcoal pencils. "Thanks. Now, let's go before she says I'm in here showing my naked body."

"Why do you say that as if it is a bad thing?"

She rolled her eyes and headed for the door. Of course, Alex was out in the parking lot, her precious Mercedes running. "You really think she was going to leave us?" Chuck whispered.

"Is today a day that ends in a *y*?"

Alex popped the trunk. "It's about time."

"Alex, why don't you allow me to drive?" Chuck asked.

She raised her right eyebrow at him and Yolanda expected to hear an explosion. Alex didn't let anyone drive her car. She didn't allow valets to park it. She drove it to the detail shop and pulled the car into an empty bay. She had cars towed when some unfortunate person parked in her assigned and marked parking spot at the bed-and-breakfast.

Granted, it was a nice car, but it was just a car.

"Thank you, Charles. The keys are already in it. So, you can drive and deal with the frustration of the rush-hour traffic that we're going to hit since we're leaving so late."

Yolanda glanced down at her watch. *Late? My sister is insane.* Yolanda fully expected Alex to sit up front and co-pilot Chuck while he drove. But she was surprised to see that her sister had gotten into the backseat. "You know Richmond better than I do," Alex said with a yawn. "I'm going to take a nap."

"You set us up!"

Alex shrugged as she grabbed her sorority throw and

covered her legs with it. "Wow," Yolanda said. "I didn't know you had it in you. Well played."

The trip to Virginia was uneventful. Chuck and Yolanda fought over the music; Alex slept. Yolanda stroked Chuck's thigh and he kept his hand in her lap; Alex pretended to be sleeping.

They arrived at Robin's town house in Petersburg, Virginia, shortly before nine a.m., because Chuck didn't believe in stopping. Alex was pleased, but Yolanda had to use the bathroom. When they pulled into the driveway of the town house, Yolanda hopped out of the car and Chuck followed. "What's wrong with you?" he asked.

"Bathroom."

"You know we need to be careful, especially since we're here."

"We're in Petersburg," she snapped before ringing the doorbell. Alex walked up to them.

"Are you two fighting after all of that hand holding on the way here?"

Yolanda started to tell Alex to shut up but Robin opened the door.

"Well, good morning," Robin said.

"Please tell me you have coffee," Yolanda groaned.

"Wait," Robin said. "Aren't you going to officially introduce me to your friend?"

Yolanda rolled her eyes and Alex stifled a laugh. The man extended his huge hand. "Charles, ma'am," he said.

Yolanda sucked her teeth. "She knows who you are. Are you going to invite us in or not?"

"I have company and I don't want to hear y'alls mouth. But I do have breakfast waiting."

"Who's here?" Alex asked as she brushed past her

sister and started toward the kitchen. Robin grabbed her arm.

"Again, Alex, I don't want to hear a word!"

Yolanda was confused when she saw Logan standing in her sister's kitchen. "Oh my fucking goodness," Yolanda exclaimed. "What are you doing here? And where is your shirt? Robin, are you sleeping with this guy?"

"You mean, my husband?" Robin said. "What kind of question is that?"

"One that needs answering, because I swear you were just crying about this asshole less than twenty-four hours ago," Alex said, then turned to Logan. "Can you put on a damned shirt?"

Yolanda ran to the bathroom because she just couldn't understand what was going on. Just a day ago, Robin was acting as if she was done with this cheating bastard and now here he was shirtless in the kitchen.

After using the bathroom and washing her hands, Yolanda dashed back into the kitchen and asked Robin what was going on. And for once, Alex didn't argue with her. They went back and forth about Robin taking Logan back until he came downstairs and jumped in the argument.

"I never did what I was accused of," Logan said as he returned to the kitchen with a shirt on.

Yolanda lunged toward him but held back. "I swear, if I wouldn't get put out of my sister's house, I'd punch you in your face."

"Yolanda," Alex said with a sigh. "Stop acting like . . . yourself."

Logan crossed over to Robin. "I've got to go. Sorry to leave you alone with all of this."

"I've been handling these two all my life. I've got this." Robin leaned in and gave Logan a quick peck on the lips. Yolanda groaned.

"What in the Twilight Zone have we stepped into?" she asked. "Where the hell is the coffee?"

Robin poured her sister a cup of coffee and Yolanda headed into the living room, where Chuck was sitting on the sofa. She watched him as he seemed to be firing off text messages on his phone.

"Chuck? You want . . . Is everything all right?"

"I don't know," he said when he turned to face her. "Why don't you go and check on your sisters?"

"Are you dismissing me?"

Chuck sighed. "Yolanda, this may be a family reunion trip for you, but keep in mind, I have to find out who's trying to kill you."

She sucked her teeth as she headed back into the kitchen. She hated it when he did that.

Chapter 30

Charles hadn't heard from Madison and he was getting worried. She hadn't answered the ten text messages that he had sent her. He called her three times and still nothing. What if she'd been found out and was in trouble now? Despite knowing there weren't many people whom Madison couldn't beat with her bare hands, he knew she couldn't stop a bullet.

He crossed over to the window in Robin's living room and looked at his phone again.

"Charles?" Robin said from behind him. "I know my rude sister probably didn't offer you anything to eat."

"Thanks, but I'm good." He smiled at her just as his phone vibrated.

"There's coffee too. I know Alex woke y'all up way too early this morning," she said with a laugh.

"That's true." Charles looked down at the phone and saw two words: *Madison Slim.* He knew his friend was all right—at least for now. Following Robin into the kitchen, he saw that Yolanda wasn't too happy to see him right now.

"Excuse me," she said as she walked out of the kitchen.

Robin handed Charles a cup of coffee. "I'm assuming you have to follow her."

He nodded as he accepted the mug and followed Yolanda. Charles found her sitting near Robin's bookshelf. That woman had a lot of books. "Yolanda," he said, "what's wrong?"

"I don't know, you tell me why you're being a complete asshole all of a sudden."

"That's what you think?"

"That's precisely what I think."

"I found out some news that may have you in serious trouble, so I'm sorry if I can't sneak kisses with you and pretend that your life isn't in danger."

Her mouth dropped open, but no words came out. Charles crossed over to her and placed his hand on her shoulder. "I didn't want you to be alarmed and . . . Yolanda, do you realize how much I love you and need you? There is no way in hell that I'm going to sit around here and forget why we were brought together in the first place."

"Is this still just a job to you?"

"You know it isn't."

She rubbed her hand across her face. "Can you tell me what's going on then?"

"I don't really know. We're going to have to wait to get an all clear from Madison, then go to the police. Do you think Alex will let us borrow her car?"

Yolanda laughed as if he'd hit the perfect joke in a stand-up comedy routine. "No."

"You know, it might be a better idea to get a rental. We still don't know for sure who's watching us."

He noticed Yolanda shiver. She was scared again and that was the last thing he wanted to happen.

Over the next couple of hours, the Richardson sisters prepared to head to Robin's old house in Richmond.

To say that Charles was on edge would be an understatement. He had hoped that they'd stay in Petersburg, where no one had any idea Yolanda would be. But whatever was happening with Robin and her husband was a big deal for her sisters to be involved with, and he already knew that asking either of them to mind their business was a mistake.

Alex decided she was going to be the one driving her car, so when they went to the Whole Foods Market he and Yolanda sat in the backseat while Alex and Robin went inside. He held her hand and leaned against her ear. "I know this is scary, but are you okay?"

"As much as I can be," she replied. "Will this ever end? What happens if they figure out that Robin is my sister and they come after her? Now, if somebody got Logan, that would be fine."

"Remind me to stay on your good side," he said with a grin. "And you really can't wish that on your brother-in-law when your sister seems to be ready to forgive him."

Yolanda opened her mouth to respond when Alex and Robin returned to the car. "This cake had better be everything you say it is," Alex said once they got in the car.

"As much as you love chocolate, you're going to enjoy this," Robin said as she shot Charles and Yolanda a questioning look. "What are you two doing back there?"

"Plotting Logan's beatdown," Yolanda quipped.

"Give it a rest, Yolanda," Robin said with an exasperated sigh.

Charles stroked Yolanda's knee. "No one is going to do that," he said.

"Speak for yourself," Alex said, shocking everyone in the car.

"I need your support right now," Robin said. "Or you can take me to get my car and I'll have dinner with my husband without y'all."

"I want to support you, but I don't understand how you can just forgive him so quickly," Alex said. "Until that woman started spouting your health issues I was in Logan's corner."

"Can we not do this now?" Robin snapped.

Alex started the car and kept quiet. Charles was equally shocked that Yolanda hadn't said much either. While everything that was going on with Robin seemed very emotional, he couldn't get caught up in the Richardson family drama. He needed to make sure Yolanda was going to be all right. Everything else they would have to handle among themselves.

When they arrived at Robin's home in Richmond, Charles's neck was aching from all the turning he'd done in the car. Every time a vehicle seemed as if it was too close to them, he'd stared at it, trying to figure out if the driver was following them or not. Luckily, no one had followed them.

When they arrived at Robin's other place, Charles's phone rang as they walked inside, and it was Madison.

"Hello?" he said when he answered the call.

"Hey. Got news. Well, I made news. I sent an anonymous tip to the Richmond police and they have recovered Danny's body and his ex-wife's."

"So, what does this mean going forward?"

Madison cleared her throat. "Danny's killer is still out there, and the police need to be put on notice. I'm going to text you a picture. This guy is lethal and I'm not sure if he has decided to disappear or continue to come after your girl."

"Thanks for the update, but are you safe?"

"For now. I'm out in Danville right now. Just to do some research and see what we're up against."

"Sounds like a good plan. Thanks for all of your help on this."

"You know I always have your back. Just wait a few days and see how things shake out before heading to the police. I think you should go check out her old shop and see if it's being watched."

He was about to reply when Yolanda walked into the living room, where he was stationed. "I'll call you back."

"Everything all right?" she asked.

Charles nodded. "Are you good being here?"

Yolanda shrugged. "Not my decision. I'm just here for the food. Speaking of, are you hungry?"

He was, but not for whatever was in a pot in the kitchen. "Yeah, I could eat."

"Really?"

"Come here," he commanded softly. "When we go to the police, we're going to put this behind us and we're going to have some decisions to make."

"Yeah. But let's not do that now while all of these people are in here doing whatever they're doing."

"What's going on with your sister and her husband?"

"Insanity. I really don't know. It's like he cheated, but he didn't. My sister had cancer, but didn't tell us. It's too much."

"So, y'all keep secrets from each other all the time?"

"Whatever," she replied.

"Have you actually come clean about what happened to you?"

"Something like that," Yolanda said.

"Um, okay."

She pinched him on his arm. "You play too much."

He was about to say something when his phone vibrated in his pocket. "Hold on," he said as he pulled the phone out of his pocket. It was Madison again. "Hello?"

"We have a problem. Can you meet me tomorrow morning?"

"Yes," he said. "But what's going on?"

"Listen, that hired killer Chase Franklin is lethal. He has never been arrested and he's filled more graveyards than a little bit. He's relentless and he's not going to stop until he thinks all of his loose ends are tied up."

"I thought you were in Danville."

"I'm on my way back. The car I was in last night had a camera and I got an image of him. Chuck, I don't think you understand how dangerous this man is."

"Where do you want to meet?" He looked at Yolanda, who was staring at him with questions dancing in her eyes.

"I'll call you at six and we'll figure it out."

When he ended the call, Yolanda started with her questions. "What's going on?" she asked.

"Let's get some food and then we can talk about it," he said.

They walked into the kitchen and grabbed two plates of food, then headed to the living room. As they took a seat on the sofa, Yolanda heard Alex yelling about the woman whom said Logan fathered her child.

"There is so much going on right now," Yolanda said. "And you wonder why I don't want to be totally honest with them."

"I get that you want to keep them safe, but maybe they should know what's going on, in detail."

"That's not what you said in the beginning. Stop flip-flopping," she said as she picked at her chicken.

"Your family is a lot closer than I realized. Seeing you all in action is something else."

"What did your source say?"

"The guy looking for you is trying to tie up all the loose ends since . . ."

She nearly dropped her plate. "And I'm a loose end?"

"I'm not going to allow him to hurt you. Madison and I are going to figure this out."

"And what am I supposed to do? I can't stay here and risk being found. What if he figures out that Robin and I are related and he comes after her? Who is this man?"

"That's not important, babe," he said.

"What the hell do you mean it's not important? He's trying to kill me, not you."

Charles set his plate on the table and took Yolanda's plate from her hand and placed it beside his. Then he took her hands in his. "When I tell you that it isn't important, trust me on that. I'm going to stop him from hurting you, no matter what."

"Even if that means you get hurt?"

"Yolanda, that's my job."

"You told me you weren't Secret Service, so that means you don't have to take a bullet for me, right?"

"I may not have to, but if it comes to that, I will."

She gasped. "No."

"Yolanda, it may not even get there. This is why I didn't want to tell you."

"Well, now that I know, what happens next?"

Alex stuck her head in the living room. "Why are you two being so antisocial?" she asked. "Robin is about to cut this cake and I'm not eating it alone."

"Give us a second," Yolanda said.

Alex shrugged and returned to the kitchen. Charles stroked her cheek. "Yolanda, this ends tomorrow, one way or another. Maybe with him going to jail or being eliminated. But Yolanda Richardson is going to be fine."

"Promise?"

"Yes. Now, let's go in the kitchen before they come back and ask why I made you cry."

Yolanda and Charles joined the rest of the crew at the table as Robin doled out slices of chocolate cake and poured glasses of wine. Charles opted for water. He watched Yolanda sip her wine and wanted to be the rim of that glass. He meant what he'd told her: He'd take a bullet for her if he had to.

Alex walked over to Yolanda and touched her elbow. "Can we talk for a second?"

Yolanda drained her wineglass and nodded. Alex pointed at Charles. "Can you come too?"

Charles knew this was about to be a moment. He just hoped it wouldn't turn into a screaming match. They crossed into the foyer and Yolanda tilted her head to the side at her sister. "What's up, Alex?"

"That's what I want to know, finally. We've had a lot of honest moments and it's time for us to have one," she said calmly.

"Fine," Yolanda replied. "But keep in mind, everything I did was because I didn't want any harm to come to you and the rest of the family."

"Why would . . ."

Charles and Yolanda exchanged a look. "Alex, someone wants to kill me. And that's why Chuck and I have been . . . It happened here in Richmond and I didn't want anyone to know. Silly me, I told Nina and she went to Dad."

"What the hell? Does Robin know?"

Yolanda shook her head and Charles ran his hand across her back. "Nina was the only one who knew a little about what was going on."

"Of course you told Nina," Alex said with a scoff.

"Well, I'm trying to tell you now," Yolanda snapped.

She threw her hands up. "Go on."

"There was a murder outside of my shop and I saw what happened," she said. "The killers, they knew who I was and I didn't want them to trace me back to Charleston and the bed-and-breakfast. Do you know how devastated I would've been if something . . ." Yolanda started crying and Alex pulled her into her arms.

"I wish you'd been honest with me before now," she said as they hugged.

"And what would you have done?"

"We could've stayed in contact with the investigators and . . ."

"No, Alex, we couldn't have," Yolanda said.

"The man Yolanda saw commit the murder is Danny

Branch, who's very connected in Richmond and it was important to make sure that whomever we talked to about what Yolanda knew wouldn't put her in more danger. Now, there is another layer," Charles said. "There is still a threat and I'm trying to make sure we neutralize it."

"I-I had no idea how much danger . . . Yolanda, I'm so sorry that . . ."

"Let's tell Robin good night before she comes over here and—" Yolanda stopped short and wiped a tear from Alex's cheek. "Please, I can't take you crying."

Alex shook her head then wiped her eyes. "Come on, let's go."

Chapter 31

After finishing dinner at Robin and Logan's place, Yolanda, Chuck, and Alex headed back to Petersburg. Alex shocked her sister again when she allowed Chuck to drive. They were halfway to Robin's other place when Alex spoke up.

"My sister is running from a killer and it's taken this long for us to find out? Charles, how are you going to fix this? How does any of this work?"

"Alex," Yolanda said quietly, "can we not do this?"

"Oh, we're going to do this. I know you're scared and you wanted to keep us out of this, but I'm scared, too. If something happens to you . . ."

"Alex, nothing is going to happen to your sister. My contact and I have a plan. That's why I'm not going back to Charleston with you two tomorrow."

"What?" Alex and Yolanda exclaimed in unison.

"Chuck, I'm not leaving you here to . . ."

"Yolanda, how much sense does it make to have you right in this killer's crosshairs? I know exactly what I'm doing," he said.

"Which is what?" Alex asked.

"Saving Yolanda's life."

A tense silence enveloped the car. Yolanda didn't want to go to Charleston and leave Chuck alone to face this killer. But what could she do? She'd shot that gun one time at the range. And she didn't even bring it with her. She just needed to be around in case something happened. What if he got hurt? What if she never saw him again?

Chuck pulled into the driveway of the town house and hopped out of the car and looked around.

"You haven't been to Milan, have you?" Alex asked as she and Yolanda exited the car.

"No."

"So, you would rather fight with me about a lie than tell me the truth?"

"You just like fighting with me because that's what you do," Yolanda quipped.

"I don't say it enough, Yo-Yo, but I'm proud of you."

Yolanda stopped walking and faced her sister. "Technically, you never say it."

"And this is why. Give me my moment, here."

Yolanda threw her hands up. "Okay, carry on."

"You had a dream, you followed it and made a success of it. Then this happened and now you're starting over. But I know your next act is going to be amazing."

Yolanda almost started crying. Alexandria Richardson had never said anything like that to her. "Maybe I should get death threats more often," Yolanda quipped.

"Don't do that! You realize that I've almost lost every one of my sisters in the last year? Robin's cancer, Nina's accident, and now this. I may never come back from my vacation," Alex said as they walked into the house. Chuck stood at the door and smiled at them.

"I thought I was going to have to come out there and get y'all." He handed Alex the spare key Robin had hidden underneath the welcome mat. "Tell your sister she shouldn't leave her keys out like this."

"I'll pass it along, but I don't think she's going to be living here much longer," Alex said as she glanced down at her watch. "I'm going to bed. Since we're leaving tomorrow, I'd better get some sleep. And you should too." She pointed at Yolanda and Chuck. "Don't keep her up too long."

Yolanda shook her head. "Classy, Alex."

Once they were alone, Yolanda flung herself into Chuck's arms. "Is this the only way?"

"Yes. Trust me, darling, this nightmare is coming to an end, all right."

"Or another one is about to start."

"I've been in war zones, I can handle this."

"You'd better, because I kind of like having you in my life."

"Good, because I enjoy being in your life." Chuck brushed his lips across her forehead. "Now, you probably should go to bed because your sister is serious about leaving early."

Yolanda groaned. "Yes, she is. But do you have to be up all night or can you join me in bed?"

"To sleep, I sure can."

She rolled her eyes at him. "You're no fun."

* * *

The bed in the guest room was small. Well, small for Charles. Yolanda went to sleep as soon as she got out of the shower, but he couldn't sleep thinking about going after Chase. Madison had sent the guy's picture over and he was certain that he was the man he'd seen outside of Yolanda's shop in Charlotte. Knowing she'd been that close to death made his blood run cold. He held her a little tighter as she snored lightly. He loved this woman more than he'd ever expected. She held his entire heart and anybody trying to hurt her would have to get through him first. She pressed her hand against his chest and a smile spread across her lips. Charles wondered what was going on in that pretty little head of hers. When he actually drifted off to sleep, Alex was knocking on the door.

"Let's go, Yolanda!"

"Alex, come on. Let's wait another hour!" Yolanda called out.

"No. I'm going to be ready in twenty minutes and I know you want to stay, but Charles said you have to go back to Charleston."

"I did say that," he whispered.

"Didn't I tell you that I don't like following orders?"

"This is one time that you don't have a choice. Get up," he said softly. Yolanda inched closer to him.

"I'll get up and get ready to leave as soon as you kiss me."

She didn't need to ask him twice as he captured her mouth in a slow and delicate kiss. Her body vibrated against his and Charles knew if he didn't let her go, she wouldn't be going anywhere—and neither would he. He pulled back from her. "Now, you have to get up," he said.

"Fine," she replied with a pout. Yolanda got out of bed and headed for the shower. Charles picked up his phone and made a reservation for a rental car to be delivered to him. Alex was true to her word: Twenty minutes after her wake-up knock, she was back at the door.

"Yolanda!"

Charles pulled his T-shirt on, then opened the door. "She's in the bathroom, Alex," he said.

She looked down at her watch and shook her head. "We really need to get going. And you need this." Alex handed him the house key. "Just bring it back when you're done. And you will be back in Charleston soon, right?"

He nodded. "I have a lot to come back for."

"And that means my sister, doesn't it?"

Charles smiled. "Yes, I mean Yolanda."

"When did you fall in love with her?"

"It's hard to pinpoint the exact moment, but I do love her. That's why I have to make sure this man is no longer around to try to hurt her."

Alex smiled and gave Charles a slow once-over. "Let's be clear about a couple of things. Yolanda and I clash a lot, but I love her fiercely. You're a big guy, but if you hurt my sister, I will be your worst nightmare."

"And I believe that, but you have to know this: I would never do anything to hurt Yolanda. Never met anyone like her before in my life and I don't even know what life would be like without her in it anymore."

"Thank you for everything you've done to keep her safe. I wish I'd known what was going on, but you're the first person, outside of Dad, who's ever kept Yolanda in check. You've already won half the battle. But if your little girlfriend doesn't hurry up, she's going to have to take an Uber back to Charleston."

"Ugh!" Yolanda said from behind them. "Why are you like this?"

Charles smiled at his woman, who was dressed in a pair of black leggings and a Spelman College sweatshirt. No matter what she wore, she was always beautiful.

"Because I hate traffic, and if you had it your way, we'd never leave," Alex said. "I'm going to put my bag in the car so y'all can talk. But I'm leaving in fifteen minutes."

Yolanda shook her head as her sister walked away. "How much of that did you hear?" Charles asked as they walked into the bedroom so that Yolanda could retrieve her bag.

"I heard nothing, other than you saying you're coming back to me." She smiled and threw herself into his arms. Charles held her tightly and buried his nose in her hair. She smelled so good and felt even better. As much as he didn't want to let her go, he knew he had to so that she could get to safety.

"Do me a favor," he said when he let her go. "Pay attention to any cars that might be following you guys when you leave."

"And if someone is following us, what am I supposed to do?"

"Tell Alex to turn off whatever road you're on and call me."

She nodded. "This is some real Jason Bourne shit here."

He stroked her cheek. "It isn't, it's some keeping-my-baby-safe shit." Charles leaned down and kissed her slow and deep. His hand rested on the small of her back as their tongues danced against each other's. Though he didn't want to let her go, he knew Alex was going to leave her.

"You'd better get going," he said.

"Wish you were coming with me."

"I'm going to see you real soon." They started down the stairs and Yolanda tugged at his hand.

"Chuck, I love you too, and I don't care what you have to do, but come back to me."

"That's the plan, Yolanda." He opened the front door and saw Alex was ready to go. "She's going to leave you."

Yolanda stood on her tiptoes and gave Charles a quick peck on the lips. "See you soon," she said, then rushed to the car.

It was five forty-five and Charles had to get ready for this showdown with Chase. He pulled out his phone and called Madison.

"What's up, Chuck?"

"You tell me. Where are you?"

"I'm in the East End. Right outside of downtown. I found out who this man really is."

"What do you mean and text me your address. I have a rental coming in an hour."

"Maybe I should come to you," Madison said. "This man is an ex-cop. I think that's how he's gotten away with all of the murders. He knows how police investigations work. How to make evidence disappear and how to be a killer in plain sight."

"I'm in Petersburg and I'm not sure you should come here because I'm at Yolanda's sister's place."

Madison sighed. "You're right, because I think he knows

who I am. Chuck, how are we going to bring him down? Even the good cops I know are scared of this guy."

"So, we're going in blind?"

"Kind of. But we can possibly surprise him," Madison said.

"Surprise him and do what?" Charles asked. "Because I know you don't think we're going to bust in on him and kill him."

"No, not unless it's necessary."

"Is there more to this story that I need to know?" he asked.

"Ugh, I hate that you know me so well. I think this motherfucker killed my sister. Chase was fired because he ran a child porn ring. He started his career in Danville. He got caught in Richmond and disappeared before an arrest."

"Wow. But what makes you think he . . . How long have you been researching this?"

Madison snorted. "I fell down a rabbit hole when I started looking for Simone Branch and things clicked."

"Is this about revenge for you?" Charles snapped.

"Like this isn't about you trying to make up for . . ."

"Don't go there."

"Chuck, we all have things that haunt our past and if I can finally get justice for Kira, then let me do it."

"You mean let you kill this man?"

"If it comes to that, don't try to stop me," she said. "I just sent you my address. Let me know when your car comes." She ended the call and Charles wondered if Madison could handle this.

Chapter 32

Charles drove to the East End in Richmond and met Madison at an apartment complex. Seeing his friend, he could tell she was mad. Dressed in a pair of jeans, a long-sleeve T-shirt, and a knife clipped to her hip, Charles knew Madison was ready for war. He didn't know where her gun was, but she had one or two on her.

"Glad to see you found your way here with no problem," she said as she ran her hand through her cropped curly hair.

"Can we talk about the plan first?"

Madison sighed. "The plan is . . . You know, I have been waiting for this for years. But I'm not a criminal," she said. He nodded and pulled her into his arms.

"I know this is tough," he said.

She pushed back from him and wiped her eyes. "Very. But justice is sweeter than revenge. I called the FBI agent who had been working my sister's case and she's getting a warrant for Chase."

"I'm guessing we're going to observe this takedown?"

"Yes, we are! Agent Greene said we just need to stay out

of sight." Madison nodded toward Charles's nondescript rental car. "And you got the perfect car for it."

"When is all of this going down?" he asked.

"Waiting for her to text me."

"And you think she will?"

Madison nodded. "Sarah wouldn't leave me hanging like this."

There was something about the way she said *Sarah* that made Charles think there was more to their relationship than just an FBI agent staying in touch with a family member on a cold case.

"Let's go get some coffee and head toward Chase's house so we can be there when this shit goes down," he said.

Yolanda hated riding in the front seat while Alex drove. She had road rage, yet she wasn't a speed demon like Nina. She drove like an auntie hauling her sister's kids. The speed limit and no faster.

Even though she'd normally talk junk about how Alex was the cause of rush-hour traffic because she did the speed limit in the fast lane, today she was following Chuck's instructions.

"Why are you staring at every car that passes us?" Alex asked.

"Just trying to make sure . . . um . . . Chuck told me to."

"My God," she muttered. And to Yolanda's surprise, Alex actually sped up.

"I had no idea you knew how to do this," Yolanda quipped.

"Do what?"

"Drive above the speed limit."

"Oh, shut up. And I was going to actually stop and buy us breakfast," Alex said. "How have you been dealing with this over all these months?"

"Not very well," Yolanda said honestly. "You know, I will probably never watch another movie where someone is murdered. Seeing that up close and personal is not healthy. It was horrifying."

"Don't take this as a judgment, but what were you doing out so late?"

Yolanda reached for her phone. "Being an artist." She pulled up the picture of the window. It seemed like a lifetime ago when she'd set up that display. Alex gave it a quick glance.

"Oh, that is cute. I hate that I never got to see your shop. I'm sure you're going to make the Charlotte store pop whenever you officially open it."

"That's the plan. And, I hope that you will stop by and let me style you for your vacation."

Alex snorted. "I don't know about that, your taste is a little too outlandish for me."

Yolanda rolled her eyes. "That's where you're wrong. I have some nice Golden Girls–like items for you. Though, I hope when you go on vacation you get you some to take the edge off."

"There you go. Don't ever change, Yo-Yo. And I am not going on vacation to have a tawdry fling."

"Why not?"

"Have you ever?" Alex asked.

"I'm going to go ahead and plead the fifth on that."

Alex shook her head. "I don't have the words to say."

"I mean this in the nicest way possible, but, sis, you need to live a lot. You spend all of your time about business. Or trying to fix whatever you think is wrong with me and Nina. When is the last time you did something for Alexandria the Great?"

Alex sucked her teeth. "I hate that little nickname of yours."

"This time I mean it, you're great. Beautiful, smart, and a boss. But if you don't start having some fun and living life as more than Dad's clone, you're going to wake up wallowing in regret one day."

"You worry about me too much. I mean, I'm satisfied with my life. I get to help Daddy build on our family legacy, I get to watch you guys do amazing things. What's wrong with that?"

"You didn't mention anything about what you do for you. It's not selfish, but you could stand to be a little selfish. And please, let somebody in that doesn't have the last name Richardson."

"All right, I'm done with this. Thanks for the advice. I might not ignore all of it."

"That's my Alex," Yolanda quipped.

By the time they made it back to Charleston, Yolanda had hoped to see a text from Chuck, but there was no news. She hoped that was a good thing.

Charles and Madison had been sitting in the car across from the address that was supposed to be Chase's house for about three hours. They hadn't seen any movement or the FBI.

"I hate this shit," Madison bemoaned.

"Our tax dollars not working. You think someone may have tipped him off?"

"I hope not. But if anyone did that, I'm sure it came from . . . Wait. Did you see that?" She nodded toward the front door of the two-story white house that looked as if a peaceful family resided there. There was a snowman flag flying from one of the pillars on the porch. The front door opened and Chase stepped out on the porch, holding a black trash bag. He didn't look like a killer or a peddler of child pornography, but that's probably what made him dangerous. Chuck gave Madison a sidelong glance as she gripped the door handle.

"Whatever you're thinking, don't do it," he said, then looked up at Chase. The man was smoking a cigar, but Chuck wondered if he was looking at them. "You're going to have to relax. This guy probably came outside because he noticed the car."

"Don't get any ideas," she said as she dropped her head in his lap. It took everything in Charles not to start laughing. He just threw his head back and followed along with Madison's playacting, but he never took his eyes off Chase. And he'd been right, the man was watching them. Madison's quick, albeit crude, act was enough to send him back inside.

"He's gone."

Madison sat up. "But where the hell is Sarah?" She picked up her phone as it vibrated against her thigh.

"Yes. The warrant has been issued and the calvary is on the way."

"We should drive around the block," he said as he saw the curtain moving on the front window.

"All right," she said, then reached into her bag and pulled out her gun. Charles put his hand on top of it.

"What are you doing?"

"Getting ready, just in case. I said I was going to let . . . Why are you questioning me all of a sudden?"

"Because I don't want you to do something you can't take back."

"Only if it's me or him."

"How is it going to come to that if you're going to leave his capture to the authorities?"

Charles started the car and drove around the block. He saw four black sedans heading toward Chase's house. He stopped on another corner and they got out of the car. Watching from the corner, they saw that the FBI was storming Chase's house. Then the explosions started. Charles and Madison ducked down as debris flew everywhere.

"Sarah!" Madison screamed as she pushed Charles off her and ran toward the flaming house. Charles tried to stop her, but he realized that he had been struck in the arm by a piece of wood. Blood dripped down his arm, but he got up and ran after Madison.

"Madison!" he called out when he saw Chase aim at her from the flaming porch. Charles pushed Madison out of the way just as Chase fired. The bullet hit him on the shoulder; then two FBI agents tackled Chase to the ground.

"Chuck! Chuck, are you okay?" She rolled him over and saw all of the blood. "Oh my God!"

"I'm all right."

Madison waved for one of the agents. "Call an ambulance! He's been shot!"

Charles started to tell her that he was fine, but then everything went black.

"Yolanda! Yolanda!" Alex called out to her sister. Yolanda had been sitting in Alex's office for two hours with her phone in her hand staring at it.

"What?"

"You're not going to get a response to your text by willing it to happen. I have a meeting soon. I need you to get out."

"Why do you think Chuck hasn't texted or called? What if . . ."

"Maybe he's busy with the police. Maybe he kicked the man's ass who wanted to kill you or maybe his phone died. But you have to get out of my office so I can do some work." Alex pointed to the door. "And don't worry, I doubt there is anything that can stop your *Chuck.*"

Yolanda wanted to smile, but she felt uneasy. She hadn't even wanted to think it. And she wasn't going to say it, but what if he was . . . Finally, her phone rang. It was Chuck.

"Chuck, you really had me freaking out."

"Is this Yolanda?" a female voice asked.

"Who is this?"

"Yolanda, this is Madison. Chuck and I were working together on your case and I don't want you to be alarmed."

"You're not doing a real good job of keeping me calm right now."

"He was shot."

Yolanda nearly fell to the floor. "Sh-shot?"

"He's all right," Madison said.

"Where is he? I'm coming to see him."

"We're at Richmond Memorial Hospital. I know you went back to Charleston, right?"

"So what? I'm coming." Yolanda ended the call, then remembered that her car was in Charlotte. She turned back toward Alex's office and saw her sister standing in the doorway.

"Did I hear you say Charles got shot? Come on, let's go."

"Thought you had a meeting? If you would just let me drive your . . ."

Alex stood in front of Yolanda and grasped her shoulders. "You're shaking like a freaking leaf. I'm not letting you drive. Let's go."

Charles sat up in the hospital bed as the pain medication began to wear off. It was funny to him that the wood that had gone through his forearm hurt more than the bullet he'd taken in his shoulder. He started to call the nurse for more medicine, but he didn't want to go back to sleep. How long had he been in the hospital and where in the hell was his phone? He needed to call Yolanda and ease her into what had happened.

He gingerly rose from the bed and walked the length of the small room. He felt dizzy after his first two steps, then got his bearings. On his second walk around the room, Charles realized that he needed to sit his ass down. Reaching for the edge of the bed, he eased down on the mattress and closed his eyes again.

It felt as if a few minutes had passed when he felt soft lips on his forehead. Clearly, he was dreaming because . . . Charles opened his eyes and saw Yolanda standing over him. Her eyes were red rimmed and filled with tears.

He reached out and stroked her cheek. "Hey, hey, don't cry."

"Don't cry, he says from a hospital bed. Chuck, what happened?"

"You're safe now. That's all that matters and I'm going to be fine," he said.

"You'd better be and we need to talk about your superhero complex. You're Clark Kent, not Superman."

"Yolanda, you're lucky that smart mouth of yours is one of the main things that I love about you."

She leaned down and kissed him slow and deep. "You wait until you get out of this hospital bed," she said when they broke the kiss. "I'm going to show you what a smart mouth can do."

Epilogue

Yolanda stood in the middle of her showroom. She'd finally made her mark in Charlotte with her boutique. Her shop had been called iconic and the place to get a one-of-a-kind outfit. Though her sister couldn't stand a certain quarterback, he was one of Yolanda's best customers. Nina figured it out when he was on television in an outfit that matched.

Tonight, though, Yolanda closed her doors early and was preparing to show Chuck Morris her latest fashion line. Things had changed so much over the last three months. She no longer had to look over her shoulders for killers, Robin and Logan were back to being insanely happy, Nina was still learning to cook, and Alex . . . well, Alex was always going to be Alex. And Chuck Morris was going to be a daddy.

The couple had been engaged for a month. After he was shot in Richmond, Yolanda hadn't wanted t
side. First, they spent a week at his home in (
where she refused to let him work. Then h
that they come to Charlotte and actually p

security system in her house and the shop. He'd also announced that he was going to open an office in Charlotte. Yolanda had been pleased and they decided to split their time between Charleston and Charlotte, which Yolanda felt was the best of both worlds, the city and the beach with the man of her dreams.

The buzzer went off when the front door to the shop opened. "Yolanda," Chuck called out. "What's all of this?"

She flipped the switch and turned on the overhead lights so the room was bathed in pink and blue. Yolanda sauntered over to him, dressed in a pink and blue sundress. "What do you think?" she asked as she did a little twirl.

"Interesting color choices. What's with all the pink and blue?"

"Well," she said as she grabbed his hand, "you're going to be somebody's daddy."

Chuck's eyes sparkled like the Emerald Coast she loved so much as he lifted her into his arms and spun her around. "I love you so much, Yolanda."

"I love you even more. And I can't wait to marry you and raise our little bundle of joy."

"You have told your sisters, right?"

"Um, not yet. I figured you should tell my dad first, see how he feels about you making him a grandfather and whatnot."

Chuck grinned. "Oh, I get to break the news?"

"It's only right—remember, he's the one who hired you."

He brushed his lips against her forehead. "Best job I've ever taken in my life. Thank you for opening my heart again."

Don't miss the previous installment in the Richardson Sisters series...

WON'T GO HOME WITHOUT YOU

A refuge in good times and bad, there's nothing the four very different Richardson sisters won't do to sustain their family's legacy—a historic bed-and-breakfast in Charleston, South Carolina. Now, as one sister celebrates new love, another's heart is sorely tested . . .

One night only—that's all Robin Richardson-Baptiste will give the husband she once adored. She thought nothing could shatter their storybook marriage—not illness or a life-saving operation that left her unable to have children. For her husband, Dr. Logan Baptiste, told her in a thousand unspoken ways their love was all he needed. But now, in the face of overwhelming evidence, his co-worker, Kamrie, claims Logan fathered her son.

Logan can't recall what happened with Kamrie—and DNA never lies. He *does* know he's never stopped loving his gentle, courageous wife. But doing whatever it takes to uncover the truth, and save his marriage, not to mention his career, will challenge them like never before. And one night of undivided attention and desire may be the only thing to heal their hearts, reveal all—or shatter things beyond repair . . .

Available from Kensington Publishing Corp. wherever books are sold

Six Months Ago

Robin Richardson-Baptiste closed her eyes and tried to forget what she'd read on the paper in her hand. The words couldn't be real. Her hands shook and tears poured down her cinnamon brown cheeks.

Logan, her husband, was a father. He'd cheated on her. He made a damn baby. She couldn't move, she couldn't speak, all she could do was stand there and cry. After everything that she'd been through. After he said that he was going to be there for her no matter what. This is what was happening? This is what he'd done?

"Robin?" Logan's voice felt like a slap in the face when he walked into the foyer of their house. "Who was at the door?"

She didn't say a word. She couldn't even look at the man she'd promised to love, cherish, and be faithful to. Obviously, she'd been the only one who'd taken their marriage vows seriously.

"Babe, what's going on? Did something happen to Pops?" He closed the space between them and reached out for her. Robin recoiled at his touch, then pressed the paper against his chest.

"Get the fuck out of here!" Anger made her voice deep like a lion's growl.

"Robin? What . . ."

She slapped him, unleashing all of the anger and sadness that had taken over her soul. "I hate you. How could you do this to me?"

Logan read the paternity results and his mouth dropped open. "You can't believe this. Robin, I've never cheated on you and I don't have a child."

She was about to pound his chest with her fists, then she took a step back. "You know, I've seen enough of these test results in family court to know that when someone is ninety-nine-point-nine percent the father that shit is real. Who is she? Who is the mother of your baby?" Robin didn't wait for an answer, which would've been another denial. She punched him in the chest, then ran upstairs to their bedroom. Robin slammed the door and locked it before flinging herself on the bed and sobbing into her pillow.

Dr. Logan Baptiste loved his wife more than life itself and he didn't understand what had just happened. Maybe he was still sleeping and this was a nightmare. But the real paper in his hand wasn't a figment of his imagination. It was a lie. Ten years ago, he married the woman of his dreams. Robin Richardson had been a quiet beauty who made his heart sing every time she walked into a room at Xavier University.

The moment he heard her say hello, he knew he was going to put a ring on it. Winning Robin hadn't been easy. While his charming demeanor and super good looks allowed him to have his choice of women, all he'd ever wanted had been Robin. Double R, he'd called her when he'd gotten into a study group with her.

She'd told the then basketball star that everyone in her group pulled their weight, and if he wasn't there to do the work, he could go ruin someone else's project. He'd been hooked.

Why would she believe that he'd do something so callous to her, when he knew she . . . He couldn't get stuck in the past—he had to get to the bottom of this bullshit and make his wife see the truth.

Logan was shocked and disappointed to see that the paternity test had been performed at the hospital where he worked and that the mother's name had been redacted. Was this just a cruel joke? As one of the lead cardiologists at Richmond Regional Medical Center, Logan took his job and reputation seriously. That had been one of the reasons why he'd started investigating the drug company that he believed was responsible for the death of several transplant patients. The more questions he asked, the fewer surgeries he'd been scheduled to perform. It didn't matter that he was one of the best surgeons on staff.

Now this.

Was he now a source of gossip because of this lie? While part of him knew he should've been pleading his case to Robin, Logan headed out the door and to the hospital. Someone was going to explain this smear job. Was this the way they wanted to move him out of his position? Hell no. He wasn't going to take this bullshit. He was going to go down fighting if he had to.

Chapter 1

Robin knew the last place she needed to be was in Charleston, South Carolina, helping her baby sister, Nina, with her wedding plans. There was so much her sisters didn't know about what was going on in her life and she didn't want to tell them while they were celebrating Nina and her fiancé Clinton's upcoming nuptials.

I can do this, she told herself as she walked into her family's historic bed-and-breakfast. The Richardson Bed and Breakfast had been the place where she learned about love as she watched her mother and father, Sheldon and Nora, live out a fairy tale romance that Disney couldn't reproduce if they tried. Granted, she knew now that there had been some hard times that probably tested their relationship.

But there were no outside babies. Robin gently patted her cheeks to stop her tears from coming. She wanted a family like she had growing up. A loving husband, three or four kids, and happiness.

But even if Logan hadn't cheated, she wouldn't have been able to have a child. Two years ago, Robin had been diagnosed with ovarian cancer. She had a lifesaving hysterectomy. Because she had her husband's support, she'd never shared with her family—especially her sisters—what she'd been through.

She didn't want pity. And she didn't want a reminder that she couldn't have the life she'd dreamed of when she'd said "I do" to Logan.

Obviously, he hadn't planned on taking his vows seriously. That's why he'd gone out and made a baby with that nurse. She'd served him with divorce papers over the summer and he'd had the unmitigated gall not to sign them. He kept sending them back to her attorney with a note: *Not signing until we talk.*

But she didn't want to talk to him, didn't want to see him—she just wanted to be done with him. And Logan wasn't making it easy.

Besides, the last conversation they'd had seemed cruel now. They had been discussing adoption and telling her family about her cancer. That, she'd told him, was going to be hard, because cancer had claimed their mother's life years ago. Back then, it felt safe to talk to him about everything. To share her fears with the man whom she'd thought she would love for the rest of her life. Robin's cancer diagnosis had put so much fear in her heart and soul because her mother didn't survive.

Logan had assuaged her fears, telling her about all of the treatments and advances in surviving cancer since her mother's death. Robin knew her three sisters would've been overly emotional if she had shared her illness with them. That's why she'd valued having Logan's strong shoulders when she was going through it.

But now, it felt as if it had been a charade. A big fucking joke.

Robin had moved out of the house in Richmond because Logan wouldn't leave. Sheldon had come to Virginia and helped her move into a town house in Petersburg. She told her dad the whole story about Logan's infidelity and the baby.

Robin had broken down and revealed her health issue. Of course, Sheldon had been shocked that she hadn't allowed her family to be there for her.

"Daddy, I thought Logan and I could handle this. He said he was going to . . ." Her voice trailed off and tears spilled from her eyes. "He said as long as we had each other, nothing else mattered. We'd make a family our way. Didn't know that meant he'd go drop sperm in a . . ."

"I could kill him. All that Pop *shit and he does this to you?"*

Robin shook her head as her tears fell. Sheldon drew his daughter into his arms and held her. "Robby, I wish I knew what to say to make you feel better."

"Did you and Mommy ever . . ."

"I never cheated on your mother, but we had our ups and downs. All marriages do."

"But how can a man take vows and break them like this? Then he keeps the lie going like I'm some kind of idiot who's going to stick around. That mother . . . Sorry, Daddy."

"No need to apologize this time. I understand that you're upset. But you're going to have to decide if you are ready to let him go and end your marriage."

"Why wouldn't I be? Logan knew I wanted a child—

children actually. He knew how . . . Daddy, this is the worst betrayal. There's no coming back from this."

Sheldon brushed a tender kiss across her forehead. "Make sure that's true. I know you don't want to hear this, but I can't wrap my head around Logan doing this to you. That boy . . ."

"People change and I can't believe you're defending him! Daddy!"

"I'm not defending him and I'm not telling you that you should go back to him, but this doesn't seem like the man who begged me for your hand in marriage and promised me that he'd never hurt you."

"Obviously people change," she said again.

"That's true, but I can't believe there . . . Robby, whatever you need from me, let me know. I'm going to follow your lead. If we have to kick his ass, then we'll do that. But if you ever decide to take him back, then I'm going to support you on that as well."

She dropped her head in her hands because she didn't know what she wanted to do.

Robin opened the door to the suite where her sisters had gathered. Planting a plastic smile on her face, she walked in and gave Nina a big hug.

Logan walked into the house he and Robin had shared for nearly a decade and was still floored by the silence. Six months without his wife had been driving him crazy. What was also making him lose his mind had been the fact that she'd moved out like a thief in the night—with Sheldon's help.

Logan knew his father-in-law was loyal to his daughters, but he thought the older man would've allowed him to plead his case. Nope. The calm and serene Sheldon Richardson actually told him to *fuck off.*

He was still shocked to hear that word come out of Sheldon's mouth. He'd even called his sister-in-law, Alexandria, who'd been a fan of his in the past. But she obviously had his number blocked. The two times he had called, the calls went straight to voice mail.

When the Richardsons closed ranks, there was no getting inside that wall of loyalty.

As much as he wanted to fight for his marriage and prove his innocence, Logan couldn't. Not until he had gotten to the bottom of the deaths that he was sure had been linked to Cooper Drugs, the company the hospital had started using for transplant patients. Then there was his career to consider. Something he'd worked so hard to build.

But is it worth losing your marriage?

The ringing of his cell phone shattered the silence and nearly made him jump out of his skin.

"Dr. Baptiste."

"Logan," a female voice cooed. "It's Danielle."

He rolled his eyes. Why was she calling? He'd just ended a twelve-hour shift and had no plans to go back to the hospital.

"What's up?" he asked the nurse.

"Your patient, Mr. Gary Cooper, there aren't any orders

for his medication this evening and I'd hate for something to go wrong."

Logan groaned, because he knew good and well that he'd left detailed notes on the man's insulin dosages. But he wasn't going to allow anything to go wrong. "I'll be there in fifteen minutes." He ended the call without saying good-bye. It wasn't as if he had anything else to do. Being alone in what had been a dream house was nothing short of a nightmare.

Speeding down the road toward the hospital, Logan thought about the days when heading into work was an exciting time for him.

Then all hell broke loose.

Kamrie Bazal. The nurse, who had assisted him through some of his biggest surgeries at Richmond Medical, had the nerve to accuse him of being her son's father. Bullshit. He'd never slept with that woman.

No matter what a flawed DNA test said. But he'd been hit with divorce papers and a child support lawsuit in a span of six months. Then there was talk of an internal investigation at the hospital about his so-called relationship with Kamrie.

That made him laugh. Outside of the operating room, he had nothing to do with that woman. Though there were plenty of other doctors who couldn't say the same thing. He thought she'd been a friend. He had been nothing but kind to her.

So, why did she pick me? He pulled into his assigned parking spot in the parking garage.

When he got out of the car, his phone rang. Seeing that it was a blocked number, he hit the ignore button.

This day was getting more annoying as the minutes ticked by.

"Logan."

Turning around, he saw Kamrie walking toward him. "What the hell?"

"I'm sorry for the subterfuge. But you won't talk to me and we have to figure this thing out."

"Figure what out?" He folded his arms across his chest. "You mean to tell me that you and Danielle don't have anything better to do than fuck with me after my shift?"

"You could get to know your son and . . . I heard your wife left you. Nothing is stopping us from being a family now."

Logan blinked, then broke into laughter. "Have you lost your mind? How are we going to be a family when that kid of yours isn't mine?"

"We're going to do this. You remember the night of the hurricane. We were all trapped here and . . ."

Logan threw his hand in her face. "You're fucking insane."

"That's not what the DNA test says. Jean is your son and I know for a fact he's going to be the only child you're ever going to have, since your soon-to-be ex couldn't give you a child."

"Watch your mouth. You're not even fit to think about her, much less say a mumbling word about her." Logan clenched his hands into fists. And though he would never strike a woman, Kamrie was a test.

"Logan, we can have the family I know you want. Jean should meet his father and have a relationship with you."

He took a huge step back. "You don't know shit about me."

She smiled, reminding him of The Grinch on Christmas day. "You keep acting as if you've forgotten that I know every inch of that amazing body. Especially . . ." She nodded toward his crotch. "Stop denying it. We're a family and you should come home, where you belong."

Logan crossed over to his car and slammed inside. He wondered if he could order a seventy-two-hour hold for that crazy bitch. *Calm down*, he thought as he pulled out of the parking garage. Logan knew he needed to find his wife. She hadn't taken his calls and her lawyer wasn't forthcoming with where he could find Robin.

Of course, going to her office was an option but it was going to be his last resort. He didn't want to cause a public scene this close to the holidays. Hell, he didn't want to cause a scene, period.

But he had to find her and they needed to talk. Robin was more than likely in Charleston, South Carolina, with her family. Maybe it was time for him to listen to the human resources director and take some time off.

All he wanted for Christmas was to win his wife back and get his life back on track. And he was going to do whatever he had to do to prove his love to Robin. That meant that he was going to have to get Kamrie to come clean about the father of her son.

Logan couldn't live without Robin and this lie wasn't going to destroy them. All he could do was pray that he wasn't too late.

Connect with Us

Visit us online at
KensingtonBooks.com
to read more from your favorite authors, see books by series, view reading group guides, and more.

Join us on social media
for sneak peeks, chances to win books and prize packs, and to share your thoughts with other readers.

facebook.com/kensingtonpublishing
twitter.com/kensingtonbooks

Tell us what you think!

To share your thoughts, submit a review, or sign up for our eNewsletters, please visit:
KensingtonBooks.com/TellUs.